A CASE IN CAMERA

A CASE IN CAMERA

OLIVER ONIONS

WILDSIDE PRESS

TO
OLE LUK OIE

Originally published in 1920 and 1921.
Published by Wildside Press LLC.
Visit us online at wildsidepress.com

PART I

WHAT HAPPENED IN LENNOX STREET

I

The tale I am setting out to tell has to do with the killing, on a May morning of the year 1919, of one young man by another who claimed, and still claims, to have been his friend. The circumstances were singular—perhaps even unique; the consequences affected a number of people in various interesting ways and byways; and since the manner of telling the story has been left entirely to me, I will begin with the breakfast-party that Philip Esdaile gave that morning at his studio in Lennox Street, Chelsea.

II

Philip had at least two good reasons for being in high feather that morning. The first of these was that barely a week ago, with a magnificent new quill pen, he had signed the Roll, had shaken august hands, and was now Philip Esdaile, A.R.A., probably the most gifted among the younger generation of painters of the pictorial phenomena of Light.

I and his second reason for contentment happened to arrive almost simultaneously at the wrought-iron gate that opened on to his little front garden. We all knew that for many months past our barrister friend, Billy Mackwith, had been tracking down and buying in again on Philip's behalf a number of Philip's earlier pictures—prodigal pictures, parted with for mere bread-and-butter during the years of struggle, and now very well worth Philip's re-purchase if he could get them into his possession again. (I may perhaps say at once that I don't think Philip owed his Associateship to his pictures of that period. It is far more likely that the artist thus honored was Lieutenant Esdaile, R.N.V.R., sometime one of the Official Painters to the Admiralty.)

A carrier's van stood drawn up opposite the gate, and I saw Mackwith's slim, silk-hatted and morning-coated figure jump down from the seat next to the driver. Evidently Philip had seen the arrival of the van too, for he ran down the short flagged path to meet us.

"You don't mean to say you've brought them all?" he cried eagerly.

"The whole lot. Fourteen," Mackwith replied. "Glad I just caught you before you left."

Esdaile and his family were leaving town that morning for some months on the Yorkshire Coast, and it was this departure that was the occasion of the farewell breakfast.

The three of us carried the recovered canvases through the small annexe, where the breakfast-table was already laid, and into the large studio beyond. There we stood admiring them as they leaned, framed and unframed, against easels and along the walls. No doubt you remember Esdaile's paintings of that period—the gay white and gray of his tumultuous skies, the splash and glitter of his pools and fountains, the crumbling wallflowered masonry of his twentieth-century *fêtes-champêtre*. There is nothing psychical or philosophic about them. He simply has that far rarer possession, an eye in his head to see straight with.

"Well, which of 'em are you going to have for yourself, just by way of thank-you, Billy?" the painter asked. "Any you like; I owe you the best of them and more.... And of course here comes Hubbard. Always does blow in just as things are being given away, if it's only a pink gin. How are you, Cecil?"

The new-comer wore aiguillettes and the cuff-rings of a Commander, R.N. He was a comparatively new friend of mine, but for two years off and on had been a shipmate of Esdaile's, and I liked the look of his honest red face and four-square and blocklike figure. We turned to the pictures again. I think their beauties were largely thrown away on Hubbard. Somebody ought to have told him that their buying-in meant a good thousand pounds in Esdaile's pocket. Then he would have looked at them in quite a different manner.

In the middle of the inspection Joan Merrow's white frock and buttercupped hat appeared in the doorway, and we were bidden to come in to breakfast. Monty Rooke and Mrs. Cunningham had just arrived, which made our party complete.

The little recess in which we breakfasted was filled with the sunlight reflected from the garden outside. Everything in it—the napkins and fruit and chafing-dishes on the table, the spring flowers in the bowls, the few chosen objects on the buff-washed walls, the showery festoon of the chandelier overhead—had the soft irradiation of a face seen under a parasol. Little shimmers of light, like love-making butterflies, danced here and there whenever glasses or carafes were moved, and the stretches of shining floor almost looked as if trout might have lurked beneath them.

And where the tall French windows stood wide open the light seemed to be focused as if by a burning-glass on the two little Esdaile boys who played beneath the mulberry that rose above the studio roof.

I don't suppose the whole of Chelsea could have shown a merrier break-fast-party than we made that May morning. For, in addition to our host's new Associateship and those fourteen wandering pictures safely back home again, we had a further occasion for light-heartedness that I haven't mentioned yet. This was the wedding, to take place that day week, of Mrs. Cunningham and Monty Rooke. Philip was generously lending them his house and studio for the summer. Monty we had all known for years, but Mrs. Cunningham I for one set eyes on for the first time that morning. Later I got a much more definite impression of her. For the present I noticed only her slender and beautiful black-chiffon-covered arms, the large restless dark eyes that seemed to disengage themselves from under the edge of her black satin turban hat, and her manicured fingers that reminded you of honeysuckle. The Esdailes had received her "on the ground floor," so to speak, and it obviously pleased Monty that Philip had called her Audrey straight away.

So we talked of the approaching wedding, and the Associateship, and the painting-cottage in Yorkshire, and so back to the pictures again. On this subject Commander Hubbard unhesitatingly took the lead.

"Well, it's certainly Art for mine my second time on earth," he good-humoredly railed, the aiguillettes swinging gently on his breast. "Fancy going out of town this weather! Taking away all that gear behind the bulkhead there,"—he jerked his head to where Philip's painting paraphernalia lay ready packed in the hall—"a few yards of raw canvas bent on battens—and bringing it back again worth twenty pounds an inch!"

Hubbard had a Whitehall job that summer, and loathed it. Esdaile laughed.

"Can't see why they didn't make me a full Academician while they were about it," he said.

"*And* he's grumbling!" Hubbard retorted. "Perfectly revolting fellow. That's too much lunching with Admirals. Listen, Mrs. Esdaile, and I'll tell you the kind of thing we mere senior officers had to put up with. A hoist breaks out from the flagship, and every glass in the Squadron is glued to it. You'd think at least we were to proceed to sea immediately. Nothing of the sort! It's the Admiral presenting his compliments to this wretched wavy-ringed fellow your husband, and would he give him the pleasure—would Lieutenant Esdaile, R.N.V.R., condescend—stoop—to take luncheon with him! The Admiral, if you please! And that's what it is to be an Official Painter!"

Esdaile laughed again. He was trying to remove in one unbroken piece the paring of an apple for Joan Merrow.

"Give him a smile now and then and he'll eat out of your hand, Mollie," he said. "Now, Joan, the last little bit—this is where a steady hand comes in—there!" He held up in triumph the wiggle of apple paring. "Throw it over your left shoulder and see what initial it makes on the floor. Here's my guess on this bit of paper under my napkin—'C for Ch' ... Ah, clumsy infant!" The strip had fallen in two pieces. "There goes your luck. Allee done gone finish. I'll have the apple myself; you'd better go and write the rest of those labels."

The Esdailes had to all intents and purposes adopted Joan Merrow now that she was alone in the world. On the day when Philip, half scared by the risks he was taking, had informed his private pupils that their tuition took up too much of his painting-time, he had not included Joan. She had continued to prime his canvases and to make use of his models at long range from odd corners of the studio; and then, during his absence on Service, she had come to live in the house, had taught and mended for the children, and had been companion and friend to Mollie. By an affectionate fiction, her former fees were supposed to cover the cost of her board, and a proper arrangement was to be come to one of these days. She was twenty, had only lately ceased to have the stripling figure that is all youth and no sex, and was already acquiring that mystery of physical shape and of mind and emotion that causes men's heads to turn behind and their lips to murmur, "Ah—in another year or so—"

There was still the faint echo of chattering schoolrooms in the repartee that came from her pretty lips. Pertly and with little tosses of her head she enumerated the duties she had discharged that morning.

"The labels are all distinctly written, with the name at the top, then a space, and 'Santon, Yorks' quite at the bottom so you can tear it off and use the label again for somewhere else. Both the taxis are ordered for one-thirty, and Mr. Rooke won't have to send on letters because they're all being re-addressed at the Post Office. The doors and windows are all fastened, and I've shown Mrs. Cunningham where everything is for after the wedding. And I didn't want the apple, and you've no business to write things about me on your horrid bits of paper!"

And we all laughed as she suddenly twitched Philip's napkin away and tucked the horrid bit of paper safely away into her bosom.

III

I have told the foregoing in some detail because I want you to see the careless and happy party into which that morning's bolt dropped a quarter of an hour later. I want you to see the contrast between our homely light-heartedness and the complex tangle of all that followed. I will now tell you what the bolt was.

Breakfast was over, and we men had gone into the studio again. Mrs. Cunningham was helping Mollie to clear away, and Joan Merrow had joined the children in the garden, and with them was looking up at an aeroplane, the soft organ-like note of which had suddenly ceased. We were having Hubbard's views on Art again.

"But that submarine sketch of yours is the pick of all you've done to my mind, Esdaile," he was saying. "Old Horne at the periscope, eh? You caught him to a hair; a snapshot couldn't have been better! And we bagged that beggar ten minutes later, Norwegian flag and all," he added with professional satisfaction.

Philip Esdaile gave a quick exclamation.

"By Jove, that just reminds me! The orange curaçao, of course! The very thing after all that fruit—corrects the acidity, as the doctors say. We'll have some."

The Commander gave him a sharp look. On the face of it there was no very evident reason why the torpedoing of a German ship flying the Norwegian flag should remind Esdaile of orange curaçao, but no doubt there was a story behind that we others knew nothing of. If ships have to be put down there is no sense in sending bottles of delectable liqueur to the bottom of the sea also.

"What!" cried Commander Hubbard, R.N. "You don't mean to say that *you* had the infernal neck to take your whack—"

A mere wretched wavy-ringed fellow to loot bottle for bottle with his betters like that!

But Esdaile, with a wink, demanded the key of the cellar from Monty Rooke, told him to get the liqueur glasses out, and was off.

It was at that moment that the crash came that seemed to bring the whole of Chelsea running out of doors.

The shrill cry of "The aeroplane! The aeroplane!" was hardly out of the children's mouths before it was upon us—I don't mean the aeroplane, but the other thing. Judging from the harsh but muffled roar, the first installment of the crash, so to speak, which was the plane itself, must have been a quarter of a mile away; but between that and the second one there was hardly time to take breath. Simultaneously, as it seemed, there came a rushing of air, a loud cracking, and a nauseating thud on the studio roof; and Joan Merrow ran in with the children, one under either arm and her head down. The street outside was a sudden clatter of running feet and short spasmodic cries.

"Good God, right on our heads!" the Commander muttered, his eyes aloft.

The next moment he was at the studio door looking for Esdaile.

Had he found him I should not be writing this story. Not finding him, he assumed command.

"All right. All over now, little fellows. There won't be any more. Mrs. Esdaile, you ladies will stay just where you are, please. Get on to the telephone, Mackwith. You other fellows come with me."

He thought it better that somebody should investigate before the women began to move about too freely.

IV

One order at any rate was superfluous—that to telephone to the police. Aeroplanes do not crash in Chelsea in the middle of the morning unobserved. Already the windows on the other side of the street were packed with faces, and every face was turned in the same direction.

This was towards the torn fabric of a parachute that had lodged partly on the studio roof, partly in the branches of the mulberry in the garden.

Hubbard ran out through the French windows and looked up. Tapes trailed and rippled and fluttered in the merry morning breeze, and the gray silk ballooned and rose and fell. But the sound of running feet warned Hubbard not to pause. He strode quickly down the flagged path, shot the catch of the wrought-iron gate in the faces of the too curious, and then hurried into the house again. He addressed Rooke, who stood by the group of shocked women.

"Here, you seem to know this house pretty well. How do we get up there?" he asked.

"Bathroom window, I should think," Rooke replied. "This way."

The bathroom lay at the end of a short passage on the floor above. The three of us dashed upstairs. Rooke tried the bathroom door, but found it locked. "Damn!" he muttered, and then I reminded him that possibly he had the key of it in his pocket.

It was oddly irritating to watch him try first one key and then another. We wanted to tell him to make haste, as if he could have made any greater haste than he was doing. Then luckily he hit on the right one. The door opened, we sprang across the cork-covered floor, and Rooke began to tug at the window-catch. The window was one of these late-Victorian windows with a colored border and white incised stars, and already the tragic huddle a dozen yards away could be seen, violently crimson through the red squares and morbidly blue through the blue ones.

Then, as the sash flew up, all was sunshine again, and the wrecked parachute and the two men enwrapped in its folds could be seen only too clearly.

Monty Rooke had a new silver-gray suit on that morning, but already he had thrown one leg over the sill.

"I'm not so heavy as you fellows," he muttered. "I'm not so sure about this gutter—give me a hand while I try it. Then I can shin up that spout over there."

Hubbard took the small, nervous hand in his own beefy fist and let him down three or four feet. "All right," said Rooke, after a moment's trial; and, spread-eagled out on the annexe roof, he began to make his way towards the higher roof of the studio beyond.

"Tapes oughtn't to have fouled like that," I heard the Commander say under his breath as we watched. "Parachuting's safe enough if you're any height at all. This breeze, I suppose, and risking the double load. Wonder they didn't go slap through."

It was, indeed, merely by inches that the two men had missed the roof-glass. Apparently the parachute, the roof-frame and the mulberry had shared the shock among them. Not that another fifteen feet would have made much difference to the poor devils, I couldn't help thinking.

The street was now a densely-packed mass of faces, all watching Rooke's progress. Even the whispering had ceased. Then cries of "Make way there!" were suddenly heard. Fifty yards away a ladder, preceded by a plump young man in a horsey check coat, was being passed over people's heads. Every hand that could touch the ladder did so, as if out of some odd pride of assistance. What anonymous mind had foreseen the need of it none could have told. Down below Mackwith opened the gate; an Inspector, followed by a couple of constables and the last relay that bore the ladder, entered; and Mackwith closed the gate again. The ladder was set up by the splintered mulberry, and the Inspector and one of the constables joined Rooke on the roof.

Five minutes later Rooke was down again. Hubbard and I had also descended. We met him as he came in at the French window.

"Well?" we both demanded at once.

He was agitated, as indeed he had some reason for being. He had had an unpleasant task. Before replying he advanced to the breakfast-table and poured himself out some water into the nearest glass. The glass knocked unsteadily as he set it down again. Then he glanced down at his clothes, made a movement as if to brush the grime from them, but gave a jerk to his tie instead.

Nevertheless his news was not all bad. In one particular it was rather astonishingly good. One of the two men, it appeared, was by no means fatally hurt—was, indeed, quite likely to pull through.

"Do you know who they are?" Hubbard asked.

Again Monty seemed preoccupied with his clothes. Then we had his tidings, jerkily and bit by bit.

The plane itself had come down somewhere by the Embankment, and was said to have caught fire. Parts of the parachute seemed to be singed too. Both men were civilian flyers; at least neither was in uniform. The other poor fellow was killed. The ambulance had been sent for, and for the present there was little more to be done. The police were seeing to the rest. This was the sum of what Monty told us.

Then we heard the voice of Mackwith, who had come up behind us.

"That's so," he confirmed. "I've just been having a word with the Inspector about that. He doesn't think anybody here will have to attend any inquiry or anything; the police evidence ought to be enough. So I was thinking, Mrs. Esdaile," he turned to Mollie, whose face was still pale and drawn and who bit the corner of her lip incessantly, "that the best thing for you to do is to stick to your program just as if this hadn't happened. You'll do no good staying here. You didn't see it,"—here Joan Merrow, from the little sofa, raised her head but dropped it again without speaking—"well, I mean that even Joan didn't see anything that five hundred other people didn't see just as well. Rooke may just possibly be wanted, but anyway he'll be here. And as for Philip—"

He broke off abruptly. Of a sudden we all stared at one another. We had forgotten all about Philip. Where was he?

If you remember, he had gone down into the cellar to fetch a bottle of wine. And in performing this simple errand he had been away for close on half an hour.

Mollie Esdaile, all on edge again, turned swiftly to Monty Rooke.

"Where is he? He did go down there, didn't he? You did give him the cellar key, didn't you? And nobody heard him go out of the house?"

Well, that was a matter that was very easily ascertained. Already Hubbard had taken a stride towards the door that led to the cellar.

But he did not reach the door. A footstep was heard behind it and the turning of a key, and Esdaile entered. In one hand he carried a stone jar of Dutch curaçao. In the other, arrestively out of place in the spring sunshine, its flame a dingy orange and its little spiral of greasy smoke fouling the air, he held a lighted candle in a flat tin stick.

<h2 style="text-align:center">V</h2>

For a moment we all gazed stupidly at that jar and candle; but the next moment our eyes were fastened on Philip's face.

Now ordinarily Esdaile's face, clean-shaven since 1914, is quite a pleasant one to look at, lightly browned, and with the savor of the sea still lingering about it. Nor was it noticeably pale now. Indeed, you might have said that some inner excitation made it not pale at all. But there was no disguising the strained tenseness of it. At the same time he was obviously attempting such a disguise. His features were set in a would-be-easy smile, but the smile stopped at his eyes. These blinked, though possibly at the sudden brightness after the obscurity below. And he spoke without pause or preliminary, as if rehearsing something he had had time to get letter-perfect but not to make entirely and naturally his own.

"Did you think I was never coming up?" The mechanical smile was turned on us all in turn. "I suppose I have been rather a long time. Just wool-gathering. I apologize to everybody. Where are the liqueur-glasses?"

There was a dead silence. Was it possible that he had heard nothing, knew nothing of what had occurred?

Monty Rooke was the first to speak.

"Do you mean to say you didn't hear it?" he blurted out.

Then, as Philip seemed to concentrate that artificial smile suddenly on him alone, he seemed sorry he had drawn attention to himself.

"And where on earth have *you* been?" Philip demanded slowly. "What's the matter with your clothes? Been emptying the dustbins? Here, let me give you a clean-up, man—"

He got rid of the jar of liqueur, not by putting it down on a table, but by the simple if unusual expedient of letting it drop through his fingers, where it made a heavy thump, rolled over on its side, and came to rest. He stepped forward.

But Rooke, for some reason or other, stepped much more quickly back. He muttered something about his clothes not mattering—it was only a few grains of dust, but damp—better let it dry before touching it—

It was at this point that I caught Cecil Hubbard's eye.

Hubbard's is a bright blue eye, with angular lids like little set-squares and a tiny dark dot in the middle of the blue. That eye may not know very much about pictures, but it knows a good deal about men and their faces. Esdaile was taking risks if he hoped to play any tricks with that eye on him.

Then, having caught mine for that moment, the eye was attentively fixed on our host again.

You see how preposterous it was already. Esdaile apparently could notice a trifle like the dust on Rooke's clothes, but he seemed to be both blind and deaf to everything else—the soft surging murmurs of the crowd outside, the voice of the Inspector in the garden, the shadows of strangers across the French windows. He just dropped heavy stone jars to the floor, talked about wool-gathering, and had not even thought of extinguishing the candle that was melting and guttering in his hand.

Wool-gathering—Philip Esdaile, the least woolly-minded of men!

Already I was certain that he was deliberately acting, and acting far from well at that.

It was little Alan, the elder of the two boys, who broke the spell that seemed to have benumbed us all. He ran forward, his blue-and-white check smock against his father's knees and his little face upturned.

"A naeroplane, daddy!" he cried eagerly. "Some men fell out of a naero-plane close to Jimmy and me, didn't they, Auntie Joan? In a parachute, bigger'n this room!" The little arms were outstretched to their widest reach. "Do come quick and look, daddy!"

And he seized his father's hand.

Again I caught Hubbard's eye. Esdaile was at it again, this time with a badly-exaggerated gesture of astonishment. He might have made just such a gesture if Alan had told him that the Grandmother in the bed was really a Wolf—good enough for children but not for anybody else. Hubbard at any rate thought that this had lasted long enough.

"Do you mean to say that you didn't feel the whole house shake half an hour ago?" he demanded.

Esdaile turned, but with a curious reluctance that I didn't understand.

"I did fancy I heard a noise of some sort," he admitted. "What about it?"

Hubbard gave it to him plain and unvarnished, for all the world as if he had been in the Admiral's office with a sentry with a bayonet at the door.

"A plane crashed, and two men came down on your roof in a parachute. One's living, the other's killed. Those are the police in your garden now. That's all—except that you seem to live in a pretty solidly-constructed house."

This time Esdaile made no demonstration. He stood listening for a moment longer, as if he thought Hubbard might add something; then, without a word, he released himself from Alan's hand and strode, not to the garden where the voices were, but towards the studio door.

VI

The studio (into which Hubbard and I immediately followed him) was a large oblong apartment, with a portion of one of its longer sides and almost the whole of the roof glazed. More or less light could be admitted by means of a system of dark blue blinds and cords running to cleats on the walls. It was to the roof-glass that my eyes turned first of all. One corner of it was darkened, as if melted snow had slipped down its slope, but the irregular triangle thus made was not so dark but that the shapes of the two heads could be seen, a little darker still. Nearer up to the ridge one thick pane was badly starred, and in the middle of the star was a small hole. This I judged to have been made by the broken branch that still brushed and played about it. A couple of pictures had fallen from the walls and lay face downward among their sprinklings of broken glass on the floor. One or two others were disarranged. Otherwise the apartment seemed to be undamaged.

Esdaile's behavior was now odder than ever. With those two men lying on the roof just over his head and the police moving about the garden outside, apparently he found nothing more urgent to do than to move displaced rugs about and to push at the bits of broken glass with his foot. And he did this with the candle, now a stalagmite of tallow, still licking and flickering in his hand.

He made no remark when Hubbard took the candle almost roughly from him, blew it out, and set it down on the table where the artist's tubes and brushes usually stood.

"We'll be rid of that first of all," he said. "Unless it's a mascot. Scaring 'em to death with that in your hand like a sleepwalker in traveling-tweeds! Now what about it, Esdaile?"

There was sudden attention in Philip's attitude, though he still looked down at the floor and pushed at a rug with his toe.

"What about what?" he asked.

"About this last half-hour."

"You mean where have I been? I went down into the cellar. I went to get that liqueur."

"That doesn't take half an hour—and it certainly didn't take this particular half-hour."

To this Esdaile made no reply.

"Come," said Hubbard again after a pause. "You admitted just now that you thought you heard something."

The words came slowly. "Did I? Yes, I remember. But it was all muffled. Honestly, I couldn't tell from the sound that it was—that it was all this."

"Was that when you were down there, or as you were going down, or when?"

"I'd just got down, I think."

"But didn't you wonder what was the matter? What kept you all that time? And what's the matter with you now that you have come up?"

"The matter?" Esdaile began once more to parry; and then suddenly his manner changed. For the first time he looked up from the floor, and the mask, whatever it was, almost dropped. "Look here, you fellows," he said almost appealingly, "you might see I'm a bit worried. I've been trying to hide it, but perhaps it wasn't much of an effort. Not so dashed easy to hide. But if you're suggesting that I've been somewhere else besides in the cellar I can only tell you I haven't. Couldn't for one thing; Rooke's got every key of this house. I had to get the cellar one from him. By the way, what's he doing now?"

"Looking out your next train. But what I want to know is—"

He broke off suddenly as sounds were heard over our heads. About the snowslip on the roof other shadowy shapes could be seen. Feet shuffled and moved, and the broken branch was dragged away. They were preparing to get the two men down.

And until they should have finished our conversation ceased.

But in the meantime Esdaile did yet another trivial incongruous thing. Moving towards one set of blind-cords he motioned to me to take another set. With short sticking tugs we drew the blinds across a foot at a time, and soon only narrow gold lozenges of sunlight showed among the rafters. All below was a dark blue twilight, as if for an obsequy within instead of for one on the roof.

Then, when from the cessation of sound all appeared to be over, Hubbard made a fresh appeal. He took the painters arm.

"Now let's have this out," he said. "No good letting a thing get way on when a few plain words will stop it. A perfectly ordinary thing's happened. Simple parachute accident. No mystery about it whatever. The mystery only begins when *you* come in carrying your damned candles and dropping jars and coming in here to tidy up instead of going outside to see what's happened. That's where the answer begins to be a lemon, my son. Listen to me. Whether you heard that crash or whether you didn't, at any rate you know all about it *now*. Then why can't you be just decently upset like the rest of us and have done with it?"

"Decently upset?" The words seemed to strike him. "Have I been behaving any other way?"

"You were behaving damnably indecently when you came up out of the orlop there—and that was *before* you were told a word of all this, remember."

At last Esdaile saw the point. His behavior *had* been extraordinary for whole minutes before the situation had been explained to him. One would have thought that during those minutes he had been deliberately trying to find out how much we knew about something or other before committing himself. When next he spoke it was almost apologetically.

"I see," he said quietly at last. "Yes, you're perfectly right. That was certainly the proper way to take it—just be decently upset. I see now. I must have looked a perfect zany.... Now look here: I want to tell you both all about it, but the trouble is that I can't just at this moment. At present it's somebody else's affair, not mine at all. Must get that cleared up first. I'm not perfectly sure of my ground either; you'll see by and by. But as regards the accident—well, that's the whole point at present. I mean anybody would say it *was* an accident, wouldn't they? It *looked* like one, I mean? It would never occur to anybody who saw it that—"

But here he broke off abruptly as his wife appeared in the doorway.

VII

Perhaps at this point I had better tell you who "I" am who write this, and also how our little circle came to choose me for the task.

As a minor actor in these events you may set me down as a working journalist. Among other things I am one of the sub-editors of the *Daily Circus*. But that is not the whole of my life. I am also a novelist of sorts. And one of my reasons for sticking to journalism when I could manage at a pinch to do without it is that in this way I escape the doom of having to produce two novels a year whether I have anything to write about or not.

But that was not their idea in asking me to put into shape the mosaic of differently-colored pieces that constitutes this Case. I believe their idea was that my two capacities might supplement one another—that I might hold fast (so to speak) to the bed-rock facts with my journalistic hand while the other was left free for the less tangible elements. I don't know that I altogether agree with this distinction. I happen to have some experience of how much fiction people swallow when they take up their morning papers, and also of how much mere hurdy-gurdy-grinding they accept as "human nature" when it comes to them in the form of a novel. But that is their look-out. I told them that with their help I would do my best.

I had to have their help. Obviously I could not always be at the side of this person or that, Rooke or Esdaile or Hubbard, throughout every winding of a complicated chain of events. But I have known Esdaile for twenty years, Rooke for a dozen, and most of the others long enough to have a fairly reliable impression of them, and their accounts are quite trustworthy. If I have any doubt about this I say so.

I cannot deny that we took a good deal of responsibility when we conspired to hush up the facts of this Case. We have no more right to come between the agents of the Law and their duty than any other set of private persons. And, though many of the beaten tracks are lost in these changing days, and new precedents are making whichever way you turn, I for one don't like making new precedents, especially moral ones. I like tradition to have my homage even when I am resolved to break it. But we are dealing with a *fait accompli*. The Case *is* a Case. It became so in spite of laws and customs and institutions. First one person acted as according to the laws of his individual being he had to act, and another did the same, and then another and so on, until the phenomenon was complete.

So, as my chief business in life is precisely those human accidentals that make us all different beings destined to different acts, perhaps they have chosen their historian more or less rightly after all.

One caveat (as Mackwith would say) I must enter, however. This is with regard to my own Services in the War that is now over. Most of these services, though as a matter of fact performed in belt and khaki, might just as well have been discharged in a dressing-gown, so unadventurous for the most part were they. Thanks to a "joy-ride," I did just see War, but for the rest I went where I was told to go and did what I was told to do. It is therefore just possible that from the point of view of those who lived in the hell I only briefly visited, one or two of my values may be a little "out." The North Sea cannot be quite the same to me that it was to Esdaile and Hubbard, the air means just what it meant to Maxwell and Chummy Smith. For this I am afraid there is no help. But there is always the chance that if I have minimized, they might have stressed a little unduly. For while our Case has nothing to do with War, War is always antecedent to it, as for a generation to come it will be antecedent to everything.

So, on this understanding, we may get on with the tale.

VIII

A slightly embarrassing little scene next took place in that breakfast-room in Lennox Street, Chelsea. Rooke had put down the Time Table, and Mollie Esdaile's face wore an expression of exasperation.

It appeared that Philip wanted to pack his family off according to program but wished to remain behind himself. For this he gave no reason—or rather he gave several reasons, all of the thinnest description.

"But how tiresome!" broke from Mollie. "Why on earth do you want to upset everything like this?"

Philip muttered something about the newly-arrived pictures needing a thorough overhauling.

"And the children all ready, all but their hats!" Mollie exclaimed.

"Better hurry them up.... At least seven of them are to frame too."

"Then there's Monty and Audrey, what about them? When you offer people a house—"

But at this one of Mrs. Cunningham's slender hands was imploringly raised. Her small mouth was parted in appeal.

"Oh, please! Don't think of that! I should be miserable if I thought that was going to make any difference!"

"But of *course* it makes a difference!" Mollie declared. "All your things will be coming here, all your things for the wedding, and anyway you won't want Philip hanging about the place. Better never have offered the house at all!"

"Oh—for a day or two—I shan't be in the way," said Philip uneasily.

But it was awkward for all that. If Esdaile had offered his house to one of his more prosperous friends he would not have hesitated to say frankly that he was sorry, but something unforeseen had happened, and the hospitality must be considered "off." But this was different. It was known that these two were the reverse of well-off. Monty as a matter of fact had already given up his rooms in Jubilee Place, and I had gathered at breakfast that Mrs. Cunningham only intended to occupy her bed-sitting-room in Oakley Street for a very few days longer. There was her story, too, which I shall come to presently. Philip's decision certainly upset a number of minor arrangements.

"Oh, it's too ridiculous!" Mollie declared again with vexation. "If it means that the wedding's to be put off I don't feel like going away at all."

But Philip only continued to mumble soothingly that it would be quite all right, and it wasn't for long, and nobody had said anything about putting off the wedding. The situation looked rather like a deadlock, and Mackwith already had his silk hat in his hand and the Commander's white-topped cap was tucked under his upper arm. Whether Philip went or stayed was a private family matter after all.

But as we were on the point of taking our leave yet another significant little trifle was added to all the rest. And again Monty Rooke provided the occasion.

Monty, I ought to say, is one of these fellows who, whenever any odd job is to do, especially a domestic one, instinctively seems to take it upon himself. I dare say his living in rooms and studios hardly big enough to turn around in has made him methodical in his habits. It was Monty, for example, who had looked out the train in the Time Table; it was Monty who had picked up the jar of curaçao when Esdaile had let it fall to the floor; and it was Monty who, just as the rest of us were leaving, wandered off towards the studio, presently returned again, sought the kitchen, and reappeared with a sweeping-brush.

"What are you going to do with that?" Philip asked, seeing him making for the studio again.

"I thought I'd just sweep up that broken glass," Monty replied.

"Better leave it," Philip answered.

Monty carried the brush back to the kitchen again, and presently wandered off to the studio once more. Esdaile must have had eyes in the back of his head, for I, who was facing the studio, had not seen Monty preparing to draw back the roof-blinds again.

"I wouldn't bother about that just at present," Esdaile called rather loudly. "Just see if there's a train about tea-time, do you mind?"

Monty, once more returning, took up the Time Table again. Philip walked with us to the door. Then another little exclamation broke from him. Monty had put down the Time Table and had asked him for the cellar key.

"What on earth do you want the cellar key for?" Philip demanded.

"To put this jar of stuff back," Monty replied. "It won't be wanted now."

Hereupon Philip broke out with a petulance that struck me as entirely disproportionate, if indeed there had been any occasion for petulance at all.

"Oh, we can do that any time. We've got all the rest of the day to ourselves, haven't we? Sit down and smoke a cigarette or something; you've done about enough for one morning—"

It was then that we left.

PART II

WHAT HAPPENED OUTSIDE

I

It may have already struck you that while Esdaile, a responsible house-holder directly interested in any unusual occurrence on his premises, had not once been into his garden to see what the trouble was, I myself, a journalist with quite a good "news story" in the wind, had shown little more eagerness. Well, I will explain that. In the first place, we have our own reporters, who do that kind of thing far better than I can. Next, however interesting things outside might have been, I had found them quite interesting enough inside. But my real reason was this:

Rooke had said that both these aviators were civilians. Well, as regards civilian flying, we on the *Circus* had something that for want of a better name I will call a policy. To speak quite frankly, this policy was a supine one enough, and merely consisted in waiting for a definite lead.

As you know, no such thing as a definite lead existed. Except for war purposes, the future use of flying was at that time the blankest of blanks. It is true we talked a good deal about it, but that was merely our highly special-ized way of saying nothing and filling space at the same time. Nobody admit-ted this lack more readily than those who had drawn up the provisional Regu-lations. These were merely experimental, any accident might change them at any moment, and, in one word, all our experience was still to be earned.

For this reason, I was just as much interested in opinion about the facts as I was in the facts themselves, and already I was looking forward to an exchange of views with Hubbard and Mackwith.

But time had flown. Both Hubbard and Mackwith had appointments for which they were already late, the one at the Admiralty, the other in the Temple. I therefore parted from them at Sloane Square Station, and, being in no great hurry myself, turned back along King's Road. What I was in search of was a representative public-house. We have all heard of "the man in the street." You often get even closer to the heart of things when you listen to the man in the pub.

I think it was the sight of a plumpish young man in a horsey brown coat that settled my choice of pub. For a moment I couldn't remember where I had seen that or a similar coat before; then it flashed upon me. A man in just such a coat had preceded that ladder that had been passed over the heads of the crowd in Lennox Street, and he or somebody very like him had managed to get inside Esdaile's gate and to secure a privileged position within a few feet of the mulberry tree in which the parachute had lodged.

I followed this coat through two glittering swing-doors a little way round the corner from the King's Road, and found myself in a closely-packed Saloon Bar full of tobacco-smoke and noise.

II

I will venture to say that the man I followed was never shut out of a tube-lift in his life, however crowded it was. He jostled through the throng about the counter as if it had been so much water. I learned presently that he had had no sort of interest or proprietorship whatever in that ladder that had been passed along Lennox Street. Seeing a ladder approaching he had merely pushed himself forward, had placed himself at the head of it, and, with energetic elbowings and loud cries of "Make way there!" had made it to all intents and purposes his own, squeezing himself in at Esdaile's gate with such nice judgment that the very next man had been shut out. He called this "managing it a treat," and I further gathered that neat things like this usually did happen when Harry Westbury was anywhere about.

The aeroplane accident had at any rate given the licensed trade a fillip that morning. When I asked for a glass of beer I was curtly told, "Only port, sherry and liqueur-brandy—three shillings." Yet many a three shillings was cheerfully paid. Nothing so stimulates conviviality as an undercurrent of tragedy. Apparently half Chelsea had given up all thought of further work before lunch, and in my Saloon Bar there were already signs that more than a few would make a day of it.

And so bit by bit I managed to edge myself nearer to Mr. Harry Westbury.

I dare say you know the kind of man. If the house had a billiard-room upstairs no doubt he had his private cue in it, as well as his private shaving-pot at the barber's round the corner. For all his freshness and plumpness, there was nothing of the jovial about him. Either he had no humor, or he did not intend that humor should stand in his way through the world. His convex blue eyes were hard and bullying, and his rosebud of a mouth never blossomed into a smile. Probably his wife had a thin time of it. But she would have as good a fur coat as any of her neighbors.

He was holding forth as I drew near on what he called this "Tom, Dick and Harry sort of flying."

"And here you have the proof of it," he was saying, his fingers pronged into four empty glasses and his hard eyes looking defiantly round. "Look at the damage to property alone! What price these air-raids? Three—million— pounds in the City in one night! That's my information as an estate-agent. Three—million—pounds! And now everybody's going to start. What I want to know is, is it peace or war we're living in? That's what I want to know!"

He also wanted to know whether it was the same again—the three-shilling brandy. He was "not to a shilling or two" that morning. It was only right that as a spectator from the reserved enclosure he should "put his hand down."

"I wasn't thinking of property; I was thinking of those two poor lads," a gray old man said from his seat near the automatic music-box. I happened to know him by sight as old William Dadley, the picture-frame maker— "Daddy" of the fledgling artists of the King's Road.

But Westbury would have no weak sentiment of this kind. There was a blood-and-iron ring in his voice as he set the brandy down.

"Poor lads be blowed!" he said. "They know the risks, don't they? They're paid for it, I suppose? What I want to know is who's going to put his hand in his pocket if they start coming down on top of those houses we're building in Wimbledon or where I live in Lennox Place there? Let 'em break their necks if they want, but not on my roof! The world isn't going to stop for a broken neck or two. I *don't* think!"

"Well, tell us all about it, Harry," somebody said; and Mr. Westbury, taking the middle of a small circle, did so.

I am not going to trouble you with all he said, but only with as much as I saw fit to make a mental note of. At this stage of our Case he was simply a vain and interfering busybody, who had had a rather better view of things than anybody else. But first of all I noted the obstinacy with which he dwelt on the fact that Monty Rooke had been first on the roof, several minutes before the arrival of the police. There was, of course, nothing in this, excepting always Westbury's dull insistence on it.

Next, he described in detail the bringing-down of the two men. There was nothing remarkable here either, except that the living one had "kept on moving his hand all the time like this"—illustrated by an aimless fluttering of the right hand, now a few inches this way, now a few inches that.

But I had an involuntary start when Mr. Westbury pompously announced that he "had offered himself to Inspector Webster as a witness in case he should be wanted." It was, of course, just what such a fellow would do, if only out of vain officiousness, and I don't quite know why I didn't like the sound of it. I had gone into that Saloon Bar to glean, if possible, what people at large thought of flying over London, what their temper would be if there were very much of this, and similar things; but instead I had apparently hit on some sort of a human bramble, who hooked himself on everywhere with a tenacity out of all proportion to the value of any fruit he was likely to bear, and who would scratch unpleasantly when you tried to dislodge him. There was nothing to be uneasy about, but the whole of the events of that morning were so far inexplicable, and to that extent intimidating.

"Yes, me and Inspector Webster will probably be having a talk about things this evening," Mr. Westbury continued with hearty relish. "We're neighbors in Lennox Place, the very street behind Lennox Street—you can see right across from my bedroom window. So I had my choice of two good views in a manner of speaking.... Five-and-twenty to two. Not worth while going home for lunch now. May as well be hung for a sheep as a lamb. I wonder if they've got a snack of anything here?"

If they had I have not the least doubt he got it.

III

Musingly I mounted an eastward-bound bus and sought my office. The more I thought things over the less able I became to shake off the sense of accumulating trifles, of gathering events. And it was as I passed through Pimlico that yet another incident, temporarily forgotten, came back into my mind. This was the curious way in which Esdaile had snapped—it had been a snap—when Rooke had wanted to sweep up the broken picture-glass, to draw the studio blinds back again, and to return the bottle of curaçao to its place in the cellar. "You've done enough for one morning," Esdaile had said. What had Monty done that was "enough"?

Now I have known Monty Rooke, as I told you, for a dozen years, and in that time I have learned not to be surprised at anything he does provided it is sufficiently out of the way, unprofitable to himself, and unlike anything an ordinary person would have done. I will give you an instance of what I mean.

A year or two before there had arrived one night at his studio a bundle of washing, fresh from the laundry. This bundle, on being opened, had proved to contain a fully-developed infant girl of a fortnight old, no doubt the pledge of some unknown laundrymaid's betrayed trust. As a joke you will see the possibilities of this, particularly in the merry Chelsea Arts Club; but don't imagine that Monty was a butt. What he did was enough to dispel that idea. He had immediately wanted to adopt the foundling, and would certainly have done so but for the strong dissuasion of his friends; whereupon he had made a drawing instead, a drawing quite singular for its wistfulness and emotion and depth, of the infant just as it had arrived, with the newly-ironed shirts and socks for its cot, deriving none knew whence, cast for none knew what part in Life, save for Monty friendless, the close of one obscure drama but the beginning of another.

That was Monty, our little friend of the warm, unprofitable impulses, the shy and easily daunted manner, but also of the quiet persistence of purpose that kept him afloat in his seas of petty difficulties and enabled him once in a while to produce a drawing or a painting that you returned to again and again, a bit of philosophy that cut clean down to the quick of things, or—an indiscretion that it would hardly have occurred to one in a million to commit.

What was there between him and Esdaile now?

IV

The moment I reached the office I rang up the *Record*, our evening sheet. But their reporters were still out, and nobody could yet tell me anything about the accident I didn't already know. Willett, my young colleague on the *Circus*, did not propose to give the story exceptional treatment.

"If the thing caught fire in the air we'll let it alone," he said. "Fire's too much of a bugbear. We want the joy-riding idiot and the lunatic who stunts over towns. I'm for letting it alone, but we'll wait and see what the others do."

He was quite right. On its merits as Publicity it looked as if we should hear little more of the Case. I settled down to my work.

I had not actually expected that Hubbard would ring me up, but I was not greatly surprised when, at about four o'clock, he did so. He wanted to know whether I could go round to the Admiralty at once. That we must have a talk at the earliest possible moment was a foregone conclusion. I therefore replied that I would be on my way in ten minutes, and, hastily swallowing the cup of tea that had been placed on my desk and telling Willett to carry on, I took up my hat and stick, sought the lift, threaded my way through the *Record's* carts and bicycles and boarded a passing motor-bus in Fleet Street.

I had no very clear notion of the nature of the job that kept Hubbard in town that spring, and that had caused him to envy Esdaile his luck in being able to get away into the country. Indeed, I can tell you very little about the organization of that mysterious Service that moves, familiar yet isolated, in our midst. I understood that originally he had been a torpedo man, but had later been drafted into the Inventions branch. It is quite possible that the scope of his work had been expressly left rather ill-defined. So many amazing extemporizations had to be hurriedly made and applied.

Still, these war-improvisations have to be overhauled afterwards, so that it may be seen which disappear with the emergency, and which are to be permanently incorporated in the strategy of the future; and I knew that one at any rate of Hubbard's tasks was to explain to a certain Parliamentary Committee a number of technical and basic facts that have a way of not varying very much however the political situation may change.

I found him alone in his room on the third floor. The screen just within the door was so disposed that, in the spot to which your eyes naturally turned on entering, the officer you had come to see was not. They are old in cunning in the Senior Service, and I had never seen Hubbard at work before. His voice came to me from quite a different part of the room, and I had the feeling that if I had been a stranger there would have been a moment in which I should have been pretty thoroughly looked up and down.

"Come in and take a pew," he said. "Hope I haven't fetched you away from anything important. But I couldn't stop to talk this morning. I only got rid of my By-election Blighters half an hour ago. Well—"

And, as I sat down in the chair at the end of his desk, he plunged straight into the matter by asking me how long I had known Esdaile.

Now how long you have known a man, in the sense of how well you know him, is not always simply a matter of time. I have told you how humdrum my own War services were. They had not included those incredible moments of intensified action that may more truly reveal a man to you than years of desultory familiarity. It was plainly something of this kind that Hubbard had in his mind now. He frowned as he trifled with a paper-weight.

"No, it's absolutely unaccountable," he broke out suddenly, putting the paper-weight down with a slap. "He's not that kind of man. It simply doesn't fit in."

"His behavior this morning, you mean?"

"Yes. It was another man altogether. Why, before I knew Esdaile well I remember I bet him a supper that he'd drop his palette on the quarter-deck when the first shell came over. Well, it came, and half the bridge was wrecked, and he never turned a hair. Just carried on with that sketch of Hopkins at the range-finder. Absolutely undefeated sportsman. So why should he behave as he did this morning?"

Hereupon—though not as throwing very much light on the question after all—I told Hubbard of my own surmise with regard to Rooke. He looked rather quickly up.

"What, little Queerfellow? He's—er—all right, isn't he? What about him? Tell me about him."

This too I told him as well as I was able. And I may say that I noted with pleasure, as perhaps the real beginning of a valued friendship, that there did not seem to be any question in Hubbard's mind as to what kind of man I was myself. He was quite content to accept my summing-up of Monty.

"So it's between 'em, you think, whatever it is?"

"Or else I give it up," I replied.

"I wonder if you're right," he mused.... "But then," he added suddenly, "what about all that time he spent in the cellar?"

From that point our conversation took for a time a curious little turn.

For Hubbard, while seeming to have no explanation that as a sensible man he must not reject as fantastic, seemed nevertheless to be reluctant to let something go. He seemed to hint and to dismiss and then to hint again, to come to the brink of saying something and then to leave it unsaid after all. And again I had the feeling that though he had known Philip Esdaile for only two years as against my twenty, in some things he might be the familiar and I the outsider.

Then again he seemed to decide to take a risk. He spoke to the paper-weight in his palm.

"You don't happen to know anything about these new sound-appliances, do you?" he asked.

"No. Which are they?"

"Oh, there are a lot of 'em," he answered again, half evasively. "There's sound-ranging, of course. Then there's the hydrophone. And as a matter of fact the best brains in the world today are trying to cut-out sound—aeroplane propellers and so on.... What I mean is Esdaile's not hearing anything. I suppose it's just possible that he didn't. All a matter of where the sound-wave hits. You remember the broken windows in the Strand when Fritz used to come over and drop his eggs? First a broken one, then two or three whole ones, then broken ones again, all along the street? Well, this might have been one of those dumb intervals. Otherwise he *must* have heard. And I should have thought he'd have felt the vibration too."

"He's admitted he thought he heard something."

"Pooh, there was no mistaking it. If he didn't recognize it we can take it he didn't hear it. If we believe him, of course."

"Don't you believe him?"

"Yes," Hubbard answered without a moment's hesitation.

"Then—?"

"Oh, I suppose it means I'm on the wrong track," Hubbard replied.

Naturally any track of that nature was totally unexplored by me; but I was far from dismissing it on that account. Here again my ignorance of modern War came in to humble me. For what is the good of saying things are fantastic and far-fetched—sound-ranging and the selenium cell and what not—when for a number of years the food we have eaten and the clothes we have worn and the roofs over our heads have depended on just such fantasies? Not for nothing were those clusters of listening cones at Hyde Park Corner and on Parliament Hill, not for nothing those wireless masts over our heads at that very moment. Their operation might be unfamiliar to me, but these things were the daily business of Commander Hubbard, R.N. He turned as naturally to them as I myself turn to those equally mysterious things, a man's motives and the operative emotions of his heart.

"For all that," said Hubbard abruptly, "I should like to have a good look at that cellar of his."

I was silent. I didn't know whether his wish to see the cellar included sound-experiments on the roof also.

"More than that," he continued slowly, "—by the way, did Mrs. Esdaile and the children get away?"

That I did not know.

"Well, what about going round this evening to see?"

"The chances are that they did if I know Philip."

"I don't mean that. I mean what about going round to see that cellar," Hubbard replied.

I didn't say so, but I had a sudden wonder, quite new and born all at once of I don't know what, whether Esdaile might want us to see his cellar.

V

However, we went, and at a little after eight o'clock rang the bell we had rung under such very different circumstances at breakfast-time that morning. The parachute still waved in the mulberry, and a few policemen were unobtrusively hanging about the street. Two of these did not move very far from the gate. I supposed that in view of pending inquiries it was important that the parachute should not be touched.

We waited so long for an answer after ringing the bell that I had almost concluded there was nobody at home. We were, in fact, on the point of turning away when Esdaile himself opened the door.

Poor devil! I learned presently that he had had callers enough that afternoon to make him wish to disconnect his bell altogether—interested parties of all sorts, a dozen of them at least. He had as a matter of fact removed his telephone receiver from the hook. He said its ringing had nearly driven him mad.

But even all this did not explain his weariness as he stood holding the door open in the still bright light of the perfect evening. My first glance at him made me wonder whether something even more untoward than that morning's sudden drama had happened. Before, his manner, baffling as it had been, had at least had a sort of hectic brilliancy, an artificial excitement that had buoyed him up and kept him going. Now it was as unlike that as possible. He was spiritless and played out. He no longer seemed to wish to keep everything and everybody at arm's-length. Indeed, we had his reason almost before he had closed the door behind us.

"Of course, you've heard who it is?" he said to Hubbard in a dull voice.

"No. Who?"

"Chummy Smith."

Only the fanlight over the door let in the last of the day, but it did not need light to reveal how the name Esdaile had spoken affected Hubbard. To me this name conveyed nothing for the moment. I heard Hubbard's indraught of breath.

"You don't say so! Good God! Which? The dead one?"

"No. The other. I happened to ring up the hospital to ask how he was going on and learned that way. That was before I took that infernal receiver off. Come in. I'm all alone."

"Your people got away, then?"

"Yes," said Esdaile. And I fancied I heard him grunt, "Thank God!"

"Who's the other chap?" Hubbard asked as we walked along the passage.

"Fellow called Maxwell. Never heard of him. Did you?"

"No."

"Well, come in. It's the devil, isn't it?"

I suppose it *is* the devil when one of your particular friends comes down like this on your roof; but it struck me even then that it would have been still more devilish if he had been killed in doing so. Yet not only had their friend Chummy not been killed, but, according to Rooke's account earlier in the day, he was in a fair way for recovery. Hence I didn't quite see the reason for Esdaile's utter dejection. I should have understood it better had their friend been, not Smith, but the dead man Maxwell.

You see, I had totally forgotten one pretty little incident of that morning's breakfast. Perhaps you have forgotten it too. Remember, then, that Philip had pared an apple for Joan Merrow, had told her to see what initial the paring made on the floor, and had shaped his own guess with his lips—"C for Ch"— as he had hidden his bit of paper under his napkin.

Philip pushed up chairs for us and pottered about in search of whisky and glasses. Then, having set out a tray, he dropped heavily into a chair. For a time none of us spoke, and then I asked if Rooke was out.

"Yes. He's taken Audrey Cunningham home," Philip replied with marked brevity, and the silence fell on us again.

If Hubbard had really come for the purpose of seeing Esdaile's cellar I could see that all thought of this had now passed from his mind. The first thing to do was to cheer Esdaile up. After all, Chummy was alive and doing well. The news when Esdaile had rung up the hospital that afternoon had been reassuring. It might be some little time before he was out and about again, but certainly the occasion did not seem one for gloom. I therefore kept silence while Hubbard pointed all this out.

And as Esdaile's spirits seemed to revive a little and things began to seem not quite so hopeless after all, I began to rummage in my memory for recollection of this Chummy Smith of theirs. I remembered now that I had at any rate heard his name. And I confess that I am a little curious, not to say jealous, about some of these intensive War friendships. It interests me to note which of them survive the quieter and more persistent pressure on the lower levels, and which fail to do so. Not every one of them succeeds. It is one thing to wait in a Mess for the overdue chum, trying not to look too often at the full glass of gin-and-bitters that by this time he ought to have come in and claimed, and quite another to meet that chum a year or two later and, as you ask him what he will have, to know that you are making the swift mental note, "Ah, *that's* him in mufti!"

But this rubicon had been safely crossed in the case of Chummy Smith. I began to piece together odd things I had heard. Philip, meeting him in Coventry Street six months before, had stopped, spoken, and had presently brought him home to a scratch supper. A fortnight later Chummy had dropped in again unannounced. Thereafter he had continued to come at fairly frequent intervals. He and myself had never happened to call at the same moment, that was all.

"Who do you say he's flying for now?" Hubbard asked presently.

"The Aiglon Company. He's a goodish bunch of shares in it, I believe. Knows his job, too. Ever see him zoom?"

He described Smith's performance of this terrifying maneuver, with the fire of the Lewis gun reserved till the last twenty yards, then the fiery bridge-clearing rafale, and the upshooting like a rocket as he cleared the rail by a yard.

"Yes, he's a dashed good youngster," Hubbard agreed. "Thank the Lord he's all right."

But Esdaile only leaned his head wearily on one hand and sat gazing moodily at his whisky-and-soda.

Then it was that the probable reason for all this depression flashed upon me. Then it was, in that moment, that I remembered that apple-paring, Joan's adorable little schoolgirl's outbreak, and her tucking away of that piece of paper into her breast. Philip Esdaile was thirty-nine, young Smith twenty-four; that is a difference of fifteen years; but a young man of twenty-four could be quite devoted to Methuselah himself if there was a young woman anywhere about. Those frequent calls after that meeting in Coventry Street simply meant that Philip's leg had been pulled. Chummy Smith was no doubt very fond of Philip, but he was even fonder of Philip's wife's help and companion.

And Joan had seen the crash.

No wonder Philip thanked God that she didn't know who it was she had seen come down.

VI

I know now the exact point up to which I was right, and also where I ceased to be right. Mollie Esdaile made a clean breast of the whole guileful conspiracy of their courtship afterwards. Here it is, for your edification and warning.

Mollie had several times been down to visit Philip in his billet at the Helmsea Station. There it was that she had first seen Chummy. At first she had not been able to single out Chummy from the rest of the uniformed mob that led such a mysterious existence down there—a world of womenless men, who paraded at all hours of the day and night, suddenly vanished by the half week together, turned up smiling again, danced with one another to the grinding of gramophones, played cards and snooker, howled round pianos and swapped yarns, Kirchners and pink gins. To Mollie their uniforms were of two kinds only, khaki and dark blue. In course of time she had come to pick out Chummy as wearing both—khaki, but with the rings and shoulder-badges of the other Service. The lad made Philip ask him to tea, and the next time, in Philip's absence, Chummy had asked her to tea.

And so to the sky-blue uniforms and the monochrome of mufti again, by which time Chummy and Mollie were firm friends.

I believe she threw the youngsters together from the moment Philip first brought Chummy home to Lennox Street. She says she didn't, and refers me to Joan. I wouldn't hang a dog on what Miss Joan says on such a matter.

For who can believe in the candor of a young woman of just twenty who, the very first time a young man is brought to the house, straightway enters into a clandestine arrangement to meet him at tea the next day, and presently can hold out her hand with a conventional "Good-by, Mr. Smith," as if the last thing that entered her head was that she would ever set eyes on him again? It takes the nerve of the modern young woman to do that. The case of Mr. Smith, observe, is entirely different. Mr. Smith, suddenly meeting the lovely young thing, may not be sure whether his feet are treading a polished studio floor or whether they have little Mercury wings on them that waft him through the empyrean; but there is this to be said for Mr. Smith—that when he is in love he doesn't behave as if he wasn't. He fidgets even if she goes out of the room for a minute. He doesn't know that she herself couldn't tell him why she has gone out of the room. He thinks she had something to go for, and never dreams that she is just sitting on the edge of her bed, knowing perfectly well that he will be leaving in half an hour, asking herself what made her so suddenly get up and leave him, and yet not even writing him a note.

The notes came later, at about the time she put a lock on her letter-case. They were numbered "1," "2" and "3" to indicate the sequence in which they should be read (a billet scribbled at seven o'clock in the evening must on no account be read before one that is dashed off at tea-time), and they were constantly on the wing.

Nor did these protégés of Mollie's choose tea-shops that Philip was known to frequent, nor cinemas the kindly gloom of which might by any chance have concealed him. Philip never noticed that his monthly telephone accounts rose perceptibly higher. True, he did ask one evening why the children had been put to bed while it was still broad day, but he was not told that he might find the reason walking hand-in-hand under the trees in Richmond Park.

It is no good asking whether Joan and Chummy were engaged. What is a young woman's engagement nowadays? No doubt Joan's father had in his day ceremoniously "waited upon" her maternal grandfather-elect and had "had the honor" and so on, but Miss Joan always reminded me of the private with the field-marshal's baton—she seemed to have come into the world with a will of her own, a latch-key and her marriage-lines all potentially complete. I remember she called an engagement an "understanding." If by that word she meant what the Psalmist meant, she certainly made haste with all her heart to get it.

Of course, Philip had sooner or later discovered what was going on under his abused roof, and now knew all there was to be known about it. And it must have occurred to him also that, with letters numbered "1," "2" and "3" flying backwards and forwards all the time, any interruption of more than a day or two would set Joan, away in Santon, Yorks, anxiously wondering what was the matter.

You are now to see how far I was right in this.

VII

The lights he had switched on were a couple of standard lamps only, that worked from plugs in the wall. Both had mignonette-colored shades, and while one shade stood a-tilt near the syphon and glasses, the other threw a soft light on Philip's little escritoire. As he sat the light crossed his breast only, leaving his face in a half-transparent obscurity. A few yards away the entrance to the studio made a dead black oblong, so completely without trace of the evening light that must still be lingering in the world outside that I judged that the dark-blue roof-blinds were still drawn.

I suppose it was these roof-blinds, and Philip's apparent disinclination to have them touched, that brought my surmises with regard to Monty Rooke into my mind again. And somehow, back again under the roof where the tragedy had happened, these surmises seemed to have grown a little more threatening. Why this alteration of values should take place in me I didn't know, but there it undeniably was, hovering (so to speak) in the spaces above the unlighted chandelier, approaching as it were to the very edge of the penumbra that crossed our host's breast, and accumulated as in some dark power-house beyond the threshold of the black studio doorway. And as this feeling grew on me lesser feelings seemed by comparison to grow less still. My hastily-seized-on explanation with regard to Joan seemed all at once insufficient. A shock of some kind she would naturally receive; that was unavoidable in any event; but what would be simpler than to write to her immediately, to tell her what had been discovered since her departure, to promise to send her daily bulletins, and to warn her that for the present, in the absence of letters, these must suffice?

I didn't know to what extent I was supposed to be privy to the Chummy-Smith-Joan-Merrow love affair, but in the circumstances I did not let that trouble me. I just said what I thought. "She'll have to be told some time or other," I finished by saying.

But for some reason or other he waved my words aside.

"Wouldn't do at all." His voice came from within the shade of the mignonette-colored lamp. "Must think of something better than that."

"But she'll be expecting letters. And she won't get them. My way's much the kindest. What's the objection?"

"Oh, heaps of objection," he answered evasively. "I don't know half of 'em myself yet."

On this I instantly fastened.

"Ah! Then you haven't seen the fellow yet you spoke of?"

I knew I had him. I could feel his mental wriggle.

"What fellow?"

"You said this morning it wasn't your affair, but somebody else's. The fellow I mean is the somebody else."

He spoke slowly.

"Do you mean Rooke?"

"You didn't mention any name. I mean Rooke if it was Rooke."

This time we had to wait a long time for an answer, but at any rate it cleared the air when it did come.

"It was Rooke. I don't remember very clearly exactly what I did say, but I meant Rooke," he admitted.

"You say he's taken Mrs. Cunningham home. He's coming back, I suppose?"

With remarkable grimness Philip replied, "You bet he is."

"You mean you told him to?"

"Yes, and I told him to be pretty quick unless he wanted to drive me crazy. I said I'd give him time for dinner at the Parrakeet, though. I was waiting for him when you came in."

"Then—well, to put it plainly, do you want us to clear off?"

"No—at any rate wait a bit," he answered irresolutely. "I don't suppose he'll be long now."

I don't know how much longer we should have continued to spar like this had not Hubbard suddenly put a question. He had evidently been thinking it over for some time, and he took care, with a preliminary "I say" and a pause, that he had Esdaile's attention before putting it.

"I say," he said quietly, "about when you came up from below this morning. Why did you want to brush Rooke's clothes?"

And that settled it. Esdaile began with one more "Did I?" but Hubbard did not let him finish.

"Yes, you did," he cut him short. "It was the very first thing you did. And he jumped back when you tried to touch him. Why?"

There was no further attempt at prevarication. Without even taking the trouble to rise, Esdaile pushed back the lamp, opened the upper drawer of the escritoire as he sat, and from the corner of it drew out and placed on the table a 7.65 mm. Webley and Scott automatic pistol.

VIII

Honestly, I don't know whether I was surprised or not. On the whole I hardly think I was. If he had produced another candlestick or jar of liqueur I think I should have felt like getting up and walking out; but here at last was something on the fuller scale. Thank heaven, we had done with broken glass and sweeping-brushes and dark blue linen blinds. We might now hope to get a little farther.

For a pistol is a pistol at all times and all the world over. No other weapon has quite so exclusively sinister a meaning. Among the honorable swords and rifles of war it is a low and sneaking thing, and in peace-time an Apache's tool, something for the common garrotter to shoot through his pocket with. Its proper place was the Criminal Museum at Scotland Yard, not in a decent artist's studio.

So Philip put the revolting thing on his desk, and for a moment we sat looking at its roughened grip, black as crape, and the glossy blackness of the rest of it. Then without a word Hubbard took it up, glanced at the safety-catch and slid back the breach. A cartridge lay ready in the chamber. Then he withdrew the magazine. Six nickel steel bullets showed through the perforations of the clip. The capacity of the W. & S. 7.65 is eight shots. One shot had therefore been fired.

Hubbard replaced the pistol on the desk.

"And where did *that* come from?" he asked with pursed lips.

Philip shrugged his shoulders. Somehow the answer was "Rooke" as plainly as if he had spoken the name.

"And where did he get it?"

"Up there." Philip's eyes made the slightest of turns up towards the ceiling.

"From one of those two fellows?"

"I suppose so."

"How do you mean, you 'suppose' so? Don't you know?"

"I'm not perfectly sure yet. You see, just at that moment Audrey Cunningham came in, and it isn't the kind of thing you discuss with women there. I thought she'd gone, or I should have waited a bit."

"Well, don't you think it's time you told us a little more now?"

This is the narrative that followed, with that beastly object still lying there in the silky light of the mignonette-shaded lamp.

IX

At first Monty had tried to get out of it by saying it was the keys. Esdaile's is not a modern house; its keys are not of the Yale kind, of which you can carry a dozen in one pocket; each of them is anything from three to five inches long, and they weigh very few to the pound. In handing over the house to Monty, Philip had given him eight or ten of these; and so at first (Esdaile said) Rooke had wanted to say it was the keys.

"I don't mean the keys," Philip had replied. "I mean the pocket on the other side that you're nursing as if it had eggs in it. Why have you been standing sideways and behind people all this time? And why did you jump when I wanted to give you a dust-down this morning?"

Esdaile's face became animated as at last he warmed up to it all. He spoke almost vehemently.

"You see," he said, "I wasn't going to have any more damned nonsense. I had quite enough of that—hours of it—all this that I'm telling you took place just after tea. So I was as short as you please. Pity I spoke quite so soon, but I really thought Audrey'd gone. And the idiot hadn't even put the safety-catch on," he added with disgust.

There was no need to urge him now. He was as resolved to tell his story as before he had been reticent. The only unfortunate thing was that until Monty should return he had so little to tell.

"So when he saw the key story wouldn't do he fetched out this pretty little article," he continued, rapping with his knuckle on the writing-desk. "Just like a kid caught stealing apples he was. I asked him where he got it, and he said on the roof. Then he told me all about you fellows going up into the bathroom, and how he'd been the one to crawl along the gutter because he doesn't weigh as much as either of you."

"But which of 'em gave it to him—Chummy or the other man?" Hubbard asked.

"Well, I'm not so sure that either of them really 'gave' it to him," Esdaile replied. "He began to be a bit of a mule when I pressed him about that. And of course I asked Monty all this before I knew it was Chummy at all, and Monty doesn't know that yet, though I don't think he ever met Chummy. No, as far as I can make out, the pistol was lying on the roof, just out of Chummy's reach, and he kept pointing to it—moving his hand like this."

The gesture Esdaile made was the very gesture I had seen Mr. Harry Westbury make in the Saloon Bar earlier in the day.

"So he just picked it up and put it into his pocket?"

"Just that. Simple, isn't it?"

"And it's been fired?"

"As you see."

"Innocent young man. What did he do during the War?"

"Camouflage," Esdaile replied. "In Kensington Gardens there. Imitation haystacks and dummy O.P. trees and gunpit-screens and painting tanks and so on. Making anything look like what it isn't. Just what he would do."

"Does he know this thing's been fired?"

"That I can't tell you. Audrey came in then."

And that was the answer to all our further questions—Audrey had then come in. Esdaile had as a matter of fact now told us all that had taken place between himself and Monty Rooke. For further information we must wait until Monty's return.

You may imagine, however, that I had now quite a lot of food for thought. In the first place, Rooke had taken it upon himself to conceal a highly material fact from the police. Whether Esdaile yet shared this responsibility was at present debatable. Audrey Cunningham's interruption half-way through Monty's story rather obscured the moral aspect of this last. One does not set weighty machinery going for trifles, and for all we knew Monty, when he arrived, might have a complete explanation. In the meantime Esdaile was probably wise to hold his hand.

A pistol, however, had undoubtedly been fired, and, as a further examination of the barrel showed, probably recently. And, if you remember, there was that small round hole in the starred roof-glass of the studio that I had at first assumed to have been caused by the broken mulberry branch. A pistol-bullet might have made just such a hole.

Next I remembered how Esdaile had been occupied when Hubbard and I had followed him into the studio shortly after his return from the cellar. He had been so engrossed in poking about the broken glass and mats on the studio floor that he had seemed to notice little else. Had he been looking for the bullet that had made that hole in the roof? And why had he had the roof-blinds drawn, and broken out on Monty when he had wanted to put them back again? This last, I admit, set me all at sea again. The drawing of the blinds would certainly hide the bullet-hole in the pane from anybody *in*side the house, supposing he wished to hide it; but what about the police who had been on the roof itself at that very moment? The drawing of the blinds inside would hide nothing from them. Why seek to conceal from the rest of us something that if they cared to investigate they could hardly fail to see?

One more thing. If that pistol had been fired on the premises, somewhere there must be, not only a bullet, but a spent case also. I mentioned this, and Esdaile gave a slight start of recollection.

"Of course!" he exclaimed. "Glad you mentioned that. I found the case in the garden. Here it is. I'd honestly forgotten all about it."

And, as he fetched it out of his waistcoat pocket and put it down by the side of the pistol, I as honestly believed he had.

"But there's no sign of the bullet?" I asked.

"I've looked high and low for it," Esdaile replied. "Low, I should say, because naturally I don't want to go hunting about the roof in the daylight. Too many eyes about. There's no trace of it."

"But it wouldn't be on the roof if it made that hole in the glass. It would be in the studio. Or possibly," I ventured, "in the cellar."

But, as Esdaile was about to reply, a bell trilled in the kitchen, and, with a "That's Rooke, I expect," Esdaile put the pistol and the empty case back into the drawer, motioned us to remain where we were, and went out.

X

Philip had described Rooke quite well when he had said that he had the air of a naughty boy caught robbing an orchard. He had a hang-dog yet defiant look as he entered, shepherded in by Philip as if we had been a tribunal empaneled for his condemnation. But there was relief in his face too—the relief of one who has got the worst over and hardly fears the rest. And, as he threw his hat on the table and looked round in search of a chair, he unconsciously emphasized his air of boyish guilt by sitting down on a low stool that stood between the empty fireplace and the escritoire.

Esdaile began immediately, as if Rooke had merely been out of the room for a few moments.

"Well, to continue our chat, Monty," he said. "I've told these fellows as much as you've told me. Shall we have the rest of it now?"

From the look on Monty's face I began to think that we might have some difficulty in getting very much more out of him, for the simple reason that, in picking up and concealing an incriminating pistol, he evidently didn't see that he had done anything at all out of the way. He seemed to think that was a natural thing to have done. I gathered also that there was something further on his mind, something that had already begun to dawn on my own and has doubtless occurred to you also. But we will come to that presently.

So Monty merely repeated what we already knew, and then looked from one to another of us as if to ask, "*Now* were we satisfied?"

"Oh, we want to know a good deal more than that," Esdaile continued. "First of all, did he speak? The man who pointed to the pistol, I mean."

"No. He'd taken too bad a toss for that," Monty replied. "He just pointed, the way I showed you, and I thought perhaps he didn't want the thing lying about, so I—well, I obliged him, so to speak."

"But it's been fired."

"I don't know anything about that. I didn't fire it, if that's what you mean."

"It's been fired recently. Did you notice if it was warm?"

"No, I didn't," said Monty, ruffling up, "and it's all very well you fellows talking, sitting down here with glasses of whisky in front of you, but I'll bet if you'd been in my place you'd have done exactly the same."

Here I struck in. I asked him what made him so sure of that. He turned his earnest brown eyes to me.

"I mean you just would. If you'd seen him, I mean—seen his face. It was the look in his eyes; I couldn't get it out of my mind for hours; I can see it now. I tell you you missed a pretty rotten job by not having to go up there, and here you go asking me if pistols were warm and who fired them and all about it as if I'd been having a fortnight's holiday up there."

I saw Monty's point. I suppose I have arrived at that stage of life when I too trust my eyes more and more as time goes on. Men may have all sorts of reasons for saying one thing and meaning another, but he is a remarkable man who can control his looks with the same facility. I have seen many eyes telling the truth while the lips beneath them have told the practiced lie. So if Monty had taken his impulse from Chummy Smith's anguished eyes in that moment, I for one did not feel inclined to blame him.

"You've heard who it was, haven't you?" I said.

"No. Who?"

Philip told him. His eyes opened very wide.

"Not the fellow I've heard you talk about?"

Esdaile nodded gloomily.

"And you mean *he* fired the pistol?"

There was an embarrassed silence. Nobody so far had ventured to express his thought quite so nakedly. We had an obscure feeling of resentment, as if Monty had been a little lacking in tact. He sat up on his stool and pursed his lips into the shape of a whistle.

"I—say! *That* makes it the dickens, doesn't it? Well, I know what his eyes looked like, I can promise you that! Poor devil! Thank goodness you were all too busy watching Philip when he came up from down below to notice me much. Nobody noticed me except Audrey, and she—"

Philip sliced his words off like a guillotine.

"You haven't told her anything about this, have you?"

Monty stared at him. "No," he replied, "as a matter of fact I haven't; but what if I had? I don't quite see—"

"Then you see you jolly well don't," Philip curtly ordered him. "Four's quite enough. You understand?"

"Four's quite enough." Do you see what was already working in his mind, and what a sudden jump forward our Case took when his lips uttered that concluding word?

For he did not say "enough" for what. The What was only just dimly beginning to appear. Perhaps I shall save time if I put what I mean into the form of a single question:

Why had Esdaile, who knew perfectly well that that pistol ought to be in the custody of the police, not himself immediately handed it over?

Why indeed did he not do so now?

That is what I am getting at. He had not only *not* handed the pistol over, but he had drawn blinds and grubbed about floors and had sought high and low, though so far in vain, for a stray bullet. Nay, he might lecture Monty on the picking up of random pistols, but what else had he himself done when he had found that little empty brass case in the garden and had slipped it into his waistcoat pocket? He had pretended to hold back until Monty should have told him everything. Well, Monty had now told him everything.

There was a telephone in the hall. Ten seconds would suffice.

Yet Esdaile did nothing.

I was conscious of a curious quickening of excitement. The whole atmosphere of our little gathering had already changed. Monty, sitting on his stool, seemed somehow less of a culprit, Esdaile something much more nearly in collusion with him. And above all it distinctly began to appear—dare I say "providential"?—that Monty had picked up that pistol.

Why?

Was it because Chummy Smith, instead of being a stranger who must be left to take the consequences of his own acts, was Hubbard's and Esdaile's friend?

XI

It is not for me to draw the hair-line that divides the heart's wish from the conviction of the rightness of the act that follows it. We are all prone to do what we want to do and to look for reasons afterwards. That was for Esdaile and Hubbard to consider. I am merely stating the Case. Personally you will always find me the broadest-minded and most tolerant of men until these lofty qualities begin to react on my own private affairs; after that I become a pattern of the narrow and the hidebound. Whether in their place I should have done as Hubbard and Esdaile did I have fortunately not to answer. What that was you will see in a moment.

For it was now clear that we were looking, without very much dismay, into the perilous face of Conspiracy. A pistol had been fired, and humanly speaking could only have been fired by one man. If the pistol, therefore, ought to have been handed over to the police, *a fortiori* ought the man who had fired it.

But that appeared to be precisely the sticking-point. It was here that I saw both Hubbard and Esdaile preparing to dig in. In a word, until they (private individuals, mark you) knew more about it, Chummy Smith was not to be given up.

Monty's attitude at about this stage began to be rather amusing. Suddenly he left the stool of repentance and began to walk about. He even swelled a little. It was he, after all, who had in a sense saved the situation, and when the cartridge-case was produced (for Hubbard and Esdaile had their heads together over the pistol-barrel again in search of further minute indications) he became almost cock of the walk. Incidentally he had one of those flashes of insight I told you he sometimes had, or at any rate it was a flash with which I myself am not without a certain amount of sympathy.

"Well, there isn't half enough murder in the world if you ask *me*," he said. "Only they're the wrong people. If you could get somebody really trustworthy to pick out the right ones no end of good would be done."

"Oh, shut up!" said Philip rudely; and happily the dangerous theory was not pressed.

But Monty had used the awkward word "murder."

And if Monty was amusing, the state of mind of the other two was now fascinatingly interesting. For you see their predicament. To put it quite plainly, they were trying to screw up their courage. Esdaile in particular was almost visibly hardening his heart. That was the fascinating part—to see exactly how much and how little homage they would pay to the decencies before they thought themselves free to go ahead.

The stages of the comedy were rapid. The first of them came when Esdaile wondered whether he oughtn't to go to the telephone, not to communicate with the police, but to ask for the latest news of Chummy's progress.

"Seems funny to think of Chummy being laid out six months after the War's all over," he said. "Remember the Jazz Band in the Mess, Cecil?"

"Red Pepper Two-Step on the Birds, eh?" said Hubbard.

(I am aware that this needs elucidation. The Helmsea Mess Jazz Band had been a noteworthy improvisation, and the Birds had been Chummy Smith's special department. They were stuffed Birds, set in cases round the walls, and the glass fronts of the cases had formed Smith's tympani. With drumming fingertips and softly-pounding wrists I learned that he had got great variety out of his instruments.)

"And the cock-fight between the razorbills?" Esdaile continued.

I could also make a guess at the kind of rag that had been.

"And the night old Pike's motor-bike broke down?"

And though this reminiscence passed over my head, it was plain that they were getting on. Very soon I might expect to be told outright that Chummy Smith was Chummy Smith and a pal, and they would be damned if they would see him in the cart till things were much clearer than they were. So I simply leaned back and amused myself with mental pictures. They were jumbled pictures, but I knew I was sharing them with the other two. I seemed to see their East Coast Base, with planes homing in the evening and the M.L.'s suddenly appearing out of the mists and dropping anchor in the tideway. I seemed to see the rubber-coated and white-muffled figures striding up the jetty to that Mess they spoke of and loudly demanding drinks and food and hot baths. I imagined the mechanics filling up the tanks and the Duty Officer swearing at the snow and slush as he stamped up and down the 'drome. And, faint and ineffectual as my pictures were, they still had a little of the magic of that life in which gayety and tragedy came so close and the chances of life and death were so intertwined.

I also guessed what a purist in the matter of picking up pistols might find himself up against if he pushed his purism inconveniently far.

Esdaile took the plunge even more quickly than I expected. I saw the little effort with which he pulled himself together.

"Well, it's no good beating about the bush," he said. "We all know how things are. The question is what's to be done."

I don't think he realized, as he pulled out his pipe, that that was now hardly the question at all. Already the question was, not what was to be done, but exactly how it was to be done.

XII

For, if he had realized, he could hardly have overlooked the immensely important point he did overlook. It was left to me to draw his attention to this point.

For when one man kills another, it necessarily follows that one man has been, killed *by* another. And it further follows that, if you decide to shield the killer because he is your friend, you are inevitably forced into an unfriendly attitude towards the victim. What about the victim and his rights in the matter?

You may believe it or not, but until this moment I don't think this aspect of the affair had occurred either to Hubbard or Esdaile. All had been Chummy. More than this: so exclusively had Chummy occupied their thoughts that they had forgotten the ordinary physical fact that a bullet fired into a man's body makes a hole—the same ugly kind of hole whether the person who makes it is your friend or not. Loyalty to friendship in the teeth of the Law is not always the simple thing it sounds. Among the various facts that faced us was one inescapable one, namely, that a man called Maxwell was at that moment lying in a mortuary awaiting a post-mortem examination.

Esdaile was frowning and clawing his jaw. The realization was sinking in now all right.

"What had you thought of doing with the pistol anyway?" I asked.

"To tell you the truth I hadn't thought," he admitted. "I should say the bottom of the river's the best place for it. But as you say, you can't drop that poor devil's bullet-hole into the river. Does nobody know anything about him?"

Nobody did. Maxwell might have been Chummy's best friend or worst enemy, a good fellow, a rotter, any one kind of all the kinds of men there are.

"Chummy was in Gallipoli. Anybody ever hear of a Maxwell with him there?"

Nobody had.

Then Esdaile took another line. For a moment it seemed quite a hopeful one.

"Well, look at it this way." He tried to evade the inevitable. "It's all very well for Monty to talk out of his hat about there not being murders enough, but what earthly right have we to assume that this was a murder at all? None, I say. Far more likely to have been an accident. Accidents do happen. Chummy wasn't the kind of man to deliberately do another fellow in. It must have been an accident."

But at this moment I remembered Philip's own words that morning in the studio: "Anybody would say it was an accident, wouldn't they? It looked like an accident, I mean? It wouldn't occur to anybody who saw it that it wasn't?" Those were rather remarkable words. They had meant, if they had meant anything at all, that even then Philip had had his reasons for supposing it had *not* been an accident. Now that a thunderclap had revealed that one of the men who had come down on the roof was Chummy, he apparently wanted it to be an accident again.

And by the way, how, at that particular moment, had Philip come to be in possession of an opinion on the matter at all? This was the point I have mentioned as being on Rooke's mind also. So far, in telling his story, Esdaile had taken as his starting-point the moment when he had got possession of the pistol from Monty; but what about the antecedent mystery? How in the first place had he discovered that Monty had the pistol? Why had he walked practically straight to Monty the moment he had ascended from the cellar? The whole series of incidents, from first to last, had passed while he had been still down in the cellar; how then could he know anything whatever about them?

Then I remembered that only a series of diversions had turned Hubbard away from his express purpose in coming to Lennox Street that evening—the purpose of seeing Esdaile's cellar. First had come the shock of learning that one of the men was Chummy Smith; then Joan Merrow's implication in the affair had sidetracked us; and then had come the pistol and Monty. These things were all very well, but they brought us no nearer to the solution of the first puzzle of all. Why had Esdaile behaved as he had behaved when he had rejoined us with a jar of curaçao in one hand and a lighted candle in the other?

But for all this we had to wait. My speculations were suddenly cut short. There was another ring at the door, and Esdaile rose. But before going to see who it was this time he took the precaution of once more putting Monty's pistol away in the escritoire drawer.

It was well for our Case, as a Case, that he did so. We heard voices in the passage, Esdaile's own tenor and a deeper voice. Then I heard him say, "Well, perhaps you'd better come in."

The next moment he stood holding the door open for a Police Inspector to pass.

PART III

WHAT THE WOMEN DID

I

For a great number of years past, innumerable reviewers have been so kind as to class me as "one of the younger novelists," and with the passing of time I have acquired a certain affection for the status. But I have to confess myself unlike my brethren in this—I don't know all about women. Indeed, twenty Philip Esdailes poking about twenty cellars are clearer to me than some of the mental processes of such a person as (say) Miss Joan Merrow. For instance, she once told me that she would be terrified to go up in a machine. She told me this (as I subsequently learned) within a very few hours of a side-slip at a few hundred feet that had fairly "put the wind up" Chummy Smith, her companion in this (by Philip) strictly forbidden adventure. Some chance remark of her own revealed all this to me weeks later, and our eyes met, mine sternly accusing, hers of limpid periwinkle blue. Then she had the effrontery to take me aside, to put her arm inside mine, and to whisper that she knew she could "trust" me!

"Trust," indeed!

So, as far as Miss Merrow is my informant for the part of our Case I am now coming to, you are warned what to expect.

II

Since it was I who discovered Philip Esdaile's painting-cottage for him I think I may claim that I know the Santon country fairly well. It is a vast and skyey upland east of the Wolds, and its edge drops in four hundred feet of glorious white cliff sheer to the sea. Everything there is on the amplest and most bountiful scale, from the enormous stretches of wheat and barley to the giant barns and huge horses and the very poultry of its farmyards. The only tiny thing about it is its church, and this stands in the middle of a daisied field, not by any means one of the largest, but that can hardly be less than a hundred acres. There is a shop-post-office, a short street mostly laithes as big as airship hangars, an opaque horse-pond, and a single telegraph wire the posts of which can be seen for miles diminishing away over the Wolds. The few trees are mostly thorn, all blown one way by the wind and as stiff and compact as wire mattresses.

And Joan herself fitted into all this Caldecott spaciousness as if she had been bred and born there. Half a mile away across the young corn you saw her white sweater at the cliff's edge, and it seemed part of the whiteness of the screaming seabirds, of the whiteness of the awful glimpses of chalk where the turf suddenly ended in air, of the crawling whiteness of the waves far below. And on the shore—but any young girl is a Nausicaa on any shore. Esdaile has drawn and painted her a score of times—young neck, fair thick yellow hair, the none-too-small white feet with the sand disappearing from them as she waded into the anemonied pools. Sometimes it was no more than a cryptic pencil-line, that, as you looked at it, suddenly became her up-lifted arm and flank, or the balance of back and hips as she moved across the unsteady white stones. Sometimes the jotting was more abbreviated still, just a dab or two of color that placed her against fawn-colored sand or ribbon-grassed water. But always it was Joan romping as it were her last between the little Alan and Jimmy she mothered and those other dream-stuff children that did not call her mother yet.

I feel fairly certain that it was not in the very least on Philip Esdaile's account that she had given instructions at the Chelsea post-office for the read-dressing of letters. Neither was it, as she had falsely said, "to save Mr. Rooke the trouble." Both Philip's stupid letters and Monty's convenience were very minor matters. The really important thing was her own letters. Some little delay her change of address was bound to entail; but if, after "1," "2," and "3" there must be a short pause, "4," "5" and the rest would arrive all in one blissful bag. And, pending her receipt of them, there was no reason why she should cease to write letters.

So, accompanied by the letter-case with the new lock on it, down to the shore she took the children on the first two mornings (which is something of a journey, by the way), and back in the afternoon she came to high tea at half-past four. On the first day she did not even trouble to walk on to the little post-office-shop. But on the second day she did, returning empty-handed to boiled fowl and white sauce, tall piles of Santon bread and Santon butter and Santon jam, pints of hot tea from the luster pot under the haystack cosy, and the children's clamor:

"I saw a jellyfish as big as a cart-wheel!"

"'N Jimmy found seven starfishes!"

"I found *eight* starfishes!"

"'N I waded out till the water came right up to here!"

"'N I saw a polar bear—"

"Oh, Jimmy, what a story! You've just made that up this minute!"

This last in bell-voiced reproof from Joan. At twenty she still corrected and disputed with them as a rather larger equal.

III

They had arrived at Santon at half-past eight on a Thursday night, and after tea on the Saturday Joan walked up to the little coastguard-station on the hill. Aeroplanes were not unknown on that wide uplifted promontory, and it would not in the least surprise her if presently, say in another week or so, Chummy, finding himself within a mere fifty miles, were to drop in unannounced. He had in fact said so, in the last letter but four. He had not been able to see her off at the station because he had had a new machine to take up with a fellow she didn't know. On Friday he was chasing off to the Midlands, where he might have to stay the night, and he did not expect to be back in London till Saturday afternoon. So he would not be within fifty miles, and even if a plane did happen to pass over it could not possibly be his.

As a matter of fact a plane did happen to pass over, and she pretended that it was his. She stood watching, eyes shaded with her hand, lips smiling and parted, and the young throat long as the flower-trumpet at the pit of which lies the nectar. Though she had been in a plane (and "trusted" me not to tell), I don't think that in her heart she regarded aeroplanes as apparatus at all. They were not things of wood and steel and oil and petrol that carried a load as a motor-car might have carried a load. All was the particular skill and daring and unaided cleverness of that Chummy of hers. I suppose he simply thought of her and flew.... But her little pretense ended in a light sigh when the plane did not circle, but with unfeeling purposefulness followed the telegraph wire over the Wolds and was lost to her sight. The young chauffeur of the air, whoever he was, knew nothing of the kiss that went after him. She returned to the cottage and the letter-case and began "7."

She knew nothing of the letter that Mollie Esdaile had already received from Philip, fortunately during her absence with the children. Nor did she know that Mollie, still in her absence, had run immediately to the shop-post-office and had telegraphed *"Wire fullest particulars immediately most anxious."* Chummy (Philip had written) had had a slight accident, nothing serious, but enough to keep him in bed for a few days. It would be better (his letter had continued) if this could be kept from Joan until she, Mollie, heard further from him. If Mollie could also glance through the newspapers before Joan got hold of them, that also Philip recommended. For the rest, he had said nothing whatever about when he himself might be expected at Santon, and Mollie further wondered whether it was to create a reassuring impression that he had passed on to tell her how he was having old Dadley round about some picture-framing, and ended with similar trivial matters. That letter had come on the Friday afternoon. Saturday had brought neither letter nor reply to her telegram. She was glad that there was a Sunday delivery at Santon, which usually awaited them on their return from Church.

(I may say now, by the way, that Philip's caution about the newspapers was needless. The paper that found its way to Santon about midday was a London paper, but a Northern edition. Minor accidents in Chelsea are seen in perspective from the North, and no account of that Chelsea accident ever did appear.)

Only Joan and the children went to Church on that Sunday morning. Mollie made some excuse about helping the village girl to prepare the midday meal. Perhaps she preferred not to read letters and have her own face read by Joan at the same time.

In the summer, when the door of that diminutive Church usually stands wide open all through the service, you can see from the back pews the postman pass on his way to Newsome's, the farthest farm. So there in Church Joan sat, watching the bees that droned in and out of the open door, the butterflies that hovered, the cattle that tried to crop inside the little wire fence. The whiteness of the daisies was faintly shed up among the old rafters, and the curate's singsong rose and fell peacefully. The postman passed with the Newsome letters, and repassed with his empty bag. Then the sluggish old harmonium droned forth the last hymn, they knelt for the Benediction, and Joan and her charges were the first to hurry forth out into the sunshine again.

And this time there was a letter for her.

But her brows were already contracted even before she opened it. She stood, in the white frock and buttercupped hat, against the musk and geraniums of the sunny window, already wondering what the quite strange handwriting of the envelope meant, already half afraid to ascertain.

"Is this all—?" she began.

Then with a nervous jerk she tore open the envelope, and a cry broke from her. The blue eyes were wide frightened rounds.

For if the handwriting on the envelope was strange, that of the shaky penciled scrawl inside was not quite familiar either. Yet it was Chummy's. He had had a bit of a spill, he said, but nothing to hurt. Rather shaken, but nothing broken. She was not to come up, as he would be out and up again before she could get there.

And that was all. There was no address at the head of the letter, and he did not say who had addressed the envelope for him, nor why.

"Oh, Mollie, he's hurt!" broke agitatedly from Joan.

Mollie was writing a letter at the little round table where the workbasket stood. Quietly she rose and passed her arm about the girl.

"Yes, darling, but he's quite all right," she calmed her.

"Have you heard from Philip, then? What is it? What does he say?" the words came with a rush.

Mollie had not heard from Philip that morning. That was why she was writing her letter. But she said she had heard from him. She meant the letter she had received on Friday afternoon.

"And somebody's had to write the address for him!" Joan's voice became more unsteady still. "Oh, that means he's badly hurt! I must go at once!"

"Nonsense, dear. Anyway, there are no trains on Sunday. May I see what he says, or—?"

Joan thrust the weak scribble into her hand. She read it, passed it back, and then began to unpin Joan's hat.

"Well, that's nothing to be alarmed about," she said. "He says just the same as Philip. And he tells you you're not to go up. We shall hear all about it tomorrow."

But she did not tell Joan that it was precisely because there was so maddeningly little in the letter she had received from Philip on Friday that, despairing of getting anything plain out of a mere man, the letter she was now writing was to Audrey Cunningham.

IV

I hope you haven't got the impression that I didn't like Mrs. Cunningham. Indeed, if half I presently learned about her was true, it would have been a hard heart that had not shown a very real and compassionate consideration for her. Young as she was, she had had a wretched story. As far as I know it it was this:

The late George Cunningham, having contracted the dangerous habit of going to bed every night comparatively sober and waking up in the morning very drunk, had one day arrived at the point when something had had to be done about it. I assume that he had tried the usual specifics to no purpose, since he had presently found himself with only two alternatives left. The first of these was to have done with specifics, to go boldly forward, and to trust to the strength of his constitution to land him high, and still dry, among the seasoned octogenarians. The other was to marry, and to trust that the pure love of an innocent young girl might work its traditional miracle.

Unfortunately, instead of choosing he had tried both courses at once. An unjailed criminal of a father had either suggested the match himself or had failed to throw Cunningham out of the window when it had been suggested. So at seventeen-and-a-half Audrey Herbert had become the wife of a man-about-town of forty-two, with a roomy house in St. John's Wood, a considerable private fortune, and a hole in every one of his pockets.

It had not taken Mrs. Cunningham long to discover that a man who goes to bed sober and wakes up drunk, frequently does so in other beds than his own. But her father, to whom she ran, advised her to continue to exercise her influence for good. He seems to have thought that as long as Cunningham did not actually strike her the rest must be accepted as part of marriage-as-it-is. He had passed out of the world in that belief a couple of years after his daughter's immolation.

Cunningham never struck her. Nor, while it lasted, did he starve her of money. Twice, when housekeeping debts had pressed, he gave her blank checks which the bank duly honored. The third time (one of his mistresses appears to have been the occasion) he gave her a considerably wider permission.... No, he had never struck her. Instead, he had merely dragged through the mud of alcoholism and unfaithfulness the hope and belief in men he had found her with, and after five years of it had died—not a day too soon, as she had discovered on going into his affairs. When his debts of honor, dishonor and at law had been paid, about a hundred pounds had remained. With this, her clothes, a few pieces of furniture bought in from the sale and her experience of married life, she had become her own mistress again at twenty-three. Most of the hundred pounds had gone in fees at a School of Dramatic Art. She was now twenty-seven and on the eve of her second marriage.

I am telling you all this because of the part that Mrs. Cunningham presently came to play in our Case. I think her unhappy history partly explained certain things. I would not go so far as to say that with the exception of Monty Rooke she disliked and distrusted all men, but I think that the sense of sex-hostility was latent and instinctive in her. This never took the form of gloom. Quite the other way. Lest it should be thought for a moment that she mourned for the cur with whom she had been kenneled, she was rather histrionically bright. She fell naturally into beautiful attitudes and gestures, which beauty her art enhanced. I think I mentioned the care she bestowed on her manicuring; in the whole of her person and dress she was the same, as if to wipe out some soilure. She was undoubtedly much in love with Monty—who at any rate was a teetotaller. And, except as I have qualified, I think she liked the rest of us well enough. But the history was always behind, and, in my experience, if you like with however natural a reservation, there is something of the same reserve in the liking you inspire.

So, in this sense I was prepared to like Mrs. Cunningham, and without any qualification whatever was sorry she had had so ghastly a time and hopeful that her marriage with Monty would expunge the memory of it.

V

And so we come to the episode of the wardrobe that Audrey Cunningham had bought in from the St. John's Wood sale.

This wardrobe, with a number of dress-baskets and other articles, formed part of the furniture of the bed-sitting-room in Oakley Street that she was now on the point of leaving, and it had been Philip Esdaile himself who had suggested, some time ago, that there was plenty of room for these belongings in his cellar. Nothing had since been said about it; Philip says that the matter had entirely slipped from his memory; and Mrs. Cunningham, having no reason to suppose that he had changed his mind, had as a matter of fact had the wardrobe put on a light cart and brought round to Lennox Street the day after the aeroplane accident, that is to say on the Friday afternoon. Philip himself, coming along the street at that moment, had found the cart at the gate and Monty and Mrs. Cunningham considering the best way of getting the wardrobe in.

"Ah, so you've got it round; good," he said. "I don't quite know where you're going to put it, but we'll find somewhere. Let me give you a hand."

"I thought you said it was to go into the cellar?" said Mrs. Cunningham.

"Eh?" said Philip. "Did I? I believe I did. Well, let's get it in first. We can settle that afterwards. Has Dadley come?"

So the wardrobe was got into the hall, where it was left for the present among Philip's corded and labeled painting-gear.

"Has Dadley come?" Philip asked again.

"Yes. He's been waiting for you for ten minutes in the studio," Monty replied.

"Bon. I don't suppose I shall be more than ten minutes, but don't wait for tea. I've had a cup as a matter of fact."

"Can't say I think much of old Daddy as a framer—" Monty was beginning; but Esdaile was already at the studio door, which he closed carefully behind him.

You may remember the name of old William Dadley. It was he who, when Mr. Harry Westbury had held forth in the Saloon Bar about the danger to property from the air, had ventured to suggest that lives too had their value. His shop was the little one in the King's Road with the alleged Old Master in the window, one half of it black with ancient grime, the other pitilessly restored; and, as Monty had said, artists who were in any hurry to see their pictures back again seldom took their framing to old Daddy. Unless they went farther afield, they were more likely to patronize the up-to-date establishment across the road, kept by the two pushing young men in the Sinn Fein hats and black satin bows and little side-whiskers and hair bobbed like girls'.

And now for the discussion on picture-framing that took place between Philip Esdaile and William Dadley, behind the closed studio door.

VI

"Was he drunk?" Esdaile asked. He was walking about, head down, frowning.

The old man stroked his grizzled beard.

"Well, I won't say he hadn't had a few. I saw him have two or three liqueur brandies. And he's a crossish sort of man when he's at home, especially when it's wearing off a bit, but he isn't easily bowled over, isn't Harry. Well, as I was telling you. He gets home about tea-time that day, and the first thing he sees is one of the children playing with something or other in his mouth. He was popping it in and out. You know what children are, Mr. Esdaile—everything goes straight into their mouths. So Westbury asked the child how much oftener he wants telling about putting things into his mouth, and takes it away from him. And what do you think it was, Mr. Esdaile? It was a bullet!"

"A bullet?" said Esdaile with a show of astonishment.

"A bullet. And it had been fired, because it was all out of shape. Well, you don't find bullets everywhere, like leaves off the trees, do you?"

"Where on earth did the child get it?" Esdaile asked.

"Ah, that's what Harry wants to know!" The gray old head was wagged a few times. "Shouts for his missis, and there's a bit of a scene. The child says he found the bullet in the bedroom. How did it get there? Harry wants to know. It seems the window was wide open to air the room a bit. Then Harry asks what the child was doing in the bedroom, and what time he went up, and what time he came down again, and I don't know what else. Then he has a bit of a sleep and a cup of tea and a wash and goes off out again. I believe he went straight to Inspector Webster with the bullet, but he won't say either Yes or No. He's very mysterious about it. A man told me, though, that he'll be an important witness when the Case comes on."

"What Case?" Esdaile asked.

"Well, Westbury he looks at it like this, Mr. Esdaile: If that bullet came in at his window it might have hit somebody, he says, and he's great on the window being just opposite this house of yours. And he's worked it out, from the time it was when his wife cleaned the bedroom and where the children were and all that, that the bullet must have come in at the same time that accident was."

"But what's a flying accident got to do with a bullet?"

"Ah, that I can't tell you; but he's very mysterious. And I know he's written a letter to the papers about dangerous flying, because I heard him reciting bits of it. He says he'll make a Case of it or his name isn't Harry Westbury."

"What paper has he written to?"

"I can't remember the name just for the moment, but it's one of the papers. And I heard him reciting one bit about three million pounds' damage. I don't suppose he's written to the papers about the bullet; that's the tit-bit, that is, and he's keeping that to himself, except for Inspector Webster. Westbury's a difficult sort of man once he gets started on a thing. Stares you down like.

You say you don't know him by sight? It was him brought that ladder into your garden—he was there when Mr. Rooke went up on the roof—"

And that (to pass on) was the gist of the discussion on the framing of Esdaile's *fêtes-champêtre*.

VII

A few minutes' reflection would have shown Esdaile that there was no immediate reason why he should have hesitated to have that wardrobe carried down into his cellar. He himself admits this. But it is easy to think of these things afterwards, and he was caught off his guard. He did allow reluctance to appear.

"Why not move this desk and let it stand here?" he said, pointing to the writing-table with the mignonette-shaded lamp on it. "It's not a bad-looking piece at all. Pity to hide it. What is it—Jacobean?"

It was either genuine Jacobean or else a passable copy, but, placed where Philip proposed to place it it would have been a little in the way of anybody passing to the French window. Mrs. Cunningham pointed this out.

"Do you think so? Let's measure it," Esdaile replied.

Measurement of the piece confirmed Mrs. Cunningham's view, and Philip next suggested that it should go into the large studio.

"Why not have it where you can get at it and use it?" he said. "I thought women complained they could never get hanging-space enough. Or what about upstairs in Mollie's room?"

But Audrey Cunningham's frocks, which she made quite wonderfully herself out of almost nothing at all, were few, and Mollie had left her plenty of room for them. Besides, there were the dress-baskets. These would hardly add to the beauty either of the annexe or the studio. For the baskets at any rate the most convenient place was certainly the cellar. And it was at this point that Philip, recognizing that further objection would look rather like obstinacy, yielded.

He confesses that he felt awkward about the whole situation. Either he had lent his house or he had not. If the former, Monty and his fiancée should have had the complete freedom of it; if the latter, or if for any reason he regretted his generosity, the position was even more obscure. To say that until the marriage he had lent it to Monty only and not to Mrs. Cunningham was mere quibbling; he had made the offer in entire good faith, and had not made a lawyer's matter of it, with clauses and reservations about this, that and the other.

Yet here he not only was, but here very much master of the house whether he wished it or not. Audrey Cunningham would of course be very nice about it, but he could see very plainly how it must strike her. He did not even pretend to be working. He was merely hanging on, for a reason unexplained and unexplainable to her. Monty knew his reason, of course; but the reason she supposed to be the truth (for she had been told that one of the men who had crashed was their friend and Joan Merrow's more than friend) by no means accounted for everything. It did not account for a quarter of his eccentricities; it did not even account for his latest inadvertence, of proposing any place in the house except the cellar for the bestowal of that nuisance of a wardrobe. What an ass he had been about that! The cellar could be made *perfectly safe* at an instant's warning; as a matter of fact it was *perfectly safe* at that moment. There was no reason whatever why Audrey Cunningham should not go down there.

But things would get worse as time went on. Presently Audrey would be living here, as Monty's wife, and it would be difficult for Philip to delay his departure after that. A honeymoon is a honeymoon even when it is spent in a borrowed studio, and newly-married couples don't commonly take in fussy and fretful lodgers. Within a week or so he or they would most certainly have to clear out.

Philip could have stated what had actually happened in one short sentence. He had offered them one house, but was now called upon to hand over to them the possession of quite a different one.

But this was impossible to explain without dragging in the thing of all things that he wished to keep from Audrey, from Mollie, and above all from Joan—that beastly episode of the pistol, with all it involved.

And here at any rate he was quite firm. Chance what might, that must be kept the men's affair only. As far as the women were concerned at present the accident was a pure accident. Well, an accident it must remain.

But what about that Police Inspector who had appeared so suddenly in our midst the night before, and for all Philip knew might be round again at any moment? Audrey Cunningham had been told nothing about that. She might have many opinions about Philip's delayed departure, but about a series of domiciliary visits by the police she could have one only, namely, that the loan of a studio wasn't worth it. In suppressing this piece of information Philip was actually doing his best to keep her in Lennox Street. To have informed her would have been much the same thing as asking her to leave.

And what exactly had passed when Philip's tenor voice, interrupting the Inspector's deep one, had said, "Well, perhaps you'd better come in"?

VIII

Of the four of us sitting there I alone had instantly realized what must have happened. Our Nosey Parker of a Westbury had been at work already. I remembered the dull insistence of the man and how he had said in my hearing that he and Inspector Webster "would be having a bit of a talk that evening." I recalled also the stupid but dangerous cunning with which he had repeated over and over again that Rooke had been the first on the scene of the accident. Well, he hadn't lost very much time. The Inspector had stood there in the doorway, and neither Esdaile, Hubbard nor Rooke had had the least idea why.

Now there are a good many of the commonly-accepted views on physiognomy that I for one don't share. One of these is about rather narrowly-set eyes. Webster, who was a very big red-and-black man, had these eyes under a sort of bison-front of close-curling hair, but I did not associate them with meanness and slyness at all. On the contrary, they had rather a kindly glint, and they reminded me of the infinitesimal slight cast that at certain moments makes some women irresistible. No, I did not set Inspector Webster down as a bad sort. At the same time there was no nonsense about him, and I should have thought twice before trying any tricks with him.

I was more thankful than I can tell you that Philip also, in spite of the emotional gamut he had run that day, still had resilience enough to sum the Inspector up very much as I did. There was no bland "Well, Inspector, and to what are we indebted for the pleasure of this visit?" nor anything of that kind. Perhaps that dangerous pistol, X-raying itself so plainly in our minds through the top of the escritoire, had forbidden any such attitude. I now know, as a matter of fact, the life-line on to which he had immediately and instinctively laid hold. Inspector Webster, whatever he had come for, was to be treated exactly as the women were to be treated, and the accident-theory was to hold the field.

So this is what had happened:

The Inspector, after a few conventional remarks about being sorry to trouble us gentlemen for the second time that day and so on, had come down like a hammer straight upon our weakest point. This was the part that Monty Rooke had played in that morning's events. First of all he wanted (with our permission) to put a few words to Mr. Rooke. I think he used the word "permission" in good faith, and not as any kind of a veiled threat.

I saw Monty moisten his lips. He has since explained the swiftness with which he also was able to come into line and to play up so really nobly as he did. Philip, if you remember, had forbidden him pretty gruffly to say one word about all this to Audrey Cunningham; it is no light matter to dictate to another man what he shall say and what he shall not say to his fiancée; and this it was that saved the situation. If Monty was to be ordered to keep his mouth shut before his fiancée he was jolly well not going to be pumped by an outsider, Police Inspector or no Police Inspector. On such hairs do our actions hang sometimes.

"Fire away," he had said.

"Well, sir, to begin with, would you be so kind as to tell me in your own words exactly what you saw on the roof this morning?"

"Certainly," Monty had replied.

And he had launched out.

From the point of view of the things he omitted I can only describe his performance as brilliant. Camouflage was certainly Monty's war-job. Not one single word was there about bullet-holes, cartridge-cases or pistols. Had there been a polar bear or a pterodactyl on the roof it might have been worth mentioning, but a pistol—no.

My only fear was lest he should be so pleased with his own performance as to undo it again out of sheer satisfaction presently.

"Thank you very much indeed, sir," said the Inspector. "I asked you for your own words and you've given them. Now I wonder if I might be allowed to ask you one or two questions?"

"Fire away," said Monty again.

But here the Inspector himself had seemed to be in some slight difficulty. Apparently for some reason he wasn't very anxious to speak of pistols either. Polar bears or pterodactyls, yes; but not pistols. I have since thought that, as a man of some penetration, he also might have had his private opinion about Mr. Harry Westbury, and thought it best to act on anything Westbury said with caution.

Nevertheless, the series of questions that had followed had all been in the very close neighborhood of pistols, so to speak. I itemize what struck me as being their real, if unuttered trend.

"About this man that's dead, Mr. Rooke. You saw his face, of course?"

(*Item: Had Maxwell been shot through the head?*)

Yes, Monty had seen his face, but so, he ventured to remind the Inspector, had he himself.

"Well, say I had other things to attend to and didn't particularly notice. You'd say he was—pretty bad?"

(*Item: So bad that there might have been a little hole on one side of his head and a big one on the other without your noticing it?*)

"Rotten," said Monty with an unaffected shiver.

"Bleeding much?"

(*Item: Or anything else scattered about?*)

"No."

"Clothes singed?"

(*Item: If not through the head, perhaps through the body?*)

"Yes. Badly. Bits of the parachute too."

"From where you were on the roof lots of people could see you?"

(*Item: If you'd done anything you'd no business to do, for instance?*)

"Any number of people I should say," Monty had replied rather faintly. "But I don't see what you're getting at. You were up there too. What is it all about?"

And here Philip had seen fit to intervene, rather quickly.

"Yes, that's what I'm wondering, Inspector. Is it a proper question to ask? And is it proper to ask you if you'd like a glass of whisky, by the way?"

The narrow eyes had twinkled. "Not supposed to, sir—"

"Right. Say when—"

And so our healths had been drunk.

"You see," Philip had resumed presently, "I understood from Mr. Mackwith this morning—you knew that was Mr. Mackwith, K.C., you were talking to, didn't you—the tall man in morning-coat and spats?"

"Was he indeed, sir?"

"Yes, that was Mr. Mackwith, and I understood from him that you had said you had all the evidence you wanted?"

The Inspector had been sitting with his cap on his knees and the glass of whisky inside it like a flowerpot in a vase. He had ruminated.

"Well," he had said suddenly, "the fact is that that was this morning, gentlemen. Since then a certain piece of information's been laid in connection with this affair. I'm not at liberty to say what this information is, nor whether we shall act on it or not, but the Law's for the protection of us all, gentlemen, and I take it all of us wants to do our best to maintain it. Even if it meant the inconvenience," he added deliberately, "of a warrant for the search of these premises."

Here the sorely-tried Philip had given a wild laugh.

"Search these premises! Search 'em now if you like. But in God's name what for?"

"Accidents aren't always what they seem, sir," Inspector Webster had replied.

IX

And now (to come out of this winding of the story into the open again) here was Audrey Cunningham with dress-baskets and a wardrobe for which the most suitable place was certainly the cellar.

"All right," Esdaile said suddenly. "Let's do it now. Monty and I can manage it if you'll hold a candle for us."

And he lighted and put into Audrey's hand the same candle he had himself used when he had gone down into the cellar to fetch the orange curaçao.

He was still kicking himself that he had made such a fuss. Now at last he saw that, although only a trifle stood between revelation and perfect concealment, this trifle was as firm as the rocks of which the mountains are built. A short flight of steepish stone steps, with a rather awkward right-angled bend half-way down, descended ten feet or so, and there was no cellar door. You stepped from the bottom step, which was a little worn and concave, and there you were, with nothing more to do but to put the wardrobe and the dress-baskets inside and to come out again.

The wardrobe was at the turn of the stairs. Mrs. Cunningham stood just above it, holding the candle for the two men to see.

"Gently—don't knock it," muttered Philip, "and mind the edge of the steps—they're pretty old—"

The wardrobe cleared the bend, and Audrey Cunningham followed it into the cellar.

It was only natural that she should look with some curiosity at the place in which Philip Esdaile had spent that unaccounted-for half hour on the morning of the day before. I did the same thing myself at a later stage. But all that she saw was the most ordinary of cellars. Hubbard himself, who seemed to have cellar-on-the-brain, would have found nothing remarkable in it. This is all that was to be seen:

A roomy, gloomy, clammy place, with old plastered walls, and neither door nor window of any kind nor other means of entry than that they had just used. Its air hit skin and nostrils like that of a grave. The light of the single candle seemed lost in its obscurity. When Audrey held the candle up above her head a couple of heavy beams could be seen, necessary for the support of the largish area of the studio floor; when she held it to one side it showed in a corner a couple of gas-meters with the usual pipes, and underneath them the improvised rack in which Esdaile kept his modest stock of wine. When she held it to the other side its light hardly reached the farther wall, but wavered over the dim objects that half-filled the floor-space. These were merely the furniture for which Esdaile had no present use, and consisted of a large couch covered with a dingy dust-sheet, a few oddments of chairs, a number of packing-cases, and in fact the usual miscellaneous collection of household lumber that one day seems hardly worth keeping and the next looks just too good to throw away. Nearest to hand on the wine-rack stood the bottle of curaçao, just where Esdaile himself had replaced it. And that was all.

"Well, where will you have it, Audrey?" said Philip. "What about over by the sofa there?"

Mrs. Cunningham was once more holding the candle over her head. Any young woman's face by candlelight always seems singularly attractive to me, especially if she is a dark-eyed woman, and she was a slight and graceful thing to have endured so much. Had Joan been holding that candle up she would have given you the impression of a statue, but Mrs. Cunningham was just the opposite—all warm and fleeting and impermanent charm, a creature depending on the varying accidents of color, even when that color was only the sooty black of her home-made dress, the candlelight on her face and the tiny reflections in her large and lustrous eyes.

Suddenly she gave a shiver and a nervous laugh.

"I don't think I should like to be shut in here alone," she said.

"Why not?" Philip asked.

But the "why not" hardly needed saying, with that same candlestick in her hand and, as she once more moved it, that same jar of curaçao seeming to advance a little out of the shadows. These things brought the shock and dread of that other morning all too plainly before her again. It was within these chill sweating walls that Philip Esdaile had done the "wool gathering" he had spoken of. What wool? She saw none. Then why, up to that very moment almost, had he shuffled so? Why had he seemed so anxious that the wardrobe should be placed anywhere rather than in the place where they now stood? Here she was. She could not imagine any kind of cellar, however earthy and tomblike, that so changed its nature or properties that at one moment it must be jealously guarded and the next thrown open for her to look as much as she pleased. She was free to look. Monty also was wandering about in the farther corner there, as greedy for knowledge as she. The only check on her freedom was that she felt that Philip at the same time was covertly watching her.

Then all at once something seemed to give way in her. She put the candle down on one end of the sheeted sofa and turned to Philip. Her hands were clasped at her breast, the honeysuckle fingers interworking.

"Oh, please tell me!" she begged. "What is it makes this place so queer? There's something—I can feel it—like eyes on me—I've a being-watched sort of feeling, as if something was wrong—"

Philip took up the candle. "Then let's go upstairs," he said promptly.

But something almost like hysteria seemed to take her. Her voice rose.

"No, I want to know! I don't feel I can come to this house unless I know! I don't want to come here if it's going to be like this! You don't want to tell me—I know you could if you wanted! Oh, I wish Mollie was here!"

"Come upstairs," Philip repeated gently. "Bring her up, Monty."

But she went on with even less and less control.

"Oh, I think it's cruel! You're all cruel! You never think of us! Joan's to go on being told nothing, and Mollie's kept in the dark—oh, I know she is— and I'm made to feel that I'm not wanted here.... I want to go back to Oakley Street, Monty. I can't stop here. I won't. Everything's been wrong ever since that accident. It's horrible. I'm going away. I dare say they'll let me keep my room on; if they won't I must find somewhere else. Please take me away."

Upstairs, she became a little calmer, but she still wanted to be taken away. Monty was soothing her where she sat on the little Empire sofa, and Philip's face was distressed as he walked up and down. Then, though there was little heart in his attempt, he tried gently to laugh her out of it.

"But of course you'll go back to Oakley Street," he said. "You're there for three days yet, aren't you? It will be all right by that time. It's just a little bit of a complication we're in. It won't be long now. Then you'll get married and come along here, of course. Pull yourself together, my dear. It's all right. There, you're feeling better now, aren't you?"

He felt a perfect brute, he says, but he didn't see what else he could do. Even if he had had the right, he doesn't see that it would have helped to tell her that, after tying herself up with a drunkard, she was now going to make a second experiment with a man who had no more sense than to go and get himself mixed up in an affair that might bring the police round at any moment. He had no such right. Just as before he had been unable to explain to Hubbard and myself until he had spoken to Monty, so now he couldn't take any further step till he had seen Chummy Smith. It might be hard on Joan and Mrs. Cunningham, not to mention his wife, but what other course could he take? When you set about to burke inquiry into a capital Case the fewer people you take into your confidence the better. Besides, who knew yet that it was a capital Case? Suppose twenty words from Chummy should somehow explain it all? Suppose some ridiculous mistake had been made? Suppose our elaborate pretenses to ourselves were in reality no pretenses at all, and that the thing really was what it seemed—just an aeroplane accident with nothing more to be said about it?

Yes, in spite of all the evidence, he would have been glad at the moment to have believed that.

"Look here, Audrey," he said at last, "I feel absolutely rotten about all this. I know I'm in the way and I oughtn't to be here at all. When I turned over this place to you I hadn't the faintest idea of stopping on like this. I'd go straight into rooms now if I could, but that wouldn't do. Don't ask me why, there's a dear. For one thing I've got to see Smith. They tell me he can be seen in a few days now. Then I'll just stop for the wedding and clear right out afterwards. Whats the matter with that?"

The matter with that appeared in Audrey Cunningham's next words, which she spoke slowly and with her eyes on the floor.

"It isn't just you. It's Monty as well. He could tell me if he wanted, but he doesn't want. I don't think I want to get married," she said.

X

The letter she wrote crossed Mollie Esdaile's Sunday morning one. It was written on Saturday, and missed the Santon Sunday morning delivery by a post, arriving there on Monday.

"Please don't think me ungrateful," Mollie read, "but all sorts of things seem to be happening, and I'm so afraid of hurting you after all your kindness. Perhaps I'd better come to the point straight away and explain afterwards. I don't think I can accept your offer of Lennox Street for Monty and myself after all."

Mollie was standing in the porch of the cottage as she read this. It was immediately after breakfast. The postman could be seen in the middle distance, climbing the stile on his way to Newsome's. Joan was upstairs, getting the children ready for the shore.

Mollie thrust the letter into her breast. If Joan knew that the postman had been she would come flying downstairs, and in any case Mollie did not wish to be seen reading a letter. This from Audrey Cunningham was all there was for her. For Joan there was nothing at all.

Quietly she slipped into the cottage, picked up a floppy print sunbonnet, and slipped noiselessly out again. The back of the cottage had no windows. Like a malefactor she skirted the palings of the little front garden and gained the security of the back. But even this was not far enough. The path up the field led to the Coast-guard Station, and, with one furtive glance behind her, she took it. She would finish Audrey's letter there.

Mollie Esdaile is still a young woman, but she looked every minute of her age that morning. She had not slept. The room adjoining hers was Joan's, and the wall between them might just as well not have existed, so little a barrier had it been to the restless mental ticking of the girl on the other side of it. A soft and tortured toss, then the creaking of the bed, then the sounds of Joan moving about her room; the striking of a match, a long silence, and then the creaking of the bed again—all night it had gone on. Mollie had not gone to her; what had there been to do or say? A hundred times she had promised, as if it had lain in her power, that there should be a letter in the morning. None had come. She felt a coward. She simply could not face Joan.

There was a merry morning wind, that ruffled the fleeces on the sheep's backs and set the halliards of the Coast-guard's mast cracking and rattling. Mollie tied the strings of the print sunbonnet under her plump chin and walked with her head a little averted in order to see round the print blinker. Beyond the waving grass-heads the sea appeared, a wide silver glitter. You cannot see the shore from that hill. The sands and the mile-long rollers lie far below that cliff's edge over which the men are let down by ropes to gather the eggs from the awful ledges.

Then, in the little sunken way that runs down to the Rocket-house, she sat down and took out the letter again.

"I don't think I can accept your offer of Lennox Street for Monty and myself after all. Our engagement is not definitely broken off, but I can't stand things as they are, and am back in Oakley Street again. They say I can stay on, but I may have to pay a little more. Monty is still at the studio."

"I *knew* it!" broke from Mollie with soft conviction. "I knew that if Philip stayed that wedding would be put off! I told him so—"

Frowning, she turned to the letter again.

"I'm trying to think it all over quite calmly," the letter went on. "Perhaps it isn't Monty after all. Perhaps it is just that men worry me. I don't know really whether I'm a man's sort of woman. Their ways seem so queer and roundabout to me. Lots of them don't seem fair. I don't want to marry and make a mess of it a second time, and I don't think Monty sees this as I do. Of course, I don't want him to tell me every little thing he does and everywhere he goes or anything of that kind, but I hate being kept in the dark as I know I am being. It all seemed to start with that horrible accident. Nothing's been the same since. Of course, they've told me about Mr. Smith and poor darling Joan, but if it was only that I could understand it. I know there's something else. I'm afraid I'd rather a breakdown yesterday, when all three of us were in your cellar putting that wardrobe of mine away. There's something uncanny about that place. Monty thinks so too, but says he doesn't know what it is any more than I do. But there is something he does know and won't tell. And now it's all over Chelsea that something not quite right has happened. Mrs. Cook hinted at it this morning when she brought my milk up, and she said the milkman had told her. I really think that if the milkman knows I might be told. The fact is that just at present I don't feel much like men and marriage. You'll understand this, because I've told you heaps of things I should never dream of telling Monty—"

Mollie's gaze wandered to the twinkling silver sea. She remembered some of those things that would never be told to Monty. It was perhaps not altogether fair to Monty that he should have to restore the whole of the credit of his sex that the late George Cunningham had so let down, but she knew how Audrey felt about it. Men *were* trials sometimes. "Queer and roundabout?" Mollie not seldom called them infants outright. Such little things pleased them, such even less things caused them to dig their hoofs into the ground and refuse to budge. Whatever Philip's tremendous reason for remaining in Chelsea might be, Mollie brushed it aside as a trifle compared with Audrey's marriage. For a moment she almost forgot Joan's distress. Philip, with his curaçao and candle-sticks, postpone Audrey's wedding? It was nonsense—not to be thought of. Mollie wouldn't hear of it. All this mystification should be put a stop to if she had to do it herself. Audrey, to be sure, was a highly-strung creature; lying there among the warm grasses and with the wind ruffling the silver sea, Mollie could afford not to take too seriously Audrey's broken sentences about uncanny cellars and whispered hints that ran all over Chelsea; but it seemed to her that there were two birds to be killed with one stone. If she were to go up to town she would be able to ascertain for herself what this Audrey-Monty trouble was all about, and also why newspapers were to be kept from Joan and how it was that Joan had first heard of Chummy's crash from Chummy himself.

She looked at her wrist-watch and scrambled to her feet. She could not go without letting Joan know she was going, and Joan would already have started with the children for the shore. There was a train at midday. She would have plenty of time to intercept Joan, to tell her she was going to leave her for a couple of days, to return to the cottage, change and pack her bag.

And she did not think it necessary to warn Philip of her intention either.

XI

"But, darling—oh, don't go on like this! Can't you see that if I go I can clear up everything in half an hour? It's *much* the best!"

Joan's manner was stony and impregnable. She stared straight before her.

"I don't mind being left quite, quite alone," was her reply.

"But I shall be back again on Wednesday, foolish child, and I'll wire you everything immediately if it costs me the whole of my quarter's pocket-money. Anything's better than this!"

"Just as you like," came the expressionless response.

Not finding her on the shore, Mollie had climbed the precipitous zig-zag path to the cliff-top again and had sat down to rest, fairly blown. Then she had seen her a quarter of a mile away, sitting motionless on a rounded sky-line over which a hawthorn hedge straggled. The children were stolidly watching her, and she as stolidly was watching nothing. The boughs under which she sat were a custard of white bloom, and white was the sun-flecked sweater in the shadow of them, and white as snow the battlemented clouds overhead. Her eyes were dry and quite consciously enduring, and Mollie was alternately comforting and scolding her.

"I shall catch the midday train, and I shall be back on Wednesday," she repeated firmly. "If the mountain won't come to Mahomet or whatever it is, very well. And *do* try to be a little cheerful, darling. I heard you last night. That does no good."

"I know you haven't had a letter this morning, either," came the dull voice.

"I haven't from Philip, but I have from Audrey. She sends her love. Of course, she knows about Chummy, and it's quite all right."

"But you won't show me the letter," Joan replied, steadfast in her misery. "I know you won't. Nobody shows me anything. I saw him fall—I was the only one who did—but nobody tells me anything."

"You shall hear every word the moment I get there."

"I saw him fall," Joan repeated obstinately. "You were all indoors, but I was in the garden. But of course I didn't know who it was—"

"Don't, darling—just to please me," Mollie begged, distracted.

"He fell like a stone, crash into the tree. You can't realize that. You haven't been up. I have. I know what it's like."

"But you've had a letter from him!" Mollie protested. "Really you talk as if he was killed!"

"I don't know where the letter came from, and I can't write to him, except to the Aiglon Company, which I've done, and there's no reply, and somebody else had to address the envelope for him. I ought to go, not you. I saw him fall."

To Mollie's touch on her shoulder she was quite unresponsive. Mollie could have shaken her. It might have been the best thing to do.

"Do run away, you boys!" she said crossly instead. "Go and pick some of those blue flowers; Auntie Joan's a little tired. Now, Joan, I'll tell you what I'll do if you're good, but not unless. He's in a hospital or a nursing-home, I expect, and I shall go straight to him; and then if he's fit to move, as I expect he is by this time, I shall bring him straight down here. Will that do?"

"I know he's not fit to move. I saw him fall. I saw him falling all last night."

"Now you're naughty and just trying to make the worst of it. That's simply willful. It's like Alan when he wants smacking; when you're as old as I am you'll look on the bright side and be thankful it's no worse. Now do try. I'm going to bring him down here, and we'll keep him for a month. A whole month—it will be lovely! Why, you've only seen him in London and Richmond Park!"

"I've been to Chalfont Woods with him four times."

Mollie seized gratefully on the diversion.

"Joan! How *could* you! You never told me that!" she scolded. "And you never told me you'd been flying with him either! Philip would be furious if he knew! And now I'll tell him, and about Chalfont too, and all those other times as well, if you don't try to be reasonable. A month in this lovely place with him, and nobody to interfere—why, you'll be glad he had a little bit of an accident!... Now get up and we'll all go back. You'll have to get dinner ready, and I shall want a few sandwiches. Alan! Jimmy! We're not going to the shore. You can play on the see-saw instead. Run ahead, boys—and you come along, darling—"

And Joan of the cinemas and cliffs, of the secluded tea-shops and the noble Santon shore, rose, still as naughty and obstinate as ever, but obediently. Already Mollie, bustling the children on ahead, was shaping in her mind the dressing-down she intended to give Philip that very night.

XII

There was no help for it, Philip has since told me. He simply had to tell her everything. She was, in fact, in possession of the whole story long before any of the rest of us.

But even she had to wait yet a little longer. When, at half-past nine that Monday night her taxi drew up at the wrought-iron gate in Lennox Street, Philip was out and the place was in darkness. She had no key.

"Go on to Oakley Street," she ordered the driver.

Audrey Cunningham was at home. Mollie found her, alone, in her first-floor bed-sitting-room, already on the point of going to bed.

"First of all give me a cup of cocoa or something," was Mollie's greeting. "I've been half the day in the train with only a few sandwiches, and I shall drop if I don't have something."

Mrs. Cunningham lighted the little gas-ring and fetched water from an adjoining room. Then, opening a little cupboard, she mixed cocoa-paste in a cup, got out bread and margarine and a plate of macaroons, and set them on a little chintz-covered stool before Mollie.

"I've an egg if you'd like one," she said.

"No, thanks. I got your letter this morning. Have you got the one I wrote yesterday?"

"No; but I don't think the last post's been yet."

"Well, it doesn't matter now. I've come to see for myself. Philip doesn't know I'm here yet, but he will presently. Now first of all, what's all this about you and Monty? What's happening?"

Her tone was that of a woman who intended to stand no further nonsense of any kind. She was dog-tired, already angry on Joan's account, and the resigned and hopeless air of the slender creature before her completed her resolve to get to the bottom of things.

But nothing appeared to be happening about Audrey and Monty. Mrs. Cunningham was still of the same mind, or no mind, that had prompted her letter.

"Where is he now?" Mollie demanded.

Audrey did not know.

"Is he with Philip?"

She did not know that either.

"And aren't you going to Lennox Street?"

"I don't think I can."

Mollie's eyes went round the room. I myself have never been in Mrs. Cunningham's bed-sitter, but I have been in many others and can picture its frugality—the gas-ring, the little cupboard with the bread and jar of marmalade in it, the chintz-covered grocer's box on which Mollie's cup of co-coa stood, probably a slightly fresher wallpaper-pattern where the Jacobean wardrobe had stood. Lennox Street was positive luxury by comparison, yet here was Audrey preferring this. Then there was Audrey herself, heavy-eyed, drained of energy, probably thinking of George Cunningham and wondering whether any experience was worth repeating. With Joan for breakfast and Audrey for supper, poor Mollie had had about enough of it for one day.

"About this marriage," she said abruptly. "Of course, it's not going to be put off. *I* shall see to that. I shall have a talk with Monty too when I've finished with Philip. You're simply run down and want a tonic."

"Oh, it isn't that," Audrey replied, sinking into an old wicker chair. "I've thought it all over. I don't think they tell young girls enough before they get married. They ought to tell them lots more. They ought to tell them quite plainly, 'You'll have to be prepared for this and that and the other. You'll have to expect to sit up half the night in the dining-room with dinner on the table wondering where he is. You'll have to learn that he hasn't really been run over or anything of that kind and that it's only their way. You must expect telegrams and telephone calls and excuses, and you mustn't be surprised if he brings somebody else with him when he does come. They're like that. And when they come home in a beastly state—'"

Here Mollie peremptorily interrupted her.

"Leave that brute in his grave," she commanded. "We're talking about Monty, not him. And I'll see Monty. Now what's all this rigmarole about milkmen and cellars and all the rest of it? Tell me as I undress you. I'm going to put you to bed."

But little that was fresh was to be learned here either. Audrey thanked her again and again for the offer of the house, but she thought she would rather be here with her gas-ring and cocoa and chintz-covered sugar-box. Mrs. Cook thought she could arrange it—it would only be half a crown more.

"Well, I'll see Mrs. Cook too while I'm about it; may as well do the thing thoroughly. Let me unlace your boots—why, your feet are cold, and on a night like this! Never mind your hair; you can do it in bed. And drink the rest of this cocoa. Really I do think I live in a helpless sort of world—there isn't enough of me to go round—there ought to be half a dozen of me. Now into bed with you, and you'd better stay there till I come round in the morning. I'm not going back till Wednesday."

She packed up the cocoa-cups and turned off the gas-ring, opened the window and wound up the little Swiss clock. As she moved about the room folding Audrey's clothes and setting things to rights her own letter of Sunday morning was brought up, but she placed it on the mantelpiece by the side of the clock, forbidding Audrey to read it till the morning. Letters didn't matter now that she was here in her own capable, practical person. Letters took too long. She was going to have things done much more quickly or know the reason why.

XIII

Philip himself opened the door to her. She gave her cheek to be kissed and then walked straight in.

"Is Monty here?" were her first words.

"No. I think he's gone out for a walk."

"A walk, at this time of night!"

Philip shrugged his shoulders. "What brings you here, Mollie?" he said.

She was busy untying her veil. "What do you suppose? Everything, of course."

"Have you had dinner or supper?"

"I had a cup of cocoa at Audrey Cunningham's, and don't want anything else. Now why didn't you answer my telegram, and why didn't you write again as you promised?" She threw the hat and veil on the table and her gloves after them and stood before Philip.

"How are the children?" he asked.

"Perfectly well."

"And Joan?"

Her only answer to this last was a long look. Then she walked to the little Empire sofa and sat down. He might stand if he wished.

"Well?" she said at last. This was after a full minute, during which time he had stood by the table idly fingering her veil. Then suddenly his fingers pushed the veil aside, and he crossed to the sofa and sat down by her.

"What is it you want to know, darling?" he asked.

"Everything—every little thing from beginning to end," she replied.

"You've seen that I don't want to tell you?"

"Yes, I've seen that."

"And that I probably have my reasons?"

"Oh—reasons!"

"Reasons that are stronger than ever at this moment?"

"Will they go on getting much stronger? If so I can only warn you that a breaking-point will come."

"Yes. I'm very near it."

"And so am I, Philip."

There was no mistaking her tone. It did not mean that if he continued to shut her out like this she would do anything violent—live apart from him, become merely his housekeeper, or anything of that kind. It meant enormously more than that. Where confidence and trust are, there are few divergences that do not presently right themselves, few differences that cannot be resolved; but where these are absent nothing is right. Every word is possible peril, every silence a hanging sword. In all my acquaintance I know of no happier marriage than the Esdailes'. You never go into their house and feel that the air is still charged with some scene that your arrival has interrupted, you never leave wondering what weapons will be picked up again the moment your back is turned. Philip is not without his tempers nor Mollie without her own purposes, but it stops at that. The rest is brave decencies, with I know not what tenderer stuff behind. This it was that seemed for the moment to be in peril.

But suddenly she put her hand on his. She did not speak; the hand spoke for her. The next moment his other hand had fallen on hers again, so that both enclosed it. Then their eyes too met.

"It would be an awful thing to risk, Phil," she said quietly.

His eyes begged her. "Won't you let me carry it a little longer alone?"

"I don't believe you can. And if you can," she added, "I don't see what we got married for."

"But it will be rotten for you too."

"When have I shrunk from that?" she asked.

"Never," he replied in a low voice.

And so Mollie Esdaile too took her portion of the burden.

"Well, where shall we begin?" he asked, with a sigh that it must be so.

"You know best. But tell me first why you didn't write."

"I hadn't seen young Smith. I haven't yet as a matter of fact. But—," he drew her head to his breast, and there were some moments during which he whispered into her ear.

For all his care and guarding it was not possible that she should not at least tremble. But she did not start within his arms. The tremor passed, and her dry lips repeated—

"Shot him!"

"For some reason or other. I don't think either of us can quite tell Joan that, can we?"

"Shot him! Chummy!"

"There's no doubt about it. It was Monty who picked up the pistol. Neither you nor I can very well tell Audrey that, can we?"

"Monty found the pistol!"

"And I picked up the cartridge-shell myself. The police were round here at six o'clock on Friday morning looking for them."

"The police! Here!"

In spite of all, Philip could not restrain a little laugh. "Oh, they didn't find anything. They don't when they've given you warning the night before. By that time both pistol and case had been at the bottom of silver-flowing Tamesis for six hours. I dropped 'em in myself from the middle of Albert Bridge. Do you begin to see what you're in for, my poor darling?"

It was doubtful whether she yet did. She could still only repeat, "Chummy shot him! Does that mean—?" Her horrified stare finished the question.

"Oh, I don't think so," he answered quickly, "at any rate not yet. Naturally both Hubbard and I have got to stand by Chummy for the present."

"Then somebody saw Monty pick up the pistol?"

"For the police to know anything about it, you mean? Well, as a matter of fact that's the purest bad luck. There happens to be a fellow called Westbury, confound him, and that beastly bullet seems to have fetched up somewhere in his house; he lives just across the way there. That's all the police have to go on now that the other things are safely in the river mud."

Slowly it was sinking into her mind. Her eyes closed for a moment as she felt the first faint strain of the weight of it. This came with the thought of Joan.

"But—but—" she said faintly, "—that poor child—?"

"Joan? I suppose she is wondering what's happened?"

"Wondering what's happened.... You may as well know, Philip—it's a mere trifle at this stage—that they're most awfully thick—far more than you've been told. You know what boys and girls are nowadays. And now comes this horrible silence, except for that one little note from him—"

"Has she had a note from him?" Philip asked quickly. "From the hospital?"

"There was no address on it. I suppose it was from the hospital?" she in her turn asked in quick alarm.

"Yes, it wasn't from a prison. When did she get this note?"

"Yesterday morning."

"Did she show it to you?"

"Yes. It simply said he'd had this spill, but was all right, and she wasn't to be alarmed."

"He didn't mention incidentally that he'd shot a man?"

"Of course not. I don't believe he had."

Philip passed this last point.

"Well, as he's written once I suppose he'll go on writing. He's heaps better as a matter of fact. So it won't be too hard on her. Anyway, she'll have to grin and bear it."

"I did hold out hopes that I might be able to take him back with me," Mollie ventured.

"You won't be able to do that," said Philip with decision. "Quite apart from his being fit to travel, we've only gone a certain way in all this, you know. He'll still have matters to explain. And till he does, I'm afraid Audrey Cunningham will have to make the best of things too, like Joan. It wouldn't do her any good to know that Monty was liable to arrest at any moment."

"But is he?" said Mollie, startled.

"Of course he is. So am I. So are you. So would she be."

"But why?"

In spite of his explanation, I don't think she understood. I don't think she understands to this day. I don't think that at the bottom of her anti-social heart any woman does. A delayed wedding or a post without a lover's letter is a far greater thing than a capital charge in which all who conspire are principals.

Then, in spite of her fatigue, her skeptical common sense came to her aid. Philip might involve himself in a web of unelucidated stuff of which one-tenth perhaps was fact of sorts and the rest pure speculation; but she knew Chummy. The thought of Chummy as a murderer was absurd beyond words. Whatever the explanation might be it certainly was not that. And, yawning as she rose, she told Philip so.

"And that's that," she concluded. "Now do let's go to bed. Of course, if you think Chummy's a murderer I quite see why you didn't write and why you don't want to tell Audrey and all the rest of it, but you'll find it's all a mistake. There's something you don't know, or else there's been an accident of some kind. If you seriously want me to believe that Chummy Smith.... What's the matter, darling?"

The last words were a quick, startled cry. She did not know what it was that lurked at the bottom of the eyes that were looking so deeply and somberly into her own, but she feared already. His head was slowly shaking from side to side.

"Philip! What do you mean?" she cried in agitation.

Still the head shook. It was impossible for her mind not to fly back to that moment, now nearly five days ago, when he had stood blinking in the doorway with a candle in one hand and a jar of liqueur in the other.

"Tell me quickly what you mean, Philip!" she cried again.

"I saw it."

She fell back. "You—?"

"It wasn't an accident, and there isn't anything I don't know."

"You—?"

The slow sideways shake changed to one single nod. The next moment his arms were about her and he was leading her to the sofa again. He sighed. There was no help for it now. If she would have it she must have it all.

"It's the only thing I haven't told you. We may as well get it over," he said.

Nor did he whisper this time. He spoke in his usual voice, using the plainest English he could.

But what it was that Philip Esdaile told his wife you must guess for a little while longer. She was the first living soul to know. And it was a very different thing from that which she had left Santon to hear.

For it was this overwhelmingly extraordinary yet stupendously ordinary thing that sent her round to Audrey Cunningham the next morning, but without comfort for her, with no plans for settling the wedding out of hand.

It was this same thing that took her back to Santon on the Wednesday, without Chummy, without help for Joan.

It was this same thing that puzzled Monty Rooke's brain as he took his midnight walk that night down Roehampton Lane, driven from Audrey Cunningham's company and sick of the sight of Philip and all his works.

And it was this and nothing else that Cecil Hubbard so much wanted to know when he knitted his honest brows over hydrophones, sound-ranging, or whatever other mysterious apparatus it was that Philip Esdaile might have hidden away in his cellar.

PART IV

THE MAN IN THE PUBLIC-HOUSE

I

As an eager and passionate student of the Life of my day there are, within limits, few places that I don't visit and few people I don't on occasion talk to. I say "within limits," since I admit that there may be grades at one end of the scale at which I draw the line, while at the other end there may conceivably be those who draw the line at me. But within these extremes, if not always familiarly, yet on the whole without constraint, I sup at coffee-stalls or dine in quite good company more or less indifferently.

I have found that the best strategic jumping-off-points for the satisfying of this curiosity about the preponderating average of Life are two. One—the Public-house—I have already mentioned. There only a glass screen may divide you from the hawker who has left his barrow for a few minutes in somebody else's charge, or from the gibused and silk-muffled figure who finds a glass of sherry a convenient way of getting small change for his taxi. The other point of vantage is the Club, where that same taxi is paid off, but where liveried chauffeurs may stand for hours by the waiting cars.

I shall come to the Man in the Club by and by. For the present I wish to return to the Man in the Public-house.

I won't say that I always love him, but I always recognize that I have him very seriously to deal with. I am not thinking of him now either as a reader of my journalism or as a potential buyer of my novels, but as a larger phenomenon. I am thinking of him—loosely I admit—very much as some political cartoonist might think of a generalized and consolidated figure that turns a deaf ear to the Bolshevist and his sinister whisperings on the one side, while the other ear is no less stopped to the honeyed blandishments of the statesman who so frequently and extraordinarily seeks to cajole him with flatteries that are both out-of-touch and out-of-date.

He is Conservative, if Conservatism means that he cynically holds his hand till he has seen what the next dodge is likely to be; and he is Liberal in the sense of believing that if everybody looks after himself then there will not be anybody who is not looked after. You have overdone it, my good friends and representatives in Parliament. He no longer believes a word you say. You offer him good and necessary things, and he glances sideways at you, and his lips shape the words "By-election." You try to keep him from rash and dangerous courses, and he wants to know what *you* are getting out of it. You ration him, but he knows where to get sugar and butter while you make the best of saccharine tablets and West African margarine; you de-control, and he knows better than you do why hens cease to lay and rabbits to breed. It is we of the cheaper Press who really have him in hand, and he cocks his ears back at us occasionally. He did so when the *Daily Circus* gave him pictures of bathing girls instead of war news; he is doing so today when—oh, lots of things—are pushed on and off the proscenium like Monty Rooke's camouflage canvas trees and linoleum sentries. He sniffs at all these things, says nothing, and calls for another glass of his country's seven-times-accursed beer.

Yet he follows, if not his leader, his neighbor. This he sometimes does to the most astonishing conclusions, just as he looks up at the sky-line because he sees somebody else doing so, or is prepared to swear that he hears a maroon because the man next to him says "Listen!" The vaguer the rumor the greater is the scope for his self-and-collective suggestion. He sees Russians, he knows that dead Field-Marshals are still alive. He can tell you from private information that such-and-such a battalion has been cut up or such-and-such a battle-fleet sent to the bottom of the sea. And not one of these larger things is half so large to him as the smaller thing that looms huge because it is in his own immediate neighborhood. We on the *Circus* provide pictures to give him at least the photographic semblance of body for his belief. But what when the very flesh and blood of the drama passes along his street every day? What when he has spoken with the chief actor himself, knows who he married, the number of his children and their names? What when he knows the house he lives in, who lived there before, why he left so suddenly, and the very words he is said to have said on leaving?

Do you see what I am coming to—those first faint whisperings of something wrong—or if not positively wrong so much the better for public-house debate on the point—with Philip Esdaile's house in Lennox Street?

II

The first that Esdaile knew of all this was from the younger of Mollie's two maids. Monty and Audrey had arranged to dispense with the services of these two domestics, but Philip, still lingering on, had wanted the younger one at least back. She had promised to come, but had not done so, and Philip had sought her out. Thereupon she had said that she would rather not come.

"Why?" Philip had asked; but she had given no satisfactory reason.

He had then turned to the second maid, but with no better result.

After all, it didn't matter. It was very little trouble for himself and Monty to make their own breakfasts. They could take their other meals at the Chelsea Arts Club, and there would be no difficulty in getting a woman one or two days a week to clean.

Then, to his extreme astonishment, on the very day after Mollie's departure for Santon, he left Monty to a sandwich-and-coffee luncheon in the studio and came out of his house to find Lennox Street almost as full of people as it had been on the morning when the parachute had descended on the studio roof.

"What's the matter? Anything happened?" he asked the nearest loiterer at his gate; but he did not learn what had really happened till he reached the Club.

Certainly the joke, if it was a joke, appeared to be "on him." Simultaneously two grinning fellow-members thrust into his hand that morning's issue of the *Roundabout*. The *Roundabout*, I should say, is the *Circus's* (much inferior) rival.

It contained a photograph of Esdaile's house, with the spot where the parachute had descended marked with a cross.

It was, of course, a thousand pities. No man likes the house he lives in held up to the idle public gaze. Had the annoying thing been submitted to my own paper I could have stopped it. Had it been a big thing I might even have stopped its appearance in the *Roundabout*, for, while we cut one another's throats in detail, we have our understandings in larger matters. Hurriedly I scanned the rest of the paper to see whether any letterpress went with the picture. None did. There was simply the photograph, with a couple of quite innocent descriptive lines underneath.

"Seems to me rather a stumer," I said to Willett. "Is Hodgson losing his grip a bit?"

"Haven't noticed it," Willett replied. "Sound man Hodgson. Doesn't often do things without a reason. I think we might go a bit slower on actresses and mannequins. This is the crash we were talking about the other morning, isn't it?"

"Yes. A wash-out I should have said."

"Perhaps he's playing the local-interest card. He's doing that just now. I don't see why we shouldn't do more of it."

"I think we'll wait for a better story than that anyway," I replied. "Well, let's get to work—"

But all that afternoon the thing worried me. It was a trifle, perhaps, but it was a trifle on the wrong side. More, unlike some other trifles, I already saw how dangerously capable of further development it was. I have told you what the attitude of the Press was to this question of civil flying. It was one of simply awaiting events. But all the time events were fermenting, so to speak. High over our heads Olympian minds were shaping and re-shaping policies and plans, and Argus eyes were tirelessly watching for indications of the receptivity of the popular mind. Had Hodgson heard something that we had not? As you sometimes see an insignificant person's affairs, of no interest in themselves, solemnly weighed by the Lords of Appeal because of some novel and far-reaching point they raise, was something in the nature of a Test Case now being sought? Had we on the *Circus* been wrong in assuming that the idea was simply to catch and make an example of the careless joy-rider and the idiot who stunted over towns? Was some more important point to be raised, and had Hodgson had wind of it?

I was inclined to think not, and for the reason I have just given. Make a thing big enough, and we hang fairly well together; but take the whips off, so to speak, and we go as we please. If it had been as important as all that we should have heard of it. Willett, who is a youngster of parts, was in all probability right. Hodgson was merely catering for the local interest.

But still I was uneasy, and my uneasiness had nothing to do with the annoyance the publication of the photograph of the house in Lennox Street must cause Esdaile. I was thinking of far graver possible consequences. Even the lightest measure of Publicity is not a thing to be trifled with. Here I know what I am talking about. The merry fellows of the Chelsea Arts Club might pull Esdaile's leg about his haunted house, and want to know whether the White Lady dropped any hairpins as she passed, or if the horrible shrouded figure with the crimson-dripping hands would make a good film; but we journalists have to take these things a good deal more seriously than that. Publicity, sometimes of the most incredibly silly kind, is our meat and drink and hourly breath. All day and every day our brains are on the stretch in our endeavors to secure it. We bring our heaviest guns to bear on the elusive thing, are sure we can't possibly miss it this time, let fly, and lo! we have missed after all. Like a pithball on a fountain, it is still dancing there untouched, and any penny peashooter may bring it down when all our trained intelligence has failed.

And what would be the effects on our Case if it came down?

Well, you can see that for yourself. In obscurity lay our hope that the thing might remain what on the face of it it appeared to be. Switch the arc-lamps of the great papers on to it, with the whole power-house of dynamic government behind them, and all was over. Not an aspect of the Case would go unprobed to the very bottom, and the hungry newspapers would find themselves, not with a mere aeroplane crash that could be dismissed in a couple of lines, but with a really fine fat, first-class Murder Case that would keep them merrily going for weeks.

And I can assure you that we all wanted very badly indeed just such a Case. We wanted it for more reasons than one. We wanted it, as we always do, in the ordinary way of our business, but much more we wanted it to take people's minds off other matters. We wanted it for the same reason that made us resolutely print those pictures of girls bathing during the blackest days of the War. We wanted it because the Man in the Public-house was restless and showed a disposition to pry into affairs in which his interference is only wanted when a General Election draws near. Bathing girls were very well in their way; a really high-class line in Divorce Cases would have outstripped them easily, if I may be permitted the unintentional expression; but the man who could have given us on the *Circus* the first Assassination in the Air could have named his own price for it.

III

The flat in which I live with the old housekeeper who looks after me is not in Chelsea at all, but a quarter of an hour's walk away, just round the corner from Queen's Gate. It is exceedingly comfortable (as indeed it should be considering the rent I am made to pay for it), I have my own furniture, and on the whole I don't ask for a much better place to work in. For, quite apart from my paper, I do work, and I don't want to give you the impression that the whole of my leisure time is given over to the investigation of what happens to my Chelsea friends.

I was, as a matter of fact, particularly busy just about that time. Day after day I was getting up at half-past six in the morning, breakfasting at my table as I worked, and continuing without interruption till it was time for luncheon and the office. Since you are probably not in the white-elephant line of business, I won't tell you which of my novels I was at work on. I will only say that I at any rate was interested in it, and, severe as was the strain of writing from seven o'clock in the morning till midday, I sometimes hated to break off. Mrs. Jardine had orders not to admit anybody whomsoever between those hours, and obeyed them to the letter.

You may judge then of my surprise when there walked into my study at nine o'clock in the morning, and not over Mrs. Jardine's dead body, Billy Mackwith.

"Don't scold the old lady," he began without preface. "I suppose she hadn't any barbed wire except that on her chin—it is rather like one of the gooseberries we used to make on the old wiring-course. I had to see you."

"Had breakfast? Have a cup of coffee?" I asked him.

"Nothing, thanks. Well, I think I saved friend Philip a certain amount of trouble yesterday," he said, putting down his hat, stick and gloves. I don't think Mackwith buys a glossy new silk topper every time he goes out, but I do honestly believe he buys a new pair of lemon-colored gloves.

"Oh? How was that?"

"At the inquest on that fellow," he replied. "And by the way, I saw the *Roundabout* too. I suppose it has its humorous side, but it's very annoying too. I should go for 'em for libel. A house can be libeled, you know. Anyway, it's a good job he's out of town."

I was on the point of saying, "A good job he's what?" when I checked myself. If you remember, I had last seen William Mackwith, K.C., when I had left him at Sloane Square Station an hour or two after that confounded aeroplane accident. He and Hubbard had gone off to keep their respective appointments, while I myself had followed our check-coated friend Westbury into a public-house. Whether either Esdaile or Hubbard had seen him since I didn't know. I now gathered that Billy at any rate hadn't seen Esdaile.

"Yes?" I said. "What trouble have you been saving him?"

"Well, I told you—I saved him the bother of stopping for the inquest."

I had of course known that there must be an inquest, but I suppose I had been busy and had forgotten it again. This began to be interesting.

"Tell me about the inquest," I said.

He took a cigarette from his case and offered me one. Then he continued between puffs.

"Well, as a matter of fact there wasn't very much trouble. One man seemed inclined to be cantankerous, but we brought it in Misadventure all right. We—"

I imagine that at this point he caught sight of the expression on my face, for he stopped suddenly.

"Esdaile did go out of town, didn't he?" he asked.

"I'll tell you about Esdaile in a moment. Go on about the inquest."

He seemed puzzled, but went on.

"Of course, that was my idea in speaking to that Inspector that morning. It would have been a pity to upset the Esdailes' plans. So I explained this to the Inspector and gave him my card—said I hadn't seen very much, but as much as anybody else—result, I was made foreman of the jury."

Here I had a little flash of illumination as regards Inspector Webster too. Esdaile, if you remember, had said to him, "Yes, that was Mr. Mackwith, the King's Counsel; didn't you know?" and Webster had answered, "Was he indeed, sir?" My respect for the Inspector's powers of giving nothing away went up several hundreds per cent. Apparently it was the Inspector who had seen to it that Billy had been put on the jury.

"Well, you were made foreman. You said one man gave trouble. Who, and why?"

"Oh, some fellow or other—Westcott or Westmacott I think his name was—I forget. Insisted on viewing the body. Wanted his money's worth I suppose. He was sorry he did though."

This was more and more interesting. I asked what sort of a man this Westmacott was.

"The sort of fellow who would be down in the cellar before his wife and children when there was an air-raid on, I should say," Billy replied. "Awful nuisance of a man. But he got his all right. He'll probably be taking solid food again this day week."

"Then you did see the body?"

"Had to, if only to keep this fellow quiet. He stuck out right to the finish too, but we got our dozen without him. Prima facie case, of course. Death by burning, and what wasn't that was general smash-up."

"Was a doctor called?"

"The divisional surgeon was there, but he quite agreed, and I saw to the rest in my capacity as foreman. There was only one man who wasn't satisfied, and he was busy—" Billy twinkled wickedly.

You may imagine how I was beginning to relish all this. The Chelsea Arts with its rags about haunted houses and White Ladies who dropped hairpins was well enough in its way, but its humor could not compare for a moment with the spectacle of a rising King's Counsel who practically forced himself on to a jury-panel, got himself made foreman, and then burked inquiry by shutting up the only juryman who had as much as a suspicion of the dangerous truth—and all this in the whitest innocence and purest good faith! I could have laughed aloud. Had he been a willing instrument in the affair he could not have done his work more efficiently and completely.

"Is the poor fellow buried yet?" I asked in a suppressed voice.

"Yesterday," said Billy.

"And he can't be dug up again?"

Mackwith gave me a sharp look. "What do you mean?" he asked quickly.

"Dug. Past participle of the verb to dig. I mean is he buried once for all?"

"Short of an Exhumation Order from the Home Secretary he is. I don't understand you."

"And that's rather difficult to get, isn't it?" I continued.

"I should say the North Pole was comparatively easy," Billy replied.

At this point my laughter really became too much for me. I remember hoping that it didn't seem too rude, but I couldn't help it. Billy let me finish, and then asked quietly, even gravely, "Now if you're feeling better, will you please explain?"

I suppose my laughter had been just a little hysterical. As I have already told you, I myself stand only on the verge of this Case; but not so my friends, and Esdaile in particular. I remembered—and deep under that rather remarkable laughter it moved me more than a little to do so—the extraordinary range and sweep of emotions that had shaken Esdaile in the course of a single day. I remembered the bright strained tension of those first minutes after he had come up out of the cellar, the shock of that telephone message from the hospital that had told him what had happened to a friend. I remembered that black depression when Hubbard and I had found him waiting alone in his house for Monty. I remembered his ache on Joan Merrow's account, our later talk with Monty, his nascent and grim resolve that in the teeth of all the world the accident theory should be maintained, his dismay when he had realized what a post-mortem examination might disclose. I ran over again his whole day, from that merry breakfast-party to the appearance of Inspector Webster in our midst at ten o'clock at night.... Well, one peril was now safely past. In the absence of the Exhumation Order of which Mackwith spoke, there remained no tittle of material evidence save a battered bit of nickel-steel in Westbury's possession or in that of the police. If only for Esdaile's sake, I felt as if a weight had been lifted from me.

And, on the top of all, Billy Mackwith's innocent complicity must have moved me to that inane outburst.

"Well, for one thing, Esdaile isn't out of town at all," I said, wiping my eyes.

"Well, I thought he was. That isn't the joke, is it?"

"Not altogether. You see—"

"Do you mean that stupid *Roundabout* thing?"

"No.... I beg your pardon, Billy. It came over me all of a sudden. Now I think I can tell you—"

And so another was added to our nicely-lengthening list of Principals in the Case.

IV

While I spoke Billy had risen, and was pretending to examine the prints on my walls. I continued to talk; talking was, in fact, my morning's work that day. I finished, and there was a long silence. I thought my barrister-friend would never have done looking at those prints.

Then suddenly he crossed over to my table and stood leaning lightly on his fingertips.

"Why wasn't I told this sooner?" he asked, his eyes brightly on mine.

For a moment I thought he meant that our neglect to inform him had landed him into this equivocal position with regard to the coroner's jury, and was beginning to explain that, being everybody's business, it had also apparently been nobody's. But he cut me short.

"Oh, I don't mean that. Leave the inquest out of it for the present. What I mean is that I could have saved our friend a good deal of mental pain if I'd known—and you too," he added, "from the way you laughed just now."

"How?" I asked.

"In this way," he replied, sitting down on the edge of my table and giving his striped cashmere trousers a little hitch. "Say that a shot has been fired...."

Philip, I take it, has been worrying about the consequences to this fellow Smith, and incidentally to Miss Merrow. Now if I'd been there to ask Rooke a few material questions I think I could have assured him that it's a thousand to one there won't be any consequences."

"Why not?"

"The state of the body," he replied promptly. "Rooke saw it, you say, or at any rate quite enough of it; I saw it too; and, shot or no shot, it wouldn't have taken me two minutes to get out of Rooke that there was no earthly possibility of proving that a shot caused death."

"You mean there were so many other good reasons?"

"Well, I'm not a doctor, but I should say at least a dozen. No wonder that fellow Westbury—ah, that's his name, not Westcott—had to make a bolt for it. Unless somebody can be produced who actually saw the shot fired there won't be the ghost of a Case, and I'm inclined to think that even then it would reduce itself to shooting with intent to kill or wound—which is a felony, of course, but not quite the same thing as murder. No, I think you can take it from me that there won't be any consequences."

I pondered this for a moment. Then I saw the flaw in it. Every man to his trade. Here was the advocate speaking, his whole acute mind trained to one single end—the getting of his man off. But I myself work in a different material and saw the Case from my own angle.

"One moment," I interposed. "When you say consequences you mean legal consequences? In other words he'd slip through your fingers simply because nobody actually saw him do it?"

"He wouldn't even be charged. That was practically a certainty before the inquest. It's overwhelming now the other fellow's buried."

"But legal consequences are not the only kind of consequences there are in the world."

"Oh, I'm not speaking of moral consequences. They're quite another matter," quoth Billy.

"Not as regards Esdaile's having a rotten time over this," I differed. "Let's look at it from another point of view for a moment. Neither you nor I know Smith. But Hubbard and Esdaile do, and there's this friendship between them. And mark you, friendship too isn't always the same thing it was before the War. There were lots of men we called friends then very much as a matter of habit; I mean it didn't often occur to you to ask what kind of a man your friend would be when it came to the pinch. We've all made new friends, and there are some of the old ones whose names we never want to hear again. You see what I mean? I mean the bond must be pretty strong for two men like Esdaile and Hubbard to take instantly to the thought of shielding Smith like ducks taking to water. I watched them—it was really exciting—you could read both their faces like books. Very well. Up to this point we're both talking the same language. When we say consequences we mean legal consequences.

"But here's where the difference comes in. I don't know what Hubbard's views are, as I haven't seen him since that night; but I do know what Esdaile's are. He's shielding Smith—but only till he hears what he's got to say for himself. He doesn't want to condemn him unheard. I admit that in the meantime he's taken certain rather risky steps, and my own opinion is that he won't find it very easy if he wants to retrace them again; the river'd have to be dredged for a pistol, for example, and Lord only knows what sort of a reason he'd give for even having interfered at all. But my point is that he's done nothing final yet. Smith's got to satisfy him, and if he can't—well, it can't be quite the same between them again after that, can it?"

"You mean their friendship's broken?"

"Well, that's not quite the way I should put it. It might break, or possibly it might not. What I mean is that a friendship with a man who's killed other men in battle isn't the same thing as one with a man who murders another in peace-time. It may be as good for all I know, as I haven't done either, but obviously it isn't the same."

"No, I suppose not," Mackwith agreed. "And as for retracing his steps, I agree with you that the best thing he can do is to keep his mouth shut. I certainly intend to about that inquest. Life's too short to go moving for Exhumation Orders."

"Well, next there's Joan Merrow. Exactly the same thing applies to her. Is she going to marry a soldier or an assassin? Is Esdaile going to let her? He's her guardian for all practical purposes, and he's got that question to answer."

The barrister laughed. "I don't think he need worry about that. Miss Merrow strikes me as a young woman who won't stand any nonsense from guardians. Well," he took up his hat and stick, "I must be getting along. I didn't expect all this when I came in, but it seems to me the Case is over now. Barring these moral consequences of yours, it practically ended when I gave in our verdict yesterday."

"I hope you're right," I replied. "I thought so myself a few days ago, though, and that evening a Police Inspector marched in."

He stopped at the door and spoke over his shoulder.

"Oh? You seem doubtful. Any reason?"

"None," I replied. "Only what women call a sort of feeling about it."

Mackwith laughed.

"We'll see about that when it comes," he said. "So long—"

V

The surface indications were of course of the very slightest. So far they consisted merely of the photograph in the *Roundabout*, my speculations whether Hodgson had anything up his sleeve, and similar trifles. But others were pending. The danger of the coroner's inquest might be safely past, but at least half a dozen other rocks loomed immediately ahead. The Aiglon Company, for example, would want to know what had gone wrong with their machine, and the manufacturers would be even more interested. The same with the parachute people. The Aero Club and the Royal Aeronautical Society both have their Accidents Investigation Committees, and it was quite likely that claims against various Insurance Offices had already been lodged. You cannot thrust a finger into the close web of modern life without stirring up all manner of complexities. I suppose it was these that I had already begun to fear.

Perhaps most immediate of all was the question of unauthorized flying. What had that machine been doing over London at all? Military machines come and go under orders, but not commercial planes piloted by civilian aeronauts. Setting such things as Murder and Manslaughter entirely on one side, was it not probable that Smith would be called to book on this account? From our point of view it was obviously most undesirable that he should be brought into Court on any charge at all; but what if we couldn't prevent it? What if, in the inhuman collision of powerful business interests behind, the lawyers were to get to work—an Insurance Company resist a claim, say, or the Aiglon people proceed against the manufacturers on a point of warranty? You may think I was seeing lions in the path, but it is never safe to reckon on meeting nothing more formidable than a sheep. And I have nothing against lawyers as a class. I don't think Billy Mackwith would pick my pocket of a single sixpence. But I do believe they are like the road-mender with the stone. He hit it with his hammer ten times without breaking it, and was then asked whether he did not think he would have a better chance of splitting it if he turned it splitting-edge uppermost. "How do you know I want to split it?" he replied. I suspect even Billy of not wanting to split it sometimes.

"Willett!" I called as I entered my office after lunch that day. "Just get me out the latest thing about Air Navigation, will you?"

"Is the new one out yet?" Willett replied, walking to the big glass-fronted cupboard where we keep the current papers of this kind; the others are on the library shelves downstairs. "I think they were withdrawn. I seem to remember sending to the Stationery Office and being told there'd been a muddle of some sort."

"There must be something in force," I said. "I want that, whatever it is."

"Just a moment—ah, here we are!"

Willett was both right and wrong. A certain issue of Statutory Rules and Orders had as a matter of fact been withdrawn, but an amended reprint was now available. He handed the slender white booklet to me. It was dated April 30th, 1919, and had therefore been in force for some days at the time of the Lennox Street accident.

I walked to my desk and settled down to the study of it.

I don't know that I was very much the wiser for my efforts. So much seemed to be in the air in every sense of the word. The paper was not even an Act, but an Order, and it seemed to me that its phrases about "contravention of these Regulations" might in practice mean almost anything. What, for example, did "stress of weather or other unavoidable cause" mean? What would happen in case of a kind of accident expressly excluded from the Order—"within a circle of a radius of one mile from the center of a licensed aerodrome"? What about the special cases permitted "by direction of the Secretary of State on the recommendation of a Government Department"? I don't mean that the intention of it all wasn't plain enough. The drafters of the Regulations had done the best they could in a new and totally unexplored field. For all practical purposes this new science was just as old as the War, and these detailed points of law had not arisen during the War. But they were coming up now, a whole body of practice still to make, and any youngster who chose could loop the loop and what little proved Law there was at one and the same time.

In fact, the only quite unmistakable paragraph I found was the one that promised proper castigation "to any person obstructing or impeding the authorities" and so forth—that is to say, Hubbard, Esdaile, myself and the rest of our little gang of law-breakers.

And, before I pass on, bear with me for one moment while I ask you to observe how all History began to loom behind our Case, ready at any moment to drive it irresistibly forward. For that four-centuries-old Upspringing of daring and glory and adventure that we call the Renaissance is come suddenly and magically into our midst again today. There are now to seek and to chart and to possess Indies and Orients, not of the unembraced and bridal waters, but of the already defeated and subject Air. Our age hears the old imperious call, and across four hundred years of time the hands of a George receive Romance from those of an Elizabeth. It may seem a far cry from this to the Man in the Public-house, but it crept and lapped about our Case like a slowly-mounting flood. Idle rumors brought with the milk to Chelsea doorsteps; a Press eager to take its lead from any momentary whiff that ruffles the popular mind; a Government that without that Press could not govern for a week; and the radiance of this new sunburst over all—this is the apparatus of our Drakes and Burleighs of today. And, so long as the mighty thing went forward unimpeded, what did any individual matter?

VI

"Foreman? You may well say foreman! But he hasn't finished with me yet! You've seen what it says in today's *Roundabout*, haven't you? Very well, young-fellow-me-lad; you watch it! They laugh best that laugh last. It isn't over yet!"

I was grinding my teeth behind my copy of the paper he had just mentioned. The thick-headed fool had done it. I was not reading the paper; I was merely using it to hide behind as I stood at the Public-house counter with one foot on the brass rail.

"Over? It hasn't begun yet!" Westbury continued, his convex eyes glaring from one face to another. "It's ventilation these things want—ventilation in the public Press—and I tell you I haven't started yet! I went into this Case out of public spirit—'Webster,' I says to our friend, 'if you want me you know where to find me'—I'm a busy man with my own private affairs to look after, but right's right and I'm not the man to hang back when forward's the word—and if they think I'm as easy stopped as all that they're mistaken, K.C. or no K.C.! The body was viewed—some of 'em didn't want to, but I saw to that—but I contend there ought to have been a proper post-mortem. And you may take it from me that if there had been this Case would have gone forward."

"Do you mean to a Criminal Court, Harry?" a voice asked.

"I said gone forward; I didn't say what Court. We'll see about Courts by and by. This Mister Smith or whatever his name is will be had up for flying to the danger of the public, and we'll see what happens then!"

Once more I vehemently cursed him. It was half-past eight at night, with nothing unusual doing at the office, and I had left Willett in charge so that I might find Westbury. It was perfectly certain that after Hodgson's leading article of that morning Westbury would not spend the evening in the retirement of his home, but would be out for what young Willett calls "gin-and-glory." As it happened, I had run him to earth at my very first attempt, in the same Saloon Bar in which I had first seen him.

You may know Hodgson's leading-article style. If we on the *Circus* don't imitate it it is not that we deny that it "gets across." It is allusive, rorty and familiar, and there is frequently common sense behind it. If the Man in the Public-house likes his news served up in that way you can't blame Hodgson for meeting his wishes. This is what he had written, no doubt sending his Chelsea sales up by hundreds of quires:

"TOM, DICK AND ICARUS.

"Our correspondent Mr. Harry Westbury is some lad. You will find his letter at the foot of the next column to this. Why, asks Harry, in these days when you may consider yourself lucky to have a roof over your head at all, should your head and that roof be brought into sudden and violent contact? Not that Harry is a jumper; he isn't going to challenge Joe Darby; but the ceiling and your occiput can establish connection just the same if the former comes down on the latter. What he really means is that aeroplanes, subject to sudden syncopes of the engines, have no business over Chelsea's pleasant roofs at all.

"H.W. does not claim that he personally suffered damage from the crash we reported last Friday. But he is a respected House and Estate Agent residing in the district and speaks feelingly. *C'est son métier*, as our gallant and Gallic Allies say. He means, we take it, that if civil aviation is to develop, corresponding safeguards must be developed side by side with it. Here we are with Harry all the way. Our Olympians may have burst a number of brain-cells over the present Regulations, but they will have to find a new wave-length. Tom, Dick and Harry we know, but we have not yet been properly introduced to Tom, Dick and Icarus. No, sir, not with building materials at their present price and the plumber rolling up in his Rolls-Ford. The pilot who came down in Chelsea last Thursday is said to have been employed by the Aiglon Company. Nuff said. If the Aiglon or any other Company is out for public support it knows what to do. In the meantime we hope Mr. Westbury won't raise his house premiums. But that is another story.

"The Man in the Public-house."

That was the whole text of it. Was it fair comment on a matter of public interest? Well, I don't say it wasn't. Was it a timely reminder that high-spirited lads who had lately been praised for their dare-devilry must now pull themselves together and fall into line with the new conditions? Very likely. Was it a legitimate attempt to arouse interest in the age's new wonder, or merely a political stick with which covertly to beat some high official dog or other? I didn't know.

For my mind was occupied with quite other thoughts. From round the edge of my paper I was trying to sum up Westbury—a young man, but unexercised; seldom drunk, as a man in decent physical condition would have been on half that he swallowed, but already habituated and inured; probably quite well-to-do, in that mysterious way that causes tradesmen quietly to acquire their own houses and to drive in their own two-seaters to places of entertainment such as that I was in; and yet in a sense a minor man of affairs as distinct from a tradesman, a cut above the shirt-sleeves-and-counter business, if not exactly entitled to style his occupation a profession. He had got over the first overweening stage of the vanity of that day's publicity; he was now a little disparaging what he wouldn't have allowed anybody else to disparage; was treating Hodgson quite as a familiar, in fact, which as far as I was concerned he was perfectly at liberty to do. A dangerous beast, I thought again, and none the less dangerous now that Billy Mackwith, as foreman of that coroner's jury, had got his back thoroughly up.

"Yes, Mr. Mackwith, K.C. or O.B.E., or whatever you call yourself," he was muttering again, "they laugh best that laugh last. If he'd even said to me, 'What's *your* opinion, sir?' I won't say but what I should have thought a bit more of him, but him and his silk hat and gloves ... you wait a bit! There's a few will be surprised before this Case is over!"

It seemed to me that he scarcely took the trouble to veil what he really meant. Nor was I surprised at the way in which his hearers evidently took his words. For, looking from his cunning yet stupid face to the six or seven other faces about him, I could make a guess at their attitude too. Remember those first faint rumors that had found their way with the morning's milk to Audrey Cunningham's doorstep. Remember what whispered currency they must have had before they had come to Audrey at all. Remember that photograph in the *Roundabout* that had filled Lennox Street with a gaping crowd that morning, a crowd that had taken a couple of days to diminish and die away. Esdaile told me later, too, that for a week he had been conscious of turning heads as he had walked along the streets.... Oh, I could have made this Case of ours a thing of pistols and parachutes only, but I wished to go a little farther than that. Not that I have any particular views on mass-suggestion at large. My business is simply to observe its working. And here I was, in a Saloon Bar, observing it in a very curious form.

For I think that every single member of the group to which I was listening behind my newspaper had more than an idea of what Westbury really meant. I think they knew perfectly well that when he spoke of flying to the public danger he meant very, very much more. I don't think there was one of them who had not heard the story of Inspector Webster and the bullet. Secretive as he was, he would be garrulous among his intimates if garrulity enhanced his self-importance. I am perfectly certain that every one of them knew all this, knew that he had been thwarted in his legitimate demand for a post-mortem examination, and knew in addition something else that I also was to know by and by.

Then suddenly something happened that placed all this beyond any doubt whatever.

Besides their own party, I was the only person at that end of the room, and I had been there long enough to have drunk three glasses of beer instead of the one that still stood only half empty on the counter at my elbow. As I listened the voices suddenly dropped. There was a minute of whispering, during which (realizing a little late that eavesdroppers must keep up appearances) I finished my beer and ordered a second glass. Then Westbury's voice rose again.

"Yes, 'corresponding safeguards or words to that effect,'" he said. "I gave my copy of the paper away. Er—"

The last was a sudden clearing of his throat, evidently intended to attract attention—my attention. I half dropped the paper and saw the convex eyes on mine.

"If that paper belongs to the house, sir, might I have a glance at it just for one moment?" he said.

VII

I had bought that copy of the *Roundabout* myself, but I knew that that was in no sense the point. Without a word I handed it to Mr. Westbury. My second glass of beer was placed before me, and as I half turned to get a coin from my pocket I felt, positively felt, their eyes on me. I also felt their removal as I took up my change and resumed my former attitude. Westbury had taken the paper with a "Thank you, sir."

"Ah, it's open at the very page. Begin here, Tom," he said. "'If civil aviation is to develop—'"

And he passed the paper to one of his companions.

I had not the least intention of leaving. I was perfectly well aware that Westbury had not wanted that paper, but had wanted to see my face. He was not likely to recognize it as that of the younger novelist whose portrait appears publicly from time to time, since in order to maintain that humorous status I have for a dozen years refrained from having my photograph taken at all; but I knew enough of my man to be sure that little had escaped him during that half hour or so when he had occupied that position of privilege outside Esdaile's French window, and that he probably remembered every face of that breakfast-party—Mackwith's and my own among the rest. That was why I had no thought of leaving. He was hardly the kind of man I should have had much to say to in the ordinary course, but if he saw fit to challenge me, well and good. In fact, I hadn't very much choice in the matter. I had only to picture to myself what sort of glances would be exchanged among them were I suddenly to finish my beer and walk out and my remaining became almost a necessity. Nay, *he* had already challenged *me* when he had borrowed my paper. My only doubt was whether, in view of that whispered conversation and of the dimensions Rumor had now attained, they hadn't all challenged me.

The next moment Mr. Westbury had gone still farther. He had also chosen the ground on which our duel, if there was to be a duel, was to take place. The Public-house has its own punctilio. I wouldn't go the length of saying that you can't ask a stranger for a match without offering to buy him a drink in return, but such invitations are given on quite slight occasions. I was not surprised, therefore, when Mr. Westbury, catching my eye, acknowledged the loan of the paper by saying, "Will you have a drink, sir?"

So I had in a sense either to eat his salt or refuse it. I did not hesitate. Certainly that beer was salt enough.

"Thank you," I replied.

"And what is it, sir?"

"I'll have another glass of beer."

He ordered it. Then, "I think we've met before," he said.

The silence of the others was suddenly very noticeable. It was for all the world as if some referee had ordered, "Seconds out of the ring."

"I'm afraid I don't quite—" I began.

"Well, I won't say it got as far as an intro," he took me up, "but weren't you at a certain house in Lennox Street when an accident occurred the other day?"

"I was, but I wasn't aware—"

"Oh, I wasn't inside the house. But I was able to be of some little assistance outside," he replied. "A very curious affair, sir," he added tentatively.

"Rather a sad one," I replied.

There was a pause. "Chelsea's very much interested in that accident," he continued.

I answered that I didn't live in Chelsea.

Then suddenly he became almost amiable; but for all his amiability his eyes were like the hard-boiled eggs on the counter, only a trifle yellower.

"Well, that's two of you gentlemen I've met now," he said. "I haven't the pleasure of knowing your name, but the other gentleman was Mr. Mackwith."

There was a certain correctness about this opening that I had reluctantly to acknowledge. He may or may not have known my name—the chances were that he had already ascertained it—but I read his thought. A few minutes ago, possibly before he had become aware of my presence, he had spoken pretty freely of Mackwith; he was now obviously asking himself whether I had overheard this. In all probability I had, but in such cases the official attitude is the best. Had Mr. Westbury been an administrator I could have imagined him penning a minute: "This does not come within the knowledge of this Department."

"Yes," he continued after a pause, "I had the pleasure of sitting on a coroner's jury with Mr. Mackwith the other day."

"Really?"

"Yes, and strange as it may seem, in connection with this very accident we're speaking of."

"That's very interesting," I said genially. "I haven't seen Mr. Mackwith since the occurrence. What happened at the inquest on the unfortunate man?"

"The verdict was in the papers, sir. And my own views are in that paper my friend is reading. They're twice over, as a matter of fact, once in a letter of mine they printed and once in the editor's remarks on it."

"Ah, then you're Mr. Westbury!" I exclaimed with feigned surprise. "I was reading both your letter and the article just now. I congratulate you. I see you're in touch with both sides."

Mr. Westbury looked at me with mistrust. "What both sides?" he asked.

"With both the men who came down that morning," I replied. "You were at the inquest on one of them, and you very properly call for an inquiry into the other man's conduct."

"I do!" he said so vindictively that he might almost have been spitting the two words into one of the sawdust-filled spittoons. "I do more than call, Mr.—" he glared.

"Oh? But how can you do more?" I asked politely. "There are certain prescribed forms in such cases, and if inquiry on those lines turns out to be satisfactory I should have said there was nothing more to be done?"

"Ah! If!" said Westbury, with the greatest intensity of meaning.

There was a palm in a copper pot behind him, and above his head a picture of a huntsman holding up a fox over the baying pack preparatory to drinking Somebody's Whisky. My eyes wandered reflectively to these objects for a moment; then I took a further step. It seemed to me too late to draw back now.

"But—well, since we are discussing this I wish you could be a little plainer," I said. "You say all Chelsea's interested in this Case, and I don't live in Chelsea. Why is Chelsea so interested?"

He replied promptly enough. "Because, sir, of certain things that don't appear on the surface of which I happen to have some knowledge."

"May I ask what things?"

He echoed me.

"And may I ask you something, and that is whether you happen to be aware that the police searched certain premises the other morning?"

"Do you mean the morning of the accident?"

"I do *not* mean the morning of the accident. I'm speaking of last Friday morning, at six o'clock, before anybody was about."

I considered a moment. Then, "But why not?" I replied. "Is there anything unusual about that? Surely when an accident takes place the police are the proper people to investigate it?"

I thought he would have jumped out of his chair with vehemence.

"Ah!" he cried. "Now you're talking! That's more like! The proper people? So they are; you stick to that! And now I'll ask you this: If that's so, why keep things back from them? Why this hushing up? Answer me that. Or bring some of your friends to answer it. That's all I have to say!"

And he flung himself back in his chair and continued to mutter softly.

It was evident that his choler against Mackwith had risen again. What had passed between the two men was no less plain. If Mackwith was right in his estimate of this fellow, air-raid nights spent in cellars are not the best of training for duties so unpleasant as those a coroner's inquest sometimes involves. Billy, on the other hand, did his bit in a Field Company and is tempered metal throughout. In any contest of wills between two such men there was no doubt which would be the victor. It had hardly occurred to Billy that there was a contest. Innocently and unconsciously, he had ridden roughshod over Westbury, and, if Westbury's mutterings meant anything, was to suffer for it.

"But," I said presently, "I'm afraid I don't understand even yet. It seems to me you're bringing a charge against somebody of interfering in a very serious matter. If anybody has interfered I agree with you that it's a public scandal and ought to be exposed. But I can't believe I've understood you properly."

He did not reply.

"And not only that," I continued, "but, if you'll forgive my saying so, you're neither bringing a charge nor leaving it alone."

Here, for the first time, a third person put in an aside.

"Tell him about that, Harry," a voice whispered.

(And, feeling pretty sure that I could guess what "That" was, I thought, "Now for that wearisome bullet story all over again!")

"I need hardly say," I went on, "that if you have any such charge to make there's not a single person who was there who won't gladly help you."

("Tell him about that, Harry," the voice whispered again.)

Then it was that Mr. Westbury "went back on" that eager group of mutes who had so scrupulously kept the ring for us. I saw their faces fall as, with a little jerk of his head to me, he rose. Whatever the "That" was they wished him to tell me, they apparently were not to be present at the telling. Looking back on the scene, I don't think he had any particular motive in this except more "gin-and-glory"; he would tell them all about it, with embellishments, afterwards. He passed down the bar and held the swing door open for me to precede him; then the door gave a "woff woff" as he followed me out.

VIII

I ask you to notice several untenable points about the position I had taken up. Twice at least I had flatly lied, once when I had told him that I had not seen Mackwith since the morning of the accident, and once when I had given him to understand that I knew nothing of the police search of Esdaile's premises. I say nothing of the greater lie, that we were all ready to help him in his efforts to get to the bottom of the Case. I count that as more the natural momentum the Case itself had now acquired than any personal untruthfulness on my own part.

Next, I now saw that as an eavesdropper my technique had been painfully clumsy. I had attracted attention to myself. I had accepted Westbury's hospitality, but (believe me, out of pure forgetfulness) had omitted to return it. Several times he had given me an opportunity, which I had not taken, of telling him my name, though I had admitted my knowledge of his. These may seem small things, but there are ways and ways of drinking a glass of beer. Within certain limits, I had a distinct sense of social failure.

And if, over and above all this, I had given him and his associates credit for too little intelligence, that I am afraid is rather a fault of mine. It may even have something to do with my position as a younger novelist. I constantly forget that one man is as good as another because he is as many.

So here I was, a clumsy, unmannerly fellow with a guilty conscience to boot, face to face with a very Chesterfield of the best licensed establishments and the whole body of law and order and public duty overwhelmingly on his side. We stood there under the unlighted public-house lamp, while the violet light of the May evening slowly faded from what Hodgson had called "Chelsea's pleasant roofs."

He was fully aware that he possessed what the correspondents used to call the initiative. This showed in his very few first words. I, it appeared, was to be forced to open the ball.

"Now, sir, you wished to see me, I believe," he said pompously.

I was on the point of reminding him that it was he who had made the proposal to come outside when he put up a peremptory hand.

"No, no. I know what you're going to say, and that don't go down. When I say you wanted to see me I mean you came here tonight for that purpose. Specially. Well, here I am."

I suppose I should have been within my rights in answering that I had entered those swing doors for a glass of beer and had not spoken to him until he had borrowed my newspaper; but obviously that line led nowhere. Moreover, from his comparative calm of manner now, I realized that while the larger advantages lay with him, at least one small tactical superiority was mine. He was quiet for the moment, but would probably flare up again immediately at the mention of Mackwith's name. So I kept Mackwith in reserve.

"Well," I said in a conciliatory tone. "I have a feeling that both of us wished to see the other, and from what you've told me with very good reason. Isn't that so?"

"How do you mean, what I've told you?" he said suspiciously.

"I mean that you've given me the impression that there's more in this Case than meets the eye."

He grunted. "Impression's good!"

"That there's some sort of a misunderstanding that ought to be cleared up."

"'Impression's' damned good!" he muttered again. "I like 'impression.'"

"Well, never mind the word. You reminded me a few minutes ago that we were all there that morning, and so I take it that we're all interested. Can't we talk it quietly over?"

I don't think I ever saw eyes capable of staring for so long without a blink. Old Dadley had been right when he had said, "He stares you down, he does." I awaited his pleasure.

"No, that won't wash either," he said curtly at last. "You came here for a purpose. Specially. I won't say the place isn't free to anybody, but it would be bad for trade if everybody stood behind a paper looking for twenty minutes at a glass of beer. I don't think there's any need to be plainer than that."

"Very well, have it that way if you like," I returned. "You tell me the whole of Chelsea is interested in this Case. Well, as I was there when it happened it's natural that I should be interested too."

"Hah!... Well, all I have to say to that is that nobody would have guessed it at the time," he answered.

"Indeed? Why not?"

"Hah! Why not? It *is* a bit of a puzzle, isn't it? But suppose we put it this way: Here's two men come tumbling on a man's roof. Bit of a bump they make, don't they? Say a thousand people watching, eh? It isn't a thing that happens every day exactly, you'd think? Very well. *Now where were all of you?* Finishing your breakfast? 'Interested,' you say. Well, you'd expect the master of the house to be a bit interested. But where was *he*? Where were all the rest of you, except him that went up on the roof? You seem to me more interested now than you did then. That's the first point that strikes me."

It struck me, too, as being both stupid and acute, at the same time hardly worth mentioning and yet unpleasantly significant. If his suggestion was that at the time of the accident we were all whispering together in some dark nefarious plot, it was too ridiculous to answer; but if he meant that it was at least remarkable that not one of us except Rooke, and Hubbard for one brief moment before his arrival, had taken the trouble to step outside to see what had happened, I could only reluctantly agree with him. You will remember that precisely the same observation had struck Hubbard and myself at the time.

"Yes," he repeated, seeing my discomfiture, "that's the first point that strikes me; where was Mr. Esdaile, for instance, that *he* didn't come out?"

I answered rather slowly. "I see what you mean. As a matter of fact that *was* very curious. I wonder if you'll believe me when I tell you that Mr. Esdaile knew nothing of that accident till it was all over?"

He stopped for a moment in his walk. Without noticing it we had begun to walk. "Why not?" he demanded.

"Because he was down in the cellar at the time. He'd gone down to fetch a bottle of wine."

He resumed his walk. "But he came up again. I saw him."

"That was some time after."

"That's right," he confirmed, as if he had been testing my truthfulness. "It was about half an hour after. Funny way to spend half an hour with all that going on, wasn't it?"

As I was entirely of his opinion, I made no reply.

"So," he continued, "what strikes me about it is that you're more interested now than you were then. Now we'll pass on to another point. All the time this is happening you're all inside except one of you, and he's on the roof. He's the only person up there till the police came—has the field to himself so to speak. Then he comes down the ladder in a very shaky sort of state."

"Do you wonder?" I interposed with a quickness that surprised myself. "You were on that jury—"

"In a very shaky state," he repeated. "Nervous as a cat, as you might say. That was the state he was in when he came down that ladder. Why?" His manner changed suddenly to truculence. "Why? Hah! That's the question, isn't it? Some of you'd like to make out you know nothing at all about it, but they laugh best that laugh last, and don't you make any error about it!"

Apprehensive as I was, I forced myself also to laugh.

"And you're doing your laughing in the newspapers? Well, do you know, Mr. Westbury, I see very little in all this. Your letter certainly raises a very interesting subject, and I'm quite of your opinion that flying ought to be better regulated; but I wonder if you'd resent a piece of advice from an older man?"

"Much obliged, I'm sure." Those were the words. The tone in which they were uttered bore no relation to them.

"But let me give it, for all that. You seem to be on the point of making charges against somebody for something or other. Well, that's never a safe thing to do, but if I were you I'd certainly think twice before I started with a rather distinguished barrister. They're usually able to look after themselves pretty well in such matters."

I said it quite deliberately. It was abundantly plain that unless I kindled his wrath again he might go on laughs-best-ing and laughs-last-ing all night. I didn't want to hear his vague and muttered menaces. I wanted to know whether that bullet was in the hands of the police, and if so, what action was to be taken. So I produced Mackwith from my sleeve.

"And another thing I'll tell you plainly," I said with something nearer real warmth. "If I were to hear any annoying whispers about myself I shouldn't have a moment's hesitation in taking any steps I thought proper. As I see this business, you force your way into a private garden under cover of an accident, pick up some cock-and-bull story or other, go spreading it about, and then, when you're very properly put in your place by a coroner's court—"

But I got no further. By this time we were in a quiet and dingy street where almost every house seemed to have an "Apartments" card over the door, and at the fury of his outbreak I expected every door to be flung open and every blind to be drawn up.

"Hah! So *that's* your lay, is it, Mister Man? We've got it at last, have we? You think you can come it heavy like your blasted barrister friend, do you? Oh yes, you're all in it together! *I* knew what you came for tonight! I forced my way into gardens, did I? And what about those that force themselves on roofs before the police come, touching things they've no business to be touching, eh? *I* pick up cock-and-bull stories, do I? And what does some others pick up? *I'm* put in my place, am I? We'll see what sort of a place some of you fine gentry's put in presently! Trying to cod me one of you was in the cellar for half an hour! A bit too much roof and cellar for my fancy! I was a shade over the odds for one of you anyway! He had to come *down* the ladder again, hadn't he? And you hold a ladder when you see a man coming down it, don't you? Very well, Mister Pry! You go prying somewhere else, and drink your beer a bit quicker next time! *My* kids aren't going to be shot at and no questions asked! The questions'll come presently. They laugh best that laugh last—"

And, as a neighboring door was opened, and a blind across the street was drawn up, and a window-sash creaked somewhere else, it came upon me in a moment what had happened.

Philip Esdaile's hands had not been the first to pat Monty Rooke's pockets that morning. Westbury, holding the ladder, had been before him.

PART V

SOME BYWAYS OF THE CASE

I

Strictly speaking, it is not on the Santon headland that Charles Valentine ("Chummy") Smith ought to make his first appearance in this story; but it was there that I myself first saw him, and I want to give you my impression of him as I received it, if at the cost of taking a slight liberty with time. So I first set these eyes on him during a month I spent with the Esdailes somewhat later in that year.

I may say to begin with that he would probably have passed unnoticed among the innumerable other young men of today who at one time looked just a little civilian in their new uniforms but now wear their mufti again with a subtle but unmistakable difference. You know the young men I mean—they still speak of distances in kilometers, can talk for hours on end about motor-bicycles, and sprinkle their conversation with the jargon of ragtime French they are proud to share with their own privates and sappers and bombardiers. A year or so ago you went into a restaurant that was brown as a beechwood with khaki; you go there today and the khaki is gone—yet still hauntingly and mysteriously there, edging (as it were) the mufti with a faint rim like a color-print a little out of register. The ghost of khaki still clings about faces, movements, speech, the glances of eyes. Or if it isn't khaki it is the navy-and-gold, or Charles Valentine ("Chummy") Smith's unbelted sky-blue with the black cap-band.

He and Joan (in this little peep ahead which I am taking) were waiting for me on the platform of Santon Station. It was a week or so before the Company's Inter-Station Flower Competition—that annual Show that makes the whole line with its tiny stations as gay with flowers as a row of Thames houseboats. Geraniums and marguerites hung in boxes from the canopies; the sills of the porters' room were a rage of bloom; and lobelia and red bachelor's-buttons and white pebbles from the shore were set in patriotic emblems all the way from the booking-office to the signal-box, which alone was bare. As the train drew up I saw them standing together on the sunny platform, with a bower of ramblers over their heads and a heaven of larkspur behind them.

Charles Valentine Smith was for taking my two bags to the trap that waited at the level crossing, but peremptorily Joan pushed him away and called a porter. The presence of the trap did not mean that Chummy could not walk yet, for with the help of a stick he got about quite well, though the cliff-path down to the shore was still too much for him. And I may here mention, quite incidentally, the rôle I was apparently cast for in advance. "Auntie Joan" was supposed to take the children down to the shore every day. Charles Valentine Smith could not yet manage the shore climb. This necessarily meant a temporary separation. Two days later *I* was taking the children down to the shore. Whether Miss Joan had urged my invitation for that very purpose I cannot tell you.

So I was introduced to our young murderer, or he to me, I forget which of us was the personage in Joan's eyes, and we sought the trap. Joan drove, and paved the way for our better acquaintance by telling Mr. Smith, in these words, that I was "still young at heart." And her pleasant young assassin called me "Sir." I suppose I am entitled to be called "Sir" by these youngsters, but I am far from standing on my rights in this respect. He had his Joan, and I saw no reason for rubbing it in. People who go about murdering other people need not lay quite so much stress on the minor conventions.

"Yes, sir, thanks—practically all right again," he said as we bowled across that high world of flaming poppies and silky corn. "But I say—I'm afraid you'll have rather a crow to pluck with me."

All things considered, I thought one crow a particularly modest estimate; but "Oh?" I said inquiringly.

"Yes. I know it's your room, sir, and any old fleabag would do for me, but it's all Joan and Mrs. Esdaile. In fact, I carried all my gear out this morning, but they've toted everything back again."

"Oh, but he *likes* that little room at the end!" Joan cooingly reassured him. "He gets the morning sun, and it's beautifully cool in the afternoons—"

"If you mean that I'm in the habit of sleeping in the afternoons I wish to inform you that I'm not," I answered her coldly. "And if the room you speak of is that little cupboard place just above where the hens are fed—"

"Yes, that's the one," she answered with a darling smile. "I call it quite large, and I've put you one or two nice books to read, and I arranged the flowers myself. Come up, Robin!"

So Smith had the room that I, the introducer of these Esdaile people to my loved Santon, had hitherto always had, and I was given the one with the morning sun. You might suppose from Joan's words that the sun shone directly in, filling it with gayety and brightness. Not a bit of it. That morning sunlight she so extolled was a greenish and aquarium-like half light thrown up from the steep bit of paddock that comprised the whole of my view. And, lest I should oversleep, an enormous bronze cock, mounting to the little sloping roof of the hen-house below, was able to sound his clarion note practically on the drum of my ear.

II

I repeat, at a first glance he was very like the rest of the young fellows of his day; but I admit there was something about him that grew on you. After watching him for a while I decided that this ascendancy was principally in his eyes. I do not wish to overwork the popular clichés of fire and flash and smolder; Smith's eyes certainly had something of this quality; but it was combined with an expression that, until I can define it better, I will risk calling discontent. I don't mean by this the discontent that is common enough among those other flashers and smolderers, the artists and poets and suchlike. That is usually little more than peevishness and incapacity, and, as one of the breed myself, I rather liked Smith's attitude towards us. With perfect sincerity he looked on us as immensely clever fellows, particularly the late Mr. Jack London and the author of *The Crimson Specter of Hangman Hollow*; but there he had finished with us. We were high and he could not attain to us. Our affairs were so little his affairs that I regret to have to say that, Malvern notwithstanding, I have heard him make use of the expression "between you and I." That is an awful thing for a nice girl to marry.

But the War has taught me, among other things, the overwhelming importance of other men's jobs and the comparative insignificance of my own. If young Smith did not express himself in the terms to which I was accustomed, he expressed himself none the less. Don't ask me how, except in a general way. Here again what he calls a "dreadfully gulf" is fixed, across which I can only gaze at the New Wonder.

For Chummy, for all his Crimson Specters and his "between you and I," his cocktails at Hatchetts' and his stuffed-bird tympani in the Helmsea Mess, was part of that Wonder that today a George takes from an Elizabeth's hands. Four hundred years ago I suppose he would have sold a farm and gone to sea; this, briefly, is what he did in our own day:

Denied admission to the Flying Corps on the grounds that he was not yet seventeen, he had made his way to London, dressed himself as a mechanic or plumber, had forced his way into a foreign Embassy under pretext of repairing the ambassadorial pipes or cisterns or something, and had actually succeeded in presenting himself before the Ambassador, demanding to be taken on in the service of a foreign country. Naturally he had been refused and referred back to his own Government. Then had ensued what Chummy cheerfully described as a hell of a dust-up. General Officers had stormed and had wanted to know "what the devil he meant by it"; the correspondence, I have been told, weighs between eleven and twelve pounds; but in the end he had received his ticket—already endorsed for improper conduct in offering his services to a foreign if friendly Power. You will believe that this endorsement had stood very little in his subsequent way. The story had run like wildfire throughout the whole of the Service. It may have hindered his promotion, but what on earth did promotion matter? Any number of civilian-ingrain business-men, turning their business talents to the Services, have obtained promotion. Few of them have attained to the distinction of such an endorsement as that which made bright young Smith's ticket.

And—to return to what I have called that discontent of his—I for one cannot see that a young man of daring and vision, elementally put down into the midst of our world today and asked what he makes of it all, must either write a stuffy book or paint a jazz picture or else be told that the fire of his personality has no expression and his chosen work no value. Very much on the contrary. I think myself that Charles Valentine Smith was a thinker so single of purpose that it never occurred to him that he thought at all. And why not a technique, an artist's technique, of the wrist and eye and nerve and indomitable heart? Is my dictation more a wonder than his zooming? Is my life so full and his so empty? I cannot see it.

III

To look at, he had not in the very least the air of a man over whose head a terrible menace hung. Indeed, I have rarely sat down at a table with a less personally odious young murderer. He was lithe and of a darkish brown complexion, a perfect anatomy of graven and incised muscle when later I saw him bathe, and with hands the movements of which were full of power and grace. Then there were his eyes. Of all his features his mouth was that which communicated the least, except when he smiled. With the rest of us I am afraid that our mouths generally communicate the most.

I knew, at the time of this our peep forward, that Philip had had his *éclaircissement* with him, but had no idea of what had passed between them. Calling at Lennox Street one midday on my way to the office I had found the house shut up and even Rooke unexpectedly gone. Therefore I half expected that Philip would tell me the whole story on the night of my arrival at Santon. In fact, I gave him every opportunity to do so, remaining behind after all but he and I had gone to bed. But he talked about anything else, and at half-past ten rose, yawned, said he thought he would turn in, apologized again for the change of my room, and gave me my candle. The same thing happened the next night.

On the third night I asked him point blank.

"Eh?" he said. "Oh, that's all right—so far, at any rate. He doesn't know anything about it."

"What!" I exclaimed. "Know nothing about it!... What do you mean—that he was too stunned or dazed or something to remember?"

"Oh, no, I don't mean that exactly," Esdaile replied. "He remembers that part of it all right. It was the other I didn't tell him."

"What other?"

"Why, that anybody else knows anything about the—accident."

"But didn't you mention the shooting to him, if there was any?"

"Oh, he admits that, of course."

"Then in that case he knows you know?"

"Of course he knows *I* know. How could I ask him if I didn't know? What he doesn't know is that you fellows know. So I told him the best thing he could do was to come down here and get fit again, and not say anything to Joan."

"And—he agreed not to say anything to Joan?" I exclaimed in astonishment.

"Certainly. What good would that do? Look here: he's here getting himself well again; I'm here painting; and you're here on a holiday. If there's any trouble ahead we can't stop it, and so it's no good worrying about it. Don't you think I'm right?"

"Oh ... very well," I said in bewilderment, suddenly ceasing my questions; and I took my candle and went up to my little room over the hen-house with somewhat mixed feelings.

Just look at a few of the ingredients of the mixture. Here was Joan, knowing nothing about anything except that her lover had had a tumble, had given her a few weeks of torturing anxiety, but was now blessedly up and about again and in her pocket all day long. Then there was this Charles Valentine Smith, also knowing nothing (for apparently a mere trifle like shooting a man and admitting that you shot him didn't count), and, with the Brand of Cain on his untroubled brow, offering Joan his blood-stained hand in the most matter-of-fact way in the world. And here was Philip, apparently accepting the whole extraordinary situation with complete calm. I admit that I found all this serenity just a little perplexing.

But look at the charm of the situation for me as a novelist! Few of us have the opportunity of studying what I think I may call the amenities of murder at first hand. I dare say that grim mutterings à la Specter of Hangman Hollow would have bored me, writhings and agonies made me uncomfortable; but this new view of murder I found full of pleasing interest. And the whole of the interest lay in seeing, hearing and asking no questions. Philip was "there painting," I on a holiday. Very well. I was content.

And, in case you have any preconceived notions about the daily trifling routine of murderers' lives, I can only wish you had been at Santon with me at that time. As far as I could see, not a cloud marred the blue heaven of these young people's days. They disappeared as soon as breakfast was cleared away and returned when they returned. I don't for a moment suppose that the intervening hours were spent in the contemplation of death, judgment or the burden of undivulged crime. Chummy enjoyed his pipe, and, as he sat at high tea, idolized by the Esdaile boys because he flew, ate as heartily as ever in his pre-murder days. If his crash on the Lennox Street roof was not mentioned, that seemed to be only because everything had ended perfectly happily and there was nothing more to be said about it. In fact, here is a bit of conversation, taken almost at random, just to show you the way to be entirely happy is to shoot somebody and say nothing to your best girl about it.

Coming down to breakfast one morning I thought it my duty to administer a sharp rebuke to Miss Merrow about the throwing of a handful of hen-corn into my window in order (she said) to wake me.

"I had been up ten minutes, I had shaved, and was more than half dressed," I said sternly. "I'll tell you what you are doing; you are trying to train those hens to come *into* my room by throwing corn in. I have now to inform you that I intend to write this morning, and so shall not be able to relieve you of your duties down on the shore."

"Oh, I say, sir—" young Smith began, but I thought fit to put a spoke into his wheel also.

"Not a word!" I ordered him. "Hen-corn has been thrown into my room. What was thrown into your room yesterday morning?"

(She had tossed up to his casement a bud of the William Allen Richardson that grew up the cottage end. Coming round the corner from an early stroll up the dewy paddock I had seen her do it, as well as the little token from her lips that went with it.)

"I don't care which room I'm given, but I will not share it with poultry," I continued firmly. "Also I object to this unfair discrimination about things thrown in at windows. So understand that I am busy writing this morning."

"Well, we're going to Flaunton in the trap," said Joan defiantly.

"Children," I said, turning to them, "Mr. Smith and Miss Merrow are going to Flaunton in the trap. The tuckshop at Flaunton is a much better one than the Santon one, and there are smugglers there. They are armed to the teeth, and they carry contraband into their echoing caves usually at about midday."

"*That*," declared Joan, "I call mean! Bringing the children in!"

"It's no worse than bringing the hens in," I retorted; and our murderer guffawed and took another egg.

I cannot say that I gained much by my protest, since, having put the idea into their heads, I had to hire the station fly and take the children to Flaunton myself. But it was a change from the sands, and it gave me the opportunity for studying the blood-stained path of their dalliance against a fresh background.

IV

But as you were. The peep-hole must be closed again. From the point of view of the unities Charles Valentine Smith is still lying in a hospital cot, writing daily but brief notes to Joan, forbidding her to come up, and receiving countless boxes of tightly-packed Santon flowers. We are in London again, during the last days of May.

One morning I had knocked off my private work rather earlier than usual (I had, in fact, been quite unable to settle down properly to it), and, to fill in the time before lunch, had walked up Queen's Gate, entered the Gardens by the Memorial, and strolled slowly along in the direction of the Row. It was a pleasant morning, and the riders were out in full force. Idly I was admiring glossy flanks and cruppers and bits jingling and flashing in the sun, when suddenly a horseman overtook me from behind and called me by my name. I turned, exclaimed, and shook hands with him.

He was a junior officer in the Australian Light Horse, and several times I had come more or less closely into contact with him during my own uneventful period of Military Service. His name was Dudley Hanson, he had been in Gallipoli, was still in uniform, and was awaiting his boat back home again and demobilization. He plays no part in this story except on this single occasion. He was riding a rather pretty little chestnut, and his hand patted the animal's neck as he leaned over the railings and talked.

"By the way," he remarked, after a little chat about men we both knew, "that was rotten luck for poor old Maxwell the other day. You saw it in the papers, didn't you?"

"Who?" I said, perhaps with rather a jump.

"Bobby Maxwell. He used to spot for our lot in Gallip. Came over here after. I thought you knew him."

"What was the rotten luck?" I asked.

"Why, he came down somewhere in London the other day—crashed—killed on the spot."

"Dud," I said, "where are you lunching?"

"Whoa, lass.... Oh, any old joint, I guess."

"Then get off back to your stable and come straight along to my Club. Come straight along. Don't stop to change or anything. I want to see you particularly."

He seemed a little surprised at my urgency, but waved his hand and was off. I continued my walk, but no longer slowly. I always walk quickly when I am interested, excited or moved by any emotion.

I was now all three. Maxwell! Dud Hanson knew him, and had even fancied that I might have known him myself!

Whatever luncheon engagement Hanson might have had that day I can assure you that I should have urged him to break it.

My Club is in Piccadilly, and I waited for him in the entrance hall with impatience. I gave his name to the porter as expressly as if otherwise he might have been denied; I set my watch by the club clock, I fiddled with the skeins of tape in the baskets. I had even a momentary scare lest I should not have pronounced the name of my Club distinctly or lest by any chance he should have misheard.

You see the reason for my eagerness. Maxwell was our unknown quantity, the one big blank in our Case. One or another of us could contribute his portion of knowledge about everybody else, but nobody knew anything of Maxwell. His function was entirely unconsidered, his rights totally disregarded. Rights? I know nothing of the law of the matter, nor whether a dead man has rights; but if he has they should be all the more enforceable because he is in no position to enforce them for himself. What would Maxwell have had to say about his own shooting? What had brought about that shooting? Was he the kind of man who, in Monty Rooke's large and equable view of the crime of murder, ought to have been shot? Or was he the other kind, whose death was a loss to the world? These were a few of the questions I wanted Dud Hanson to help me to answer.

He appeared, and we made our way to the dining-room at once. I gave the order for the whole of the lunch so that we might be interrupted as little as possible, and then I came straight to the point.

"First of all," I said, "you say you knew Maxwell. Do you know the fellow who came down with him—C. V. Smith?"

"Smith? Smith? Yes, I think I do, if he was Bobby's pilot out there. Smith's a pretty common name. Slightish build, but tough as they make 'em—dashing sort of chap with very lively dark eyes?"

At the time I could not verify this physical description. "Well, were they friends?" I asked.

"I guess a pilot and his observer are like the little birds in their nests—it's dangerous to fall out," Hanson replied. "What's *to* all this?"

"The position's this. They happened to crash on the roof of a friend of mine and this fellow Smith's. Smith's still in hospital, and neither my friend nor I knew Maxwell. So I want you to tell me about him—anything you know about the pair of them."

"Right you are...."

But if it was evidence of ill-feeling between the two men I was after he could give me none. Indeed, the probabilities were all the other way. In other Services the bond between man and man is strict, but there is still room for preferences and aversions. Your mess, for example, is yours, and you are filled with a jealous pride if an outsider has anything to say about it; but within its circle you pick and choose your friends. The ward-room forces you into the closest physical contacts, but you can still please yourself about the other intimacies. Even in a submarine, where the death of one is likely to be the death of all, you may yet like one man more than another. But two men in an aeroplane are twins in a womb. The very pulse of one must be the pulse of both, their senses, glances, thoughts, such a unison of coöperation as the former world never saw. For one to harm the other is not assault, but semi-suicide. Rarely need you even "look for the woman." Gloriana both serve, but they hardly quarrel about lesser mistresses.

Yet is it not possible that this extraordinary attachment, this association somewhat in excess of that of natural and aeroplaneless man, may by its very nature have its own reactions? The closer the tie the bitterer the quarrel when it does come. And here an artificial element is superadded. For, in spite of Joan, who thought that Chummy simply thought of her and flew, man does not naturally fly. If nothing else forced him into accord the mere mechanical risks would be enough to do so. I remember Smith told me that at one time—whether this is still the case I cannot say—an observer was not allowed to be trained as a pilot also, lest, seeing his comrade doing something he himself would not have done and conscious of the functioning of a different mind, he should lose his head at a critical moment and instinctively seize the controls. Had there been such a dissolution of unity on that morning of the break-fast-party? Had hand hesitated, this factitious identity suddenly failed? Of all men living Charles Valentine Smith was the only one who could answer these questions with authority; but I wanted to get all I could out of Hanson.

"Had Maxwell his pilot's ticket?" I musingly asked him presently.

"Couldn't say. Lots of them have flown hundreds of miles without a ticket at all."

"Was he an Aiglon Company man, by the way?"

"Dunno. If he was he probably had his ticket. I can't see what use a commercial Company would have for a bomb-sight specialist."

"Oh, they might. You never know."

"Well, perhaps so. I'm sorry, old son, but you know as much about poor old Bobby as I do now."

Summarized, this was all the information I got in exchange for my lunch:

Maxwell was four or five years older than Smith, in civil life a surveyor, unmarried, not (so far as Hanson knew) engaged to be married, nice fellow, reasonably abstemious, quite sound in wind and limb.

Hanson didn't think that Maxwell had spotted for any other pilot than Smith during the time the two of them were in Gallipoli.

Maxwell didn't strike Hanson as being a sort of man to lose his head in an emergency; had indeed rather a cool head and steady nerve.

In conclusion, Maxwell had always seemed particularly attached to Chummy Smith.

"But what's worrying you? Going to put it in a book?" Hanson asked.

I shook my head. I had no idea at that time that I should ever be writing this book.

V

On that day when I called at Lennox Street and received no answer to my ringing I stepped back from the door and looked up at the house again. Little trace of the accident now remained. The broken mulberry branch had been neatly sawn off and the smaller branches trimmed. The blinds were drawn, the French window clamped up, and quite obviously there was nobody there. This, as I have said, surprised me, since, even if Esdaile had gone away without letting me know, I had certainly expected to find Rooke.

Then, as I walked down the path again, a thought struck me. Rooke, if I remembered rightly, ought to be getting married just about then—ought as a matter of fact to have been married three days before. I had had no news of this. True, he might simply have neglected to inform me, but I did not think this likely. Was he married? Suddenly I found myself wondering and doubting.

In the King's Road, to which I walked, a blue and white telephone sign hanging outside a grocer's shop caught my eye. I walked into the shop. I have a good many friends at the Chelsea Arts, and one or other of them ought to be able to tell me something about Rooke.

I got through at the second or third name I asked for. It was Curtis. He asked me to go on to the Club, but I told him that I couldn't spare the time, and he next wanted to know where I was speaking from.

"Then you're hardly a stone's-throw from him," Curtis replied. "He's back in his old rooms in Jubilee Place."

I was on the point of asking Curtis whether Rooke was married, but already I had a divination. If he was not, to ask why he was not would only make talk, and, if he was at home, I could ascertain for myself at little more trouble than walking across the road. I thanked Curtis, hung up the receiver, and turned my steps to Jubilee Place.

I say I had a divination already. At the very outset of this book I told you that the Case affected a number of people in various and curious ways and byways, and I was now beginning to think that the descent of that parachute on Esdaile's roof had left not one single member of our group unaffected. I must remind you again that at that time I actually knew far less than I have already told you; but except by collation, rearrangement and boiling down I could not have set down these facts at all. I had, for example, seen Esdaile's shocked expression on discovering that the stranger who had come down on his roof was none other than his friend Chummy Smith, but up to that time I had not set eyes on that unruffled young criminal himself. I had guessed what this discovery must presently mean to Joan, but was unaware of that head-strong dash of Mollie's up to London, and her lagging return to Santon. I had heard Hubbard's fantastic speculations as to the nature of the mysterious apparatus Esdaile kept in his cellar, but did not know that both Rooke and Mrs. Cunningham had actually been down in the cellar. I had enjoyed the spectacle of a rising barrister unconsciously frustrating the aims of a coroner's jury, but had had to pump Hanson for even the meagerest scraps of information about the subject of that inquest. And twice or thrice I had unblushingly lied to a Chesterfield of the Saloon Bars, but without a suspicion when I had done so that this very person, seeing another prime actor in our Case descending a ladder, had had the curiosity to know what made his pocket so lumpy and the deftness of hand to ascertain.

So I had begun to look with a good deal of apprehension at our Case. The beastly thing was like an egg, that hatched out one creeping thing after another. And, as I paused at the end of a long concrete-floored passage and knocked at Rooke's door, I wondered if Rooke would give me news of still another.

VI

He did. His face did so before ever he spoke. In a moment I knew that something had happened about that wedding—certainly that it had been put off, possibly worse. Still without speaking he showed me in.

He was lunching, or rather making a combination meal of lunch and breakfast in one. A single glance round the room told me a good deal about the state of mind of its occupant. I have been hard-up myself, and know these symptoms of negligence of body, mind and surroundings. He was fully dressed, but he wore yesterday's collar and his boots had not been cleaned. His bed was unmade, his furniture undusted, his floor unswept. He seemed to have got up late, to have wondered what after all there was to get up for, and not to care much whether he stayed up or went back to bed. It was all extraordinary unlike his former orderliness and neatness and precision, and I made up my mind that there were several things I intended to say to him before I left him.

"Well, how are you?" he asked perfunctorily. "Have some cocoa. I'll wash another cup."

"No, thanks. You carry on with your breakfast. I've just been round to see Esdaile. Is he away?"

"Went off on Tuesday," Rooke replied.

"Where, to Yorkshire?"

"Yes. Took that fellow with him—you know—the flying fellow."

"But why aren't you at the studio?"

He answered evasively. "Oh—I chucked that idea."

"But listen to me. You were to have got married, weren't you?"

"Oh—Audrey chucked that," he replied, pushing his cup away.

"Chucked it altogether, do you mean?"

"Looks like it," he grunted. "Let's talk about something else."

But, looking round the untidy room again I wondered whether it would not be better for him to talk about precisely that. Even an active smart was preferable to sloth and helplessness of that kind, and there is something very lovable about Monty at his best.

"No, no," I said. "Much better get it off your chest. And look here, my friend, you haven't shaved this morning. That sort of thing doesn't help. Talk about something else? No, let's talk about this. Where is Mrs. Cunningham?"

"I think Buxton this week. Haven't looked at the *Era*. She's on tour if you must know."

"But why? Why are things—like this? Surely there's a reason?"

"Oh, she said she just couldn't stick it," he answered with an off-handed but tremulous little laugh.

"Stick what?"

"Everything."

I knew what he meant by "everything." He meant, simply, this confounded Case. Now, it appeared, it had power to break off an engagement and to bring Rooke down to dirty table-cloths, unmade beds and marmalade out of the grocer's pot.

"Look here, Monty," I began, touching his sleeve, "we've been friends for quite a number of years now—"

"Oh, don't," he interrupted me petulantly. "Leave a fellow alone."

"No, I'm not going to leave you alone like this. I want you to tell me why you left the studio, and why Mrs. Cunningham's gone off on tour, and a number of other things."

Well, it took time, but bit by bit he yielded. In sullen, resentful sentences he began to talk.

"What do I mean by everything?" he said. "Well, I mean everything. Nothing's gone right. Nothing at all. Everybody's fed up to the back teeth, Esdaile too. And all that stupid business last week just about put the tin hat on it."

"Do you mean that photograph in the papers?"

"Yes, and those idiotic crowds, and all their senseless talk. Who wants a streetful of fools gaping at his windows for two or three days on end like that? Then they started pulling his leg at the Club. So he just waited till this chap Smith was fit to be moved and then cleared out. I don't blame him."

"Yes, I can understand Esdaile's being annoyed; but that's over now, and I don't quite see why you should leave and come back here."

"Well, Audrey wasn't going there anyway," he answered. "She'd had enough of it. Got it into her head there was something uncanny about the place, and so there is. Too much mystery altogether. That was Esdaile. He keeps you on the jump the whole time."

"What do you mean by keeping you on the jump?"

"All sorts of ways. There's that cellar of his for one thing; he was never in the same mind about that for half an hour together. We were going to take a cupboard or something down there one day; it was his own suggestion; but he twisted and wriggled and tried to cry off till I was about at the end of my patience. You'd have thought he wouldn't have us down there at any price. And then suddenly he turned round and said we could go down if we liked. Idiotic I call it."

"Did you go down?"

"Yes. And there was nothing whatever to make all that fuss about as far as I could see. I admit I'd wondered once or twice whether there was anything queer, but I went into every corner and there was absolutely nothing to see."

"You're thinking of that other morning when he was down there all that time?"

"Yes. I can't make head or tail of that yet, but I can't see it's anything to do with the cellar. And just listen to this. After making all that fuss he came up again and didn't even bother to take the key out of the door. It was there when I came away. One day he nearly jumps down your throat when you ask him for the key, and the next thing he goes and leaves it in the door! I'm sure he did it on purpose too. It was just like saying, 'Go and live down there if you like.' Well, I wasn't going to be messed about like that. I'm not going nosing round other fellows' places. I'm not a policeman. So I cleared out. Would *you* have stopped after that?"

Again his voice shook a little, and I could guess at the meaning behind his words. He meant, Would I have continued in a house the offer of which had promised so much happiness that one moment's happening had turned to discord and misunderstanding? I cannot say that I should.

VII

In my anxiety to set him talking after his own fashion I had not yet asked him anything about what had passed between Esdaile and Smith; but I intended to do so. For, just as Monty himself had been the first obstacle to Philip's letting us into the heart of his mystery straight away, so Smith, you will remember, had since blocked the current of disclosure. Philip had had to see Smith before taking the next step, and, as I had pre-figured the matter, he would go to the hospital one day as soon as Smith had sufficiently recovered, would ask for his account of the affair, and would then take the rest of us into his confidence or not, as the case might be. In other words, it depended on Smith's explanation whether Philip and the rest of us continued our efforts at suppression or—did the other thing.

But now Esdaile seemed to have taken neither course. As far as I could gather he had calmly evaded the whole situation by carrying Smith off into the country out of our sight and hearing. I admit that, since the assassin was taken into the bosom of Esdaile's own family, it looked as if he had succeeded in making out some sort of a case for himself; but I also remembered the strong bias of friendship and the practically instantaneous resolution both he and Hubbard had taken that their Chummy was to be stood by till the last possible moment. That is not the most judicial frame of mind imaginable. Loftier, if chillier heights are conceivable. Esdaile alone of us had asserted from the beginning, and had stuck unwaveringly to it, that as a matter of plain unvarnished fact Smith had shot Maxwell. All along his manner had proclaimed that the accident theory, which was good enough for the women and the police, was vamped up and a lie. Was he now going to have the face to say to us, "Well, I've seen him, and he admits everything, but he had his reasons—unfortunately they meant putting a bullet into a fellow, but to hang Chummy won't bring t'other chap back to life—better let the whole thing drop"?

How beautifully simple!

But at the same time how very unfortunate that an outsider, laboring under a sense of grievance, should have patted Monty's pocket as he came down the ladder that morning!

Monty had risen, a little shamefacedly I thought. But for my call I fancy he would have left his breakfast things as they were, washing up the next cup when he wanted it. Now he began to stack them together for a general washing-up. He went into the little lobby place that held his taps and I heard the running of water into a basin; then he turned to his tumbled bed and began to re-make it. He muttered something about my not minding his carrying-on. I was far from minding it.

"But look here," I said as he moved about, "about Smith. You say Philip's seen him. What did he say about it?"

"Who, Philip or Smith?"

"Well, both of them. Didn't Philip tell you?"

"He didn't say much. He wasn't gone much more than half an hour—couldn't have had more than ten minutes with him—and then he came back and said he was taking him away the next day but one."

"Then that was while you were still at the studio?"

"Yes. It was then I told him I'd had enough of it and was coming back here. He told me not to be an ass, but I don't call that being an ass. I don't mean there was a row, but I'd got my back up a bit, and I didn't feel like asking him questions. I was sorry for him too in a way. You see, that morning after his wife came up—"

"What!" I exclaimed in surprise. "Has his wife been up since she left that morning?" (This, as I have told you, was the first I had heard of it.)

"Yes. She turned up late one night. I was out—I'd gone for a walk Roehampton way just to think things over—that was before Audrey'd told me she—" He stopped, as if distrusting his voice.

"Yes?" I gently urged him.

"About his wife coming up. I didn't see her till next morning. I expect she was tired out with the journey; anyway, her face was as gray as that Michelet paper there. And Philip was done in too. That's why I didn't want to make any bother. I couldn't help feeling sorry for him. I don't know what's happened to us all."

I could have told him. It was the Case that had happened.

"Mrs. Esdaile too—she was just the same—"

Naturally. The Case was the same.

"I hadn't very much talk with her. Of course, I asked her how Joan was—"

Yes, Joan was in the Case too.

"And she told me she'd seen Dawdy the night before. Dawdy was all a bundle of nerves, and Mrs. Esdaile put her to bed. She told me that if she were me she'd go round there at once and tell her—tell her—"

But here he broke down suddenly and completely. He sank on the edge of his bed and buried his face in his hands. He shook with sobs.

"Oh," he broke out uncontrollably, "it's all that beast—that beast Cunningham—"

"Oh no," I thought; "it wasn't Cunningham; it was the Case."

"You don't know the life that brute led her," he went on. "Drunken blackguard—women all over the place—and Dawdy, Dawdy at home! I hope he's in hell! Killed her heart he did. Can you blame her for not wanting to chance it again? I hardly had the heart to beg her, I was so broken up. She admitted she'd nothing against me. She just wanted to be right away from all men. So I pay for that beast. Somebody always has to pay, I expect. If only I'd seen her before he did—"

Presently he was better. He got up and began to move about again. "Sorry," he said shortly. "But what would you do?"

"Well, I should shave for one thing," I said quietly. "And for another, I don't think I'd make up my mind that everything was entirely hopeless. You never know what'll happen. It may be all right presently."

"I suppose you're right," he admitted. "No good chucking your hand in like this. Sorry. But it is a bit upsetting, you know."

Could I at that moment have added to his troubles by telling him about Westbury, the ladder and the pistol in his pocket?

Perhaps I could have done. Anyway, I didn't.

VIII

I recognized the more readily the separate and inhuman vitality this Case of ours was beginning to assume when I carefully considered its action upon myself. My connection with it was slight by comparison with that of some of the others, but I was aware of its operation. The attitudes into which it began to constrain me were not quite natural attitudes. It exercised pressure. What pressure?

Well, to begin with, this pressure—that I began to find it difficult to leave it alone. Both at home and at the office of the *Daily Circus* it intruded between me and the work I ought to have been getting on with. Little fleeting pictures began to interpose themselves. Sometimes I would find myself looking fixedly at a galley-slip or a page still damp from the proving-press and seeing, not the thing in my hand, but Joan Merrow running in with the children from the garden again; at home my page of manuscript would blur and there in a doorway Philip Esdaile would stand, his eyes dancing with a stilly excitement, the curaçao and the candle once more in his hands. And this, in my curious trade, is a serious matter. Out of precisely these insubstantialities I have to contrive to pay my rent and income-tax and to provide my bread-and-butter. I will not go so far as to say that I dreamed of the Case at night, but it began to play the dickens with my work. Unable to settle down to it, I found the Park drawing me instead, and even in the afternoons, which in ordinary commercial honesty were not my time at all, I began to put in the briefest and most perfunctory appearances at the office. I contented myself with the appearance of busyness, and wondered how long it would be before my chief caught me out.

In this frame of mind I happened one afternoon, by the merest chance, to run across Cecil Hubbard. I had dropped into a Technical and Scientific Exhibition of some sort, and I had thought I had seen Hubbard's white-topped cap and foursquare back in the downstairs rooms, but had lost them again. It was upstairs, a quarter of an hour later, that I found him.

He was watching another man, evidently an attendant or official of the Exhibition, who wore a double telephone-receiver about his ears and was slowly turning the handle of an instrument that at a first glance resembled an overgrown typewriter. Hubbard was peering into the mechanism. Then, at the invitation of the other man, he removed his cap and clasped the receiver about his head. The official continued to turn the handle.

"Hallo!" I said, coming up. "May one ask what it is?"

Hubbard turned. "Hallo, what are you doing here?" was his greeting. Then to the attendant, "What do you say the thing's called?"

It was the optophone, and perhaps you may have seen, or rather heard it. It is an instrument for enabling a totally blind man to read a page of ordinary print. I myself had never heard of the thing, and am not sure that I give a technically correct description of it now, but, as I understand it, the page travels along the carriage in such a way that each letter in turn passes over a tiny ray of light that is directed through a morsel of selenium. The letter causes an interruption; a lower-case "l," for example, which is a straight line, making one kind of break, but an "i," which is the "l" with the dot cut off the top, a different one; and so with the other letters. The transmutation is of light into sound, and the official assured us that with a very little practice the ear learns to distinguish the minute variations in the telephonic receiver without difficulty.

Remembering Hubbard's former (to me lunatic) conjectures that day when I had called on him at the Admiralty, I thought it an odd chance that I should come upon him examining such a thing as this optophone seemed to be; but our talk did not begin with that. Leaving the instrument, we turned away between glass showcases of fabrics and British glass and brilliant dyes and crystals and approached a window-bay that looked out on a gray court-yard.

"Well, what are you doing here?" he said again cheerfully. "It's a long time since you looked me up."

I told him that I went to all sorts of places in search of a little clowning for the *Circus*, and added that it was precisely the same distance from his place to mine as from mine to his. He laughed.

"I should have thought this was out of your line," he replied. "Well, what's the news?"

It was not likely that Hubbard had forgotten incidents so remarkable as those of that Lennox Street breakfast-party. Moreover, I could see he was sorry he had met me at this dead hour of the afternoon; he always talked better over lunch at Simpson's, with a Bronx or a Martini to start off with. Failing these, there was nothing for it but a cup of tea to wash down our chat, and as a matter of fact it was at a Slater's place in the Strand, with a rather good little band of violin, 'cello and piano that, a quarter of an hour later, we settled down.

"Well, Esdaile's taken your friend Chummy away," I observed when our teapots had been brought.

"Oh, he has, has he?" said Hubbard. "Queer business that, wasn't it? Have you made anything of it all yet?"

"I can't say I have; but then I'm rather at a disadvantage in not knowing your friend. Tell me something about him."

"Well—what, for example?"

"As I know nothing you can't go far wrong," I replied.

Music is one of the Commander's passions, and, as I say, that Slater band was not too bad. I think it was the "*Valse Triste*" that sent him off into a reverie. The young creature who played the fiddle had bobbed hair and was rather an attractive sort of sylph, and the Commander's blue eyes with the dark dots in them were fixed on her intricately-moving fingers.

Then he came out of his musing with a sudden jerk. What I especially like about Hubbard is that he usually knows what you want to know, and does not cease to feel the working of your mind even through a longish silence.

"Extraordinary thing," were his words as he came out of that silence. "It seems to be like the wind—blows whither it listeth. You look for it where you'd expect it and it isn't there, and then up it pops in a place you'd never think of looking for it."

This sounded to me rather like some of my own Publicity conclusions; but "What does?" I prompted him.

"Oh, the fluence—the gism—the real stuff—the thing you know when you see it but haven't got a name for," he replied off-handedly. "I suppose you writer-fellows call it genius.... How old's Smith? Twenty-four I should say, so it isn't a matter of accumulated experience. He couldn't be more dead right if he was a hundred-and-four."

"Right about what?"

"Well, about his job. Aviation. What it's for, just as much as ever now the War's over."

"Tell me—but remember I'm a journalist."

"All the better," he replied promptly. "The more you rub it in the better. The War only ended a few months ago, but a good many people seem to be trying to think there's never been one. That's right enough from the economic point of view, of course—gets people back to work again—but there is the other side, and I wish you would rub it in."

"Well, what do you want rubbed in?"

The eyes that had caught mine in Esdaile's studio rested on my face again now. Then he pulled out a fat cigarette.

"Civil aviation's for War, of course—the next War," he said almost contemptuously. "You're not one of those who think it's for express-letters, are you? Or carrying a cheap-jack Bradford agent to make a dicker in wool? That's where so many of you newspaper fellows make the mistake. You're all so clever at disguising the truth. You don't take people into your confidence enough."

Professionally this began to interest me. The public, its interests and its confidence are supposed to be my business.

"Go on," I said.

"Well, you don't," Hubbard repeated. He has rather a rapid and abrupt manner of speech that enables him better than anybody I know to carry off the things men are usually a little shy about. "The Bradford man has his affairs, I know, and it may sometimes be an advantage to get a letter there a couple of hours quicker, but that's not the point. There are two points, as a matter of fact. One's the training of your men, and the other's continuity of manufacture. If this country forgets either of 'em it may as well chuck its hand in. Why," he exclaimed in a phrase that arrested me in a quite remarkable way as chiming in so exactly with my own private observations, "look at the Elizabethans! What did *they* do? They wanted ships and they wanted sailors. So they developed the North Sea fishing industry. Gave 'em all sorts of bonuses and rebates and privileges. Not for the sake of a few dead fish. Not on your life. It was to keep the men in training and the shipyards running and the Spaniard out. And it's the same with civil aviation today."

I won't say that I had never thought of this before. But one thinks of all sorts of things that evaporate in the thinking, so that for practical purposes they might just as well never have been thought. It was his energy and certitude and single-mindedness that gave it all its force. And although I am a journalist, that is why I think that all our print is dead and cold until it is vivified by the heard and passionate voice. Oh, I know the stock argument—that for one that is reached by the human voice a thousand are influenced by the printed word. Well, so they are, until a contradictory word is printed and both messages jam to a standstill. But you can't jam the pentecostal flames that give the prophets utterance. I am inclined to think that if there is one indestructible thing in the world it is the Uttered Word. Naturally I refrain from dwelling too much on this in the office of the *Daily Circus*. But it lies behind every word of our print for all that.

"Another thing," Hubbard continued. "I don't know much about the Elizabethans, but I'm prepared to bet that a good many of 'em were youngsters. While old Burleigh was nodding, some infant just out of his cradle was getting away with it. At all events, there's no reason that I can see why he shouldn't as well be twenty as ninety—every practical reason why he should, in fact."

"Do you mean young Smith's like that?" I suddenly asked.

Perhaps it wasn't quite fair. When a man has the pluck to talk on these lines it is rather a cold douche to bring it all down to one finite and fallible human being. Even the pentecostal flame may flicker at times. But I noticed that Hubbard did not say No. Indeed, he did not answer me at all. His eyes were on the child with the fiddle again and the living, climbing fingers.

"Clever hands, aren't they?" he said. "Wish I could play the fiddle."

It was a little later, when we came to speak of the optophone, that I found him to be still firmly rooted in the conviction that Esdaile's cellar contained the solution of at least a portion of our mystery. He was quite unshakable on this point. I will not trouble to re-state his recapitulation of the events of the morning of the farewell breakfast. Of subsequent events, I may say, he knew little.

"Well, I won't pretend to understand you," I said at last. "If you seriously think that Esdaile's got some sort of an optophone in his house—"

He waved his hand impatiently, as if to beg of me not to be an ass.

"Oh, cut that out. I'm not given to melodrama any more than you are. Of course he hasn't; that's infantile. But what is there to prevent there being something peculiar about the ordinary acoustics of the place—perfectly ordinarily and naturally, but one of these freakish effects—there are such things—an echo's the commonest example, of course—then there *are* these whispering effects—vagaries of sound—" He tailed off.

"But he heard no sound," I objected, "or at any rate so little that we decided he couldn't know what it was. He certainly didn't hear what we heard. You've got the whole thing turned round."

"I know," he mused. "And yet he gave you the impression of a man who knew more than all the rest of us put together. In fact, he practically admitted he did."

"But—if you will have it it's the cellar—two people have been down since."

He turned quickly. "Who are they?"

"Rooke and Mrs. Cunningham."

"Well, and what had they to say about it?"

I had to admit that, according to Rooke, something about the place had brought Mrs. Cunningham to the verge of hysteria, while Rooke himself had found the place inexplicably uncanny.

"Then as far as it goes that bears me out?"

"As far as it goes. But they found nothing out of the ordinary. Esdaile even left the key in the door, and there was nothing to prevent them from rummaging to their hearts' content."

"Did they rummage?"

"Rooke didn't. Said he wasn't a policeman to go scratching about other people's houses. I thought it rather decent of him."

"Well—it's possible they didn't know what to look for."

"Do you?" I parried.

"No," he confessed,—"not unless he keeps a tame ghost down there."

"In that case the Chelsea Arts Club would be right," I laughed; and we went on to speak of other things.

X

Then one morning I had a letter from Joan Merrow, which I give you without the alteration of a single word. If you yourself have a modern young Anthea who may command you anything and does not hesitate to do so I accept your sympathy in advance. The letter ran:

"Dear Old Thing,

"Do be an angel and do one or two little things for me. I'd rather ask you than anybody else because you're the *kindest* person I know. If you're too busy of course you'll say so straight out, but what I want first of all is for you to get me the addresses of a few nice small houses or convenient flats."

In course of time I had recovered my breath. This, remember, was in 1919. It was not the Crown Jewels her ladyship wanted, merely "a nice small house"; not the sun, moon and stars, only "a convenient flat." I think my nerves might be spared shocks of this kind at my time of life.

"Of course, I know rents have gone up," she continued, "but Chummy thinks there ought to be plenty of quite nice little places for about £70, but you could go up to £75 for a really nice house with a garden, rates and taxes included, of course. There are some sweet little houses right on the edge of the Heath at Hampstead with trees all round them and dear little brass knockers on the doors, but I don't know if any of those are empty, but you might ask."

I seemed to remember those sweet little houses. If I am right, your father puts his name down for one of them on his coming of age, and, with luck in the matter of intervening deaths, your son may end his days there. I have never had the impiety to ask the rent of them.

"There wouldn't have to be any premium, and there *must* be a telephone. Speaking of telephones, I do wish you could persuade Philip to have that one of his moved, as where it is everybody can hear every word you say. The house needn't be Hampstead, of course, Wimbledon or Richmond would do if you wouldn't mind having a look round. If you went on the top of a bus you'd be out in the fresh air and the blow would do you good. Then there would be the question of a maid, but we shouldn't want her for a month or two yet."

At this point a little fanning with the letter refreshed me considerably.

"And now," the joyous thing continued, "if you happen to be anywhere near Regent Street it would be so kind if you would call at Morny's and get me some soap, I like Chaminade best, and some tooth-powder, any good sort. I know how busy you are, but it is so difficult to get things here. I tried to get some Petrole Hahn the other day, but they'd never heard of it. I'd ask Mrs. Cunningham, but I hear she's away, and you carry colors so well in your head. That's why I wonder if you'd call at that little bead-shop in Oxford Street, nearly opposite Frascati's, and see if they have any amber beads, not the real amber, of course, iron-amber I think they call it. Chummy wants me to have some because of my hair. Not the huge ones, please, but from about the size of a pea to as big as a marble."

"Or a 7.65 mm. bullet," I murmured to myself.

"The weather here is lovely and we're out all day long, and I do wish you were here. But my bathing-costume is a perfect rag. I hate the skirted ones and always wear a plain club one, either navy blue or black; but I'm afraid it won't run to a silk one, though you might ask the price. And now here's something that isn't for me at all. You know Hamley's, either in Regent Street or Holborn, but they have a better selection in Regent Street. The boys want two pairs of water-wings, and they'd better be of different colors or they'll get them mixed up and be always quarreling. And oh, Chummy says it's awful neck, seeing he doesn't know you, but there are some pipes, 'Captanide' they're called, and you get them at Loewe's in the Haymarket. There are two sizes, and he would like the smaller size, two of them, please. You can add them to my bill as they're my present to him and he's giving me the beads, and he'd better have some tobacco for the pipes. His number at Dunhills' is 06369. A pipe is better for him than cigarettes, though I allow him six cigarettes a day and you can only get gaspers here. Any nice kind would do as long as they're Turkish. Thanks so much. How is the novel getting on? We're both so looking forward to reading it. Is it a love story? I do hope it is, as I'm sure you'd do that so beautifully. Do be a pet about the house. I'm sending you some flowers tomorrow.

"Joan."

With a light sigh I folded the letter and put it into my pocket. At any rate, there seemed to be two people on whom our Case did not weigh too heavily.

PART VI

THE MAN IN THE CLUB

I

I always have the lurking feeling that Democracy would be all right but for its numbers. I am aware that this sounds paradoxical, and that in its numbers is supposed to lie its strength, but I do not see how that can ever be a properly directed executive strength. There are too many cooks. Taken one at a time, how admirable are its impulses, how just in the main its judgments! But block-vote it—! Take away its trust in Princes and put it in Polls—! Convert its votes, not into effective action, but into arid deserts of statistics—!... Two men can make a holy friendship; among three there can be a useful understanding; but ten will ever winnow the wind with talk, and a hundred are a mere arithmetical obstruction in the way of ever getting anything done at all.

I am moved to these reflections (as no younger novelist ever dares to say) by a series of occurrences that began at that time so to harass me and to put me so completely off my private work that, like poor Monty Rooke, I might almost as well have stopped in bed till midday. These were the occurrences that I had already dimly foreseen when that photograph of the house in Lennox Street had so suddenly appeared in that morning's issue of the *Roundabout*. By an unforeseen fluke the peril of the coroner's inquest had been safely passed, but I had felt in my bones that others were gathering.

Well, they gathered. I learned, no matter how, that the Scepter Insurance Company was consulting its solicitors and its solicitors were instructing counsel. The plane and parachute people, as I had expected, were investigating scraps of twisted metal and pieces of scorched fabric, and the Accidents Investigation Committees were getting to work.

Understand that none of these happenings were official happenings. If the Scepter wanted to resist, it had its ordinary remedy at civil law. The Committees had no authority whatever except to draw up reports for their own information and satisfaction. The interests of the owners and manufacturers were likewise purely private ones.

In fact, as far as I could see, the only charge that could lay Charles Valentine Smith *directly* by the heels would be one under those half-baked Orders that so far were the best that could be done towards solving an entirely new problem with totally unascertained powers.

But there are wheels within wheels, and it is the little wheels that are the devil. We still speak of things being "official" long after that imposing word has ceased to have much significance. If only for the arithmetical reason mentioned above, Government works ever more and more through channels that are not official and votable on at all. Many a private concern has a Minister, or at any rate a Minister's adviser or an influential Member, safely tucked away in its pocket, and you may invert this if you wish in the sense of an understanding. This is why bright-eyed secretaries, fresh from a dinnertable or a conference that has let them into the very heart of some secret matter, are not supposed to be asked what knowledge they have in their extrasecretarial capacities; and this is what the Man in the Club understands and what his brother in the Pub does not. He thumps no tub, enunciates no "first principles." A name, a glance, a shake of the head, and block-votes are put back where they belong. "I'm told Glenfield doesn't wish it" is more to him than twenty parliamentary returns; "I wonder whether So-and-So has quite the power he thinks he has," and three months later the public is surprised to see that a newspaper has changed its policy.

But let me hasten to reassure you. I am not going to invite you to follow our Case into quagmires either legal or political. I know too little about these things myself. Recent as the judgment on Appeal was, I have to stop and think for a moment before I can remember whether the Scepter people won their case or lost it, and I have only the vaguest idea what the findings of the Accidents Investigation Committees were. For most of these things I have taken Billy Mackwith's word. But he was briefed in one case, and has followed up the others with just the same pertinacity he showed when he tracked down and brought triumphantly home again those early prodigal pictures of Philip Esdaile's.

And, as I had begun to see it, Charles Valentine Smith, whether on oath in the Scepter case or at the invitation of one or other of the private inquiries, was engaged on something enormously more important than the immediate results of an aeroplane crash. He was contributing his mite to something that would live when he and all else about him had been forgotten—to the labor and knowledge and unparalleled discovery of his time.

II

Whitaker, in its "list of London Clubs," describes my own as "Social": that is to say, that I and my fellow-members have no common bond of occupation or interest other than that of pleasant good-fellowship. We are drawn from all professions, and this gives me an opportunity I value highly, namely, that of hearing scraps of the "shop" of other men when I am bored to death with my own. Saturday nights, when there is no morrow's issue of my paper to "put to bed," usually find me in the smoking-room behind my *Pall Mall* or *Evening Standard*, with a few other non-weekenders sitting rather widely apart also behind their papers, none of us so engrossed in the news that we are unaware of each other, but using the journals as protective cover. Occasionally we all drop them to converse; more frequently two or more will engage in conversation with the others interjecting sniping-shots across the room; and it is all rather interesting and quite unexciting and very much go-as-you-please.

On a Saturday evening early in June I was sitting after this fashion, half reading, half listening to Ronald Mowbray's remarks on some boxing match or other. Mowbray's talk about boxing is sometimes rather good. He was a known man of his hands long before the sport (if you can always call it that nowadays) became quite so deadly intensive both physically and financially. Moreover, his training as a sculptor has given him a good deal of knowledge of the fundamental mechanics of the human framework, and how a slight prolongation of the heel-bone can make a Deer-foot or length of humerus a lightning hitter.

"Just at present I don't think Nature's provided the world with a real heavy-weight," he was saying. "Not the real John Hopley kind, I mean. It takes more than size. You see, it doesn't matter how hard you *could* hit the other fellow if he gets his in first."

"But surely Wells is quick enough for you, isn't he?" said Jack Beresford. His newspaper was on his knee.

"Oh, yes, Wells is fast. I'm not saying that speed's everything. But it's nearly everything nowadays, even for a heavy. That's why half these giants would be simply at the mercy of a comparatively light fellow like Carpentier."

Over against the window bay a *Globe* was dropped an inch. Cyril Turner's eye was seen over it. He is in the Home Office, quite high up, and is an untrammeled sort of spirit when he leaves Whitehall for the freer air of Piccadilly.

"That's true of other things besides boxing," he interjected.

Mowbray turned. "What is?"

"What you're saying about weight and speed. Labor's discovered it too."

"I don't quite know what you mean, but if I've said something wiser than I intended—" said Mowbray, claiming it if he had.

"Well, Labor has discovered it. Look at the way they strike nowadays. The New Strike's as different as chalk and cheese from the Old. Totally different methods—more scientific altogether. Masters and men used to stand up foot to foot like Smithfield Butchers and slog till neither of them could stand. Pure battering-ram principle, and the fellow who won wasn't much better off than the one who lost. But now it's all swiftness and surprise. No warning—just what you'd call a lightning punch where it's going to hurt most and then dance away again. That's why they go for the transport and postal services and all the distributing machinery instead of stopping production. It paralyzes just the same. Solar plexus business. And swiftness is the secret, as you say, not brute strength any more."

Another paper was lowered. It was Hay's *Evening News*. Hay is a retired Major of Gunners, and I have bought very good cigars from him and very passable port.

"And that isn't all either," he said. "It goes far beyond strikes."

"War?" said somebody. Everybody in the Club knows Hay and his talk.

Hay nodded. "You'll see where speed comes in *then*—speed and the absence of warning. The nation that can get a thousand bombing-planes into the air first will be able to do what it likes with the others."

"Oh, come, Major!" somebody laughed. "That's rather looking for trouble, isn't it?"

"No good shutting your eyes to it," Hay returned. "Turner said something about transport just now. They're talking a lot about relieving London's traffic congestion. Well, it wants relieving; but do you know how I'd relieve it? I'd dig new ways ... well underground. Big ones, to hold plenty of people. Tube Stations won't be much good the next time. And I'd start digging them now."

"Hay's had a hint from the League of Nations."

"Well, I'm a League of Nations man up to a point. Up to this point— that the next show's going to be so unutterably ghastly that a generation that leaves anything undone to prevent it ought to be wiped off the map— *any*thing undone, you understand, whether you personally believe in it or whether you don't. We're only at the beginning of the New War, and it will be far more 'lightning' than any of Turner's New Strikes."

"Democracy'll prevent it."

"As it's doing in Russia, eh? Just as likely to make it. Democracy's got such damnably high-falutin ideals and so little sense of ordinary decency. For an inhuman thing that belongs to everybody and pleases nobody give me the Will of the People. If you read your history you'll find that hot air's usually followed by bloodshed. And they won't stick at much. Personally I prefer a King's war with guns to a democratic one with black typhus germs."

"Sunny soul, our Major, isn't he?" somebody laughed again.

"Well," said Hay, disappearing behind his paper again, "a thousand bombing-planes will do it the next time. I hope we aren't forgetting how to make 'em, and use 'em. Waiter, bring me a whisky-and-soda, please."

III

For a time nothing was heard in the smoking-room but the rustle of the turning papers and the clink of a coffee-cup in a saucer. Sluggishly—for the idleness that had latterly overmastered me tired me to my very marrow—I was comparing Hay's words with what Cecil Hubbard had said on the same subject. "Continuity of manufacture and the training of men"—you might call this "civil" aviation if you liked, but according to both men it was indistinguishable from the question of national defense. And, further, Hubbard, unless I was mistaken, had allowed young Smith some portion of vision in the matter. "It doesn't matter whether he's twenty-four or a hundred-and-four"—"The wind blew whither it list"—"While the old Burleighs had been nodding some youngster had been getting away with the job."

Well, I myself, no longer very young, could only sigh and agree that it seemed to be a young man's business. In other fields of action youth, the cutting-edge, was directed by the experienced hand and the wise head that too has been young in its day; but in this field none but youth has or has had the experience. Its time is short, it reaps its harvest in its Spring. We in the August of our lives may say, "Thus and thus should be done," but a young head shakes and we are silenced. The judgment of an infant answers us. A Samuel speaks, and our lips are closed within our beards. We administer, advise, finance, organize, but his is the mounting heart.

In the midst of my meditation I became aware that I was being spoken to by Mowbray. I told you he was a sculptor. He is no great intimate of Esdaile's, but naturally they are not unacquainted.

"I beg your pardon. What were you saying?" I said.

"This Scepter action. I see it's down on the List. You're a friend of Esdaile's. I suppose it won't affect him in any way?"

"What's the action about?" I asked.

"Here you are. '*The Aiglon Aviation Company v. The Scepter Assurance Corporation.*' The Scepter people are resisting the claim on the grounds that the machine had no business to be where it was. They also allege negligence on the pilot's part, or so at least McIlwaine tells me. He's briefed. Is it true you were at Esdaile's when it happened?"

"Yes."

"Do you know the pilot?"

"No. I believe he's away with Esdaile in the country at present."

"Well, he can be getting ready to come back to town. It's down for Trinity term. I should say the whole action turns on him. Worrying sort of thing to have to go through on the top of a bad crash, but the Scepter's got to fight it. If flying ever comes to anything the position's got to be made clear."

"*If* it comes to anything?" I queried idly....

"Apart from Hay's point of view, I mean. I don't see myself that it's achieved very much yet outside war. Too risky and uncertain altogether. There isn't a flyer on the Rhine at present who'll take his leave by aeroplane; he might lose a day. And if this Atlantic flight does come off it'll be rather like Channel-swimming—done once and then not again for another forty years. Just a record. I can't see there's much more in it yet."

Here Atkinson's voice struck in. I hadn't heard him enter.

"Yes, but what about other places—Australia, for instance? It's catching on there all right from what I'm told. Say you've a station ninety miles from your front door to your back. An aeroplane'll do in an hour or two what it would take you two or three days to do in a buggy. Any number of these fellows are running their private planes now. And we're making the machines."

"And there isn't much doubt they'll be having a go at the Cape-to-Cairo route presently," somebody else remarked. (I am giving this desultory conversation very much as it happened, since I felt exceedingly desultory myself and it all contributed to the impression of Chummy Smith and the nature of his job that was slowly building itself up in my mind.)

"Well, that's a different thing again. I should say the value of that would be largely scientific, at any rate at first. Like the Shackleton and Scott expeditions."

Mowbray laughed. "Are you one of those who think those were primarily scientific?" he asked.

"What else were they?"

Whereupon we had the matter from the point of view of Ronald Mowbray, ex-amateur champion and still the soundest of referees.

"Pure sport and adventure, of course," he replied promptly. "Oh yes, I know somebody put up the money for a lot of instruments, and they took all sorts of observations and kept journals and all the rest of it. I know all that. Quite useful too in its way. But when you get right down to brass tacks those fellows did it because they jolly well wanted to and for no other reason on earth. What's better? Chuck in your science and 'contributions to the sum of human knowledge' as a make-weight if you like, but they weren't just out for that in cold blood. No, nor science books nor lecture-tours either. It was just an epic lark. After all, a fellow's got to have a go at something."

There was a general laugh. It was so very like Mowbray himself. Both in his boxing and his sculpture he was in the habit of "having a go." And that was the end of that rambling conversation as far as I was concerned. One of the waiters approached and bent over my shoulder.

"Lord Glenfield would like to speak to you at the telephone, sir," he said.

IV

Besides being Ringmaster-in-Chief of the *Daily Circus* and of a good many other journals, Lord Glenfield is a very good friend of mine; but he had never rung me up at my Club before. He was speaking from his house in Portman Square, and he wanted to know whether I was leaving the Club immediately, and if not whether he might come round. I was a little surprised, but told him to come by all means; and he said he would be along in twenty minutes.

Now Glenfield is a very much feared man, and with reason; but I speak of him as I have always found him. Before I knew him better I had the vanity to think that he had offered me my comfortably-paid job for the sake (such as it was) of my literary name; but I was soon undeceived. It appeared he was so good as to like me. Certainly he has always shown me the greatest consideration, and I am going to ask you to notice how he added to it that night.

His car glided up to the club door in exactly the twenty minutes he had mentioned, and we sought a padded alcove at the head of the stairs. He is a big and handsome man, hardly yet gray, and had I needed a leg-up in my own Club it was certainly a distinction to be seen with him. I drew a heavy curtain for the sake of privacy, and then asked him to have coffee and a liqueur.

"I will. In fact, that's why I rang you up instead of sending for you," he said with a certain pleasant grimness. "Understand?"

"Not quite."

"Well, if you're to be had up on the carpet I prefer that it should be your own carpet."

I saw, and I hope you too see the kindliness and delicacy of his action. Apparently I was in for a wigging, which was to be, not less, but still more of a wigging that I, his subordinate, was permitted to act as his host. As he said, he could have summoned me to his office or house, dressed me down, and dismissed me again; but Glenfield knows men and how to bind them to him by accepting things at their hands. It is so easy for Glenfield to give.

"Well, can you guess?" he said, nodding to me over his liqueur.

"Perhaps I can," I answered.

"Then what about it? Are you getting tired of the job?"

"Not," I answered slowly, "of the job. But I'm tired—very tired."

He diagnosed me with a swift look.

"South of France any good to you? Or Norway? Or anywhere else? I suppose young what's-his-name—Willett—could carry on?"

"Oh, of course he's been running the whole show for weeks," I admitted. Then, "Look here, Glenfield; I'd better resign."

"Don't be an ass," he replied promptly. "If I'd meant you to resign do you suppose I should have come here tonight? I sack men in my office, not while I'm drinking their liqueurs. Now tell me what's wrong. You haven't been yourself for some time."

I frowned, hardly knowing what to reply.

"This is most awfully good of you, but I hardly think it's a case for a holiday," I said at last with some embarrassment.

"Well, tell me about it. Is it working double tides, or just post-war slump? We've all got that more or less."

I mused and shook my head. "I wish you'd let me resign," I said again.

He has an imperious eye, and I did not attempt to meet it. "Why?" he demanded....

I did not answer. Willett had loyally covered my too frequent absence and neglect, but I knew and Glenfield knew that I had let my paper down. The Circus was slipping backward. Possibly there was something in Glenfield's suggestion about post-war slump. Now, when all the world should have been working as it had never worked before, so little work seemed worth the doing. The *Circus*, which after all is a vastly important instrument of democratic government, seemed to me a thing of stunts and japes and cynical mockery of the recent stupendous years; my own work, once so much to me that I had sacrificed to it the joy and ease of half a life, seemed a thing that the world could do perfectly well without. I missed my timber and gun-cotton and cordage and corrugated iron. My real books were my stores-ledgers "A" and "B," the Regulations for Engineer Services my only Muse. I feared—nay, I almost hoped—that I should write no more novels. My bolt seemed shot. It is a depressing thing to have been a younger novelist and to have wasted your life.

But I could not honestly take the way out that Glenfield suggested. Over and above the burden that I shared with everybody else, I *had* let my private affairs come between me and the work Glenfield paid me to do. The infernal Case had cramped itself on my shoulders and was making a slacker and a fraud of me. I wished that Glenfield had taken any way but this kindly one. There was only one answer to make to him.

"Well?" he said at last.

"Oh—let me send in my resignation," I growled. "I've let you down and will take the consequences."

"Consequences my eye," he replied bluntly. "The drop's nothing—a thousand or two—we can pick that up in no time. It's you I'm worrying about, not the paper. You've something on your mind. What is it? I've a bit of a pull here and there, you know, and I may be able to help."

To hear Lord Glenfield describe his appalling power as "a bit of a pull here and there" was almost comic; nobody living knows where his power ends. I consider it the most singular phenomenon of a democratic age that it gives to a few men such power as no ancient emperor ever dreamed of. Indeed, if one's conception of democracy is that it is the age's ailment, it seems to carry within itself hope of its own cure. Few men have been so bitterly attacked as Glenfield, but in my opinion he is the natural corrective to our new disease of numbers, our malady of stultifying votes.

"Of course, I'm assuming it's a purely private affair," he went on.

"Oh, it's public enough—or looks like being—that's part of the trouble—"

"Yes?" he said invitingly....

V

Let me see, how many does that make—I mean when, half an hour later, I had given him as much as I then knew of the outline of this story? How many people were parties in greater or less degree to the highly important public matter that we were struggling to keep from the light of day?

There were the five men at our breakfast-party: Esdaile, Rooke, Mackwith, Hubbard and myself. And the three women: Mrs. Esdaile, Mrs. Cunningham and Joan. Westbury, and an unknown number of his associates; and Inspector Webster, also an unknown quantity. And of course there was Charles Valentine Smith himself. I am not including Hanson and old William Dadley the picture-frame maker. Call it certainly eleven. Lord Glenfield made the twelfth. We were getting on.

He took my narrative quite lightly. Indeed, parts of it seemed almost to amuse him. He asked if he might have a second liqueur, and then sat back in the padded alcove smiling at his glass.

"Well," he said at last, "it would make quite a neat prize competition, wouldn't it?" Tremendous force as he is, he can never quite shake off his interest in prize competitions.

I asked him in what way.

"I mean the position of your painter-friend. As you've told the story it strikes me that he's the key of the whole situation. And I should say that he intended to remain so."

"What makes you say that?"

"Well, you say he has his talkee-talkee with the flying-fellow, doesn't give you a single word of explanation, but simply carries him off into the country. It looks as if he thought he'd already told you too much and was pulling out again. *I* don't think he intends to say anything more. You take a short holiday, go down there, and see if I'm right."

(How far he was right you already know. As I have told you in anticipation, I did go down, waited for a couple of days, then tackled Esdaile about it, and found he had taken the very line Glenfield indicated.)

"So it's really publicity you're all scared of?" he continued presently. "Well, I told you I had a bit of a pull here and there. Publicity's rather my line of country, you know."

"Yes, but hardly against the law of the land," I objected. "You can't go about suborning judges and telling the police their business—even you."

"Good gracious, man!" he cried energetically, staring incredulously at me. "Don't tell me I've been employing an editor who doesn't know any more than *that*!"

"Than what?"

"Than clumsy work of *that* sort! Suborn judges! Meddle with the police! I've been entrusting the *Circus* to a man who talks like *that*!... Hurry up that waiter!"

"But isn't that what it comes to?"

"You haven't got to *let* it come to that—not within a hundred miles of it! You shock me! Tell me now what you do when you find yourself all balled up and unable to meet a Case?"

"That's precisely what I want to know."

"Then I'll tell you. You attack. You manufacture a totally different Case and then proceed to demolish it. First of all you make hay of charges that were never made, and then you carry the fight over to the other fellow. If somebody says this flying-fellow's been getting gun-work in, you simply sidestep, come back, and want to know what's wrong that he hasn't been recommended for a K.B.E. *Never* defend, my boy. *Always* go for your man. What is it that Boche philosopher wrote? 'Every attack is a victory.' You've got a beauty of an opening.... You say this fellow Smith really is the goods—thinker, live wire—genuine national-importance sort of fellow?" he demanded.

"So his friends seem to think."

"Then what's simpler than for you to take a column in the *Circus* and say so? And then take another column and damn the other side? Pack of shirkers who bolted underground while your friend went up and kept the Hun off London? The old tricks are always the best—that's why they're old. Do it on general lines, of course; keep off *sub judice* cases and all that. As regards his being over London, you've got to make a molehill out of that mountain, if it is a mountain. What are the Regulations exactly?"

I told him what they were, not exactly, but in all their unavoidable inexactitude. At one of them he suddenly stopped me.

"Ah, there you are. A Secretary of State has power to except him, has he?"

"Hardly after the fact, I should say."

"Oh, don't be so dashed pedantic about it! Nothing would ever get done at all if everybody talked like that! I'm not suggesting this as his *defense*; it's his *attack*, so that he shan't be charged at all, don't you see? And if you know a better 'ole go to it.... Now you get those articles written. Write them so that they'll start correspondence. I don't quite see the *Daily Circus* being put in the cart by a Chelsea auctioneer. Then take a month's holiday.... Now tell me how the novel's going on."

This last I did over our second liqueur.

VI

I quite realize that we can't all be Glenfields. I don't suppose it would do to have the world so over-oxygenated—for he is the oxygen as against the democratic nitrogen of our modern atmosphere. He was probably right in calling my scrupulous objections pedantic, but I confess that his power would affright me did I not trust him in the main to use it rightly. If he chose to send a note to a Secretary of State requesting that special permission for a civilian to be excepted from the Regulations should be given and slightly antedated, it was highly unlikely that he would be refused. That at any rate need no longer be a weight on my mind. As far as the Regulations were concerned Charles Valentine Smith had now probably very little to fear.

But was the contravention of the Regulations the real point of our Case after all? By keeping Smith out of Court were we not in reality making the larger issue quite dreadfully simple? Had Smith killed Maxwell any the less dead that certain strings could be conveniently pulled on his behalf? And why had Glenfield been so certain that my painter-friend, who twice had been on the point of taking the rest of us completely into his confidence, had now changed his mind, was "pulling out," and intended to tell us nothing at all?

On this point I was to receive still further mystification during that very week-end.

For, returning home that night, lighter of heart than I had been for many days, I found a small registered packet from Esdaile himself. The packet contained a key. His request, after Joan's house-and-servant-hunting commissions, was quite a modest one. He wanted me to go to his house, to post on to him a certain set of sketches the locality of which he minutely described, and then when I had a moment of time to go on to Dadley's, in the King's Road, and to ascertain for myself how he was getting on with the framing of a couple of pictures. He was sorry to bother me, but Rooke had behaved rather like an ass, and Mollie and the kids sent their love.

His commission was no bother to me; indeed, I found the latter part of it rather interesting. I had no desire to exchange further words with the "Chelsea Auctioneer," as Glenfield had described Westbury, but I confess that I had a curiosity about him. I had probably queered his pitch if he hoped to get Smith into Court on a technical point and then to fly off at score about bullets, pistols and pocket-patting at the foot of ladders; but I did not know what other means of making himself a nuisance he might not have. Old Dadley might be able to tell me. Dadley probably knew Inspector Webster as well.

But I could not now see Dadley till Monday, and as for the visit to Lennox Street, Sunday afternoon would do for that. Sunday morning I intended to spend in writing the first of those articles for the *Circus*. I went to bed, slept well, rose early, and was at my desk betimes.

Those two articles, and the numerous subsequent ones I wrote, need not detain us here. Indeed, just as you will have to take the legal aspects of our Case largely on Mackwith's word, so for the journalistic side of it I refer you to Lord Glenfield and his group of papers. But it is possible that you may remember something of the wave of opinion we set in motion, for it is not so very long ago. Deliberately I sought, and successfully obtained, correspondence—a correspondence that embraced, directly or obliquely, practically every side of the subject, from the personality of famous pilots to the constitution of the new Ministry of the Air. We have, of course, the general balance of our papers to consider, but within those limits I fairly let myself go. And if you tell me that I did all this to save Charles Valentine Smith from the hands of justice, I answer that I did it because ten short years have made the air and everything connected with it as important to us as the sea. If you tell me that I did it because I was Philip Esdaile's friend, I reply that I did it because I was just beginning to see on what a hair our destiny might hang if a new and gigantic industry, suddenly hung up in mid-career, should be left unsupported, unrecognized, unencouraged. If you charge me that I did it because of Joan and her happiness, I retort that I was by this time wholly convinced that Hay and Hubbard were right, that the next attack on one nation by another would come with appalling swiftness, would be directed at civilian nerves as much as at uniformed bodies, would be the beginning of the thousand years in which the Devil is to be unchained, and the sooner the public realized the situation the better.

So I wrote my first article, read it over, decided that it was pretty much what was wanted, and lunched lightly at home, as is my Sunday custom. Then, at about three o'clock, I put Esdaile's letter into my pocket and set out for Lennox Street.

VII

As I walked along the Cromwell Road I could not but be put in mind of the last occasion when I had called at Esdaile's studio—that midday when I had found all locked up, Rooke departed, and had run him to earth in his old quarters in Jubilee Place. I have spoken of Mrs. Cunningham as an enigmatic sort of person, possibly as much an enigma to herself as to others, and inspiring more of compassion and kindness than of that other feeling that is supposed to be akin to these. Now I could not help wondering about her again. What had made her so suddenly break off with Monty? Had she had a reason, or none? I suppose there are these sensitive plants whose own interior moods and feelings outweigh all the logic of outward events, so that a flurry of nerves becomes a motive, and an intuition grounds for immediate action.

Monty had spoken of her as having been on the verge of hysteria on that afternoon when her Jacobean wardrobe had been carried down into Esdaile's cellar. It was within a few days of that that she had definitely announced her intention of not marrying again. I repeat, that as I left the Cromwell Road and turned down by South Kensington Station, I could not help remembering all this and wondering. I was still wondering when I turned into Lennox Street.

It was a sunny afternoon, now well on towards summer, and as I walked up the path I noticed that Esdaile's grass already needed cutting. I remember thinking how jolly it must be at Santon that afternoon. Inside, as I opened the door, I found the floor strewn with the usual clutter of leaflets and circulars, coal-merchants' post-cards, announcements of dairies and window-cleaning firms. I turned them over and found nothing of importance among them. Then I passed to the annexe and the studio.

Before he had left, Esdaile had evidently set the place more or less in order, but, judging from the veil of dust that lay over everything, he had made no arrangements for having his house visited in his absence. I suppose Mollie's two maids had found fresh jobs by this time. The shuttering-up of the French window gave the alcove a vacant and dreary sort of look, which was not improved by a slight fall of soot that had come down the chimney and lay spread out over the hearth. In the studio the dark blue blinds were drawn, pictures stood with their faces turned to the walls, and those on the easels were wholly or partially covered with hanging valances of newspapers.

The sketches I had come to fetch formed a small separate parcel which I had no difficulty in finding. Nevertheless, to make sure they were the right ones, I sat down in an old double armchair with a frayed tapestry seat and unfastened the string that bound the brown paper. They were the required ones, and I replaced the paper and tied the string again. Then I continued to sit in the chair, not consciously thinking, with the bundle of sketches on my knees.

I dare say it was the indigo twilight in which I sat that brought back to me the last time I had seen those blinds drawn. You will remember that I had myself helped to draw them when the shuffling of feet on the roof had warned us that the police were about to carry the two men down into the garden. I gave a slight shiver, but as much at the rather drowsy air of the place as at the recollection itself. The studio would certainly be none the worse for half an hour's ventilation and sunlight. I was in no great hurry to leave. I rose from the tapestried chair, unfastened the blind-cords from the cleats, and began to pull back the blinds. The first one I drew back showed me that the broken roof-pane had been replaced by one of a different make of glass. I pulled back the remaining blinds, and then sought the long hooked pole that was used to draw down the upper portion of the wall-window.

It was as I crossed to the corner where this pole stood that my foot caught on the corner of a loose rug, tripping me slightly. As I did not fall I took no notice of this for the moment, but found the pole, pulled down the window, and let in the needed air. Only as I was replacing the pole did I notice the small round hole in the floor that the turning up of the rug had disclosed.

Now there are times when one does not so much think as leap to an instantaneous conclusion. Be it a right one or a wrong one, it possesses you like a flash for the infinitesimal portion of time it endures. In this merest flash of time my eyes had flown aloft. A hole in the floor, and another hole in the roof!... A new roof-pane might have been put in since, but I knew accurately in which portion of the old pane that shattered star with the small round hole in the middle of it had been. In that moment of time I saw the whole picture again—the star, that gray snowslide made by the bodies of the two men, the little wavering, creeping shadows of the broken mulberry branch. The hole in the middle of the star had been approximately over the hole in the floor that the moving of the rug had revealed.

"Then why," I cried excitedly to myself, "didn't he find the bullet? How did it come to be found in another house? If it went through the floor it ought to have been in his cellar—if he looked—if he isn't lying—"

And then, in another almost simultaneous flash, "Could there have been *two* bullets? There were seven left in the pistol—the magazine carries eight—but you can get a ninth in if you place it in the chamber itself—"

All this, I say, crossed my mind in one hundredth part of the time it has taken you to read it.

And then came the drop. I was all wrong. That hole in the floor wasn't a bullet-hole at all. You can get a clean round bullet-hole in glass, but not in a floorboard. Neither does any pistol make a hole with a neat little rim of yellow metal glinting inside it.

I assure you I was already on my hands and knees by the side of that hole. It was five-eighths of an inch in diameter, perfectly round, with, as I say, that lining of what I at first took to be brass. I inserted my little finger, but the lining was firmly fixed. It did not run through the thickness of the board, but occupied perhaps an eighth of an inch about a third of the way down it. And the removal of my finger, clearing away a little grime, revealed something else. I lay down with my eye close to the hole. The ring was not of brass, but of gold.

Breathlessly I rose and looked about for an instrument. A screwdriver on the window-ledge caught my eye. Yes, a screwdriver would do. I seized it and crouched on the floor again. I worked for perhaps a minute. At the end of that time the slender circle of metal was loose in the palm of my hand.

Even without the tiny initials engraved inside it I should have known it. Tightly as it had been wedged, not one of its three little emeralds had been wrenched out. It was the engagement-ring I had seen on Mrs. Cunningham's finger on the morning of our breakfast.

VIII

Fantastic as had been the thoughts that during that fraction of time had whirled through my brain, the little gold circlet lying in my palm seemed to propound questions more fantastic still. How in the name of all that was inexplicable had Mrs. Cunningham's engagement-ring come to be there? Each momentary explanation at which I grasped seemed more lunatic than the rest. Had she simply lost it, sought for it and been unable to find it? Had it rolled of itself into that little five-eighths hole? Absurd, since even if by a miraculous chance it had rolled exactly there I had had to take a screwdriver to prise it out. Had she put it there, and for what reason? Ridiculous again, since ladies on the eve of their weddings do not use their rings for the jeweling of holes in one-inch floorboards. Yet if she had not put it there, what idiot had, and why? And what was the hole itself?

Again I was down on my hands and knees, examining the hole. Round—as perfectly round as if it had been drilled with a brace and bit—but not recent. It might at one time have given passage to a gas-pipe, a wire, a cord; it might have been a knot-hole. I peered down it. Nothing but blackness. I explored it again with my finger, and learned nothing new. Just an old hole, now scraped and jagged a little by the screwdriver.

Suddenly I rose, left the studio, and strode through the annexe. Rooke might have had his scruples about prying into the nooks and corners of another man's house, but I assure you I now had none. I was bound for the cellar. If others could go down there so could I. Rooke had said that Philip had left the key in the door. "Right you are, Philip," I muttered to myself. "If Rooke won't I will. Glenfield says you're pulling out, but so am not I. I'm for Hubbard and the optophone theory now. I've an hour or two to spare, and your cellar's going to be examined as it hasn't been yet. Here goes."

But I had all the moral guilt of my intention to abuse his roof-tree with none of the advantages. The door that led to the cellar was once more locked and the key had gone.

Slowly I went back to the studio and the frayed tapestry chair. I wanted to think quietly and at length. Now I pride myself on being rather a methodical sort of thinker when I really give my mind to a thing, and I was resolved to get to the bottom of this if I could. That almost insultingly grotesque discovery of the ring had put me on my mettle. One thing seemed clear, if anything in the whole business was clear: for whatever reason, Mrs. Cunningham had not shared Monty's delicacy about peering and pottering. Of this there seemed to be several indications. Again and again she had insisted that there was something uncanny about the place; she had had an access of hysteria and had had to be brought up from the cellar; and rather than live there she had broken off her engagement. But she had not done this last immediately. Days, if not a week or two—I did not know how long—had elapsed. I was now convinced that during that interval she had made some kind of a discovery. The ring was evidence enough of that. And she had had an advantage in her investigations that I had not: she had had access to the cellar. Then, her discovery made, apparently she had cleared out.

So much for Mrs. Cunningham. Now for the apparatus, all I knew of which was the ring in the knot-hole.

Deliberately I began to reconstruct the events of the morning of the accident from the moment when Esdaile had returned from his unexplained half hour in the cellar. I put pressure on my memory so that not a single detail should escape me. And I experienced a little thrill when, by dint of concentrated thought, I evoked Esdaile's image again at the moment when Hubbard and I had followed him into this very studio. He had been standing with bowed head, poking with his foot at fragments of broken glass and—yes—at the rug on the floor. I could see his foot again, pushing at that very mat over which I had stumbled. The mat had covered the hole then as it covered it now. Esdaile, to all appearances lost in abstraction, had—I began to feel it in my bones—been intently engaged in *covering up* that hole.

Then, having covered up the hole, what had he done next? Instantly I saw another vivid picture. I saw again those gray moving shapes on the roof, saw Esdaile suddenly stride to the blind-cords, saw the movement with which he had bidden me do the same, and the little bright gold rhomboids of light in the rafters as the deep blue blinds had been shut.

And half an hour later he had sharply forbidden Rooke to touch the blind-cords and had petulantly refused him the key of the cellar.

I felt excitement growing on me. My whole body began to glow with it. I felt myself getting nearer—nearer—

Hubbard was both right and wrong—

He was wrong in his insistence on what Esdaile must have *heard*—

But he was right about the apparatus—

Esdaile had not heard—he had *seen*—and there was no more mystery about it all than there is in putting your eye to a keyhole.

IX

And yet, approaching the truth as I felt myself to be, I had a deep-down feeling that at the same time I was wrong. Carefully I begun to examine the objections to my suddenly-formed theory, and instantly I was impressed by them. In the first place, take an inch board with a five-eighths hole in it, peep through, and see how much, or rather how little, of a field of vision your eye commands. Next, consider the awkwardness of peering through that hole, not in a vertical wall or door, but in horizontal planking some feet above your head. Then, most important of all, weigh the extreme unlikeliness of it that Esdaile, who had merely gone down for a bottle of wine and had no reason whatever to dream that calamity was imminent, should have had his eye at that hole at that particular moment of time. It was preposterous. All had happened so quickly. He would have had to stand on something, probably to pile up furniture; even with a pair of household steps ready in position he would have had to mount them—nay, he would first have had to *think* of mounting them. I had no means of telling if he had previously known of that hole in his floor, but say that he had: does one, on hearing an unaccountable noise, instantly run over in one's mind every chink and cranny of one's dwelling and select one of them as an observation-post? He could have dashed upstairs again and seen for himself what was the matter in half the time.

No; in the very moment when I thought I had got it, it eluded me again. Those perfectly ordinary considerations, of time, position and common sense, seemed to dispose of my notion completely. Or almost completely. There remained the hole. My conviction that the hole, in one way or another, had something to do with it was shaken, but not destroyed. And, as I was denied access to the cellar, I rose from the chair in order to make a further examination of the studio.

And again, though the roof-plane was no longer there, I seemed to see that circular hole in the middle of its cracked star. I remembered, too, Esdaile's assumption that it was a bullet-hole and his search "high and low" for the bullet that had made it. But was it necessarily a bullet-hole at all? Bullets are not the only things that make holes. When a heavyish mass like two falling men hits something else *en plein fouet*, can every neighboring scratch or fracture be assigned its proper cause? There was no getting away from the fact that the bullet had been found elsewhere. Might not some object have fallen from a pocket? Or some portion of the plane itself have dropped off? With the pane replaced it seemed useless to speculate.

Nor did my further explorations add much to my knowledge. They consisted of estimating distances and relative positions of things, in an endeavor to arrive at the physical significance of that hole in the floor. It was no longer in the studio at all that I was interested; all my thoughts were in that locked chamber below. I felt as annoyed as Monty himself had been at all this juggling with the key. But I hardly felt myself at liberty to break my friend's doors.

Nor—this too presently occurred to me—was I quite sure what I ought to do with that ring. Merely to put it back where I had found it seemed rather crass, and whether it should be returned to Rooke or to Mrs. Cunningham herself was a niceish sort of point. I ended by putting it into my waistcoat pocket.

PART VII

THE KING'S ROAD

I

When Philip Esdaile had put into old William Dadley's hands the framing of two of his pictures I think he had done so largely on compassionate grounds. As you have seen, his real reason for having the old man round to Lennox Street that afternoon a few weeks ago had had remarkably little to do with pictures, but quite a lot to do with a bullet that a child had been found popping in and out of his mouth. But having made framing his pretext, I suppose he felt bound to give Dadley a job. I became sure of this when, calling at the dusty little shop at eleven o'clock on the following Monday morning, I saw the pictures themselves. I knew enough about Esdaile's work to see in a moment that there was no urgency whatever, and that probably he had not wanted the pictures framed at all. Certainly he could be in no hurry for them. The autumn, or for that matter the following autumn, would be quite time enough.

This being so, I wondered for a moment that he had troubled me about them, but I did not wonder for very long. A former suspicion was renewed in my mind. It seemed to me to confirm Glenfield's prophecy, that Esdaile, having made as it were impulsive and unconsidered advances to the rest of us, was about to draw in his horns again. Yet at the same time he had the appearance of wishing to be on both sides at once—of keeping his own counsel, but also of endeavoring to "pump" those from whom he was now withdrawing his half-extended confidence. In a word, without expressly asking me to spy out the land for him, he wished me to do so, and trusted to my interest, garrulity or whatnot to report to him anything I might discover.

Well, had I happened to call on old Dadley before that Sunday afternoon I had spent so remarkably in his studio I dare say I should have done as he wished. But that hole in the floor put a very different complexion on matters. He knew about that hole, but he had no suspicion that I now shared his knowledge. Therefore if he proposed to act independently I did not see why I should not do the same. He would make use of me, would he? Very well. It rather amuses us to be made use of when we guess the intention, to allow our legs to be pulled with the knowledge that at our pleasure the position can be reversed. I am very fond of Philip and he of me, but there is no mush about our friendship. We take it keenly and with relish, even to our long rivalry at the billiard-table. Undoubtedly he knew something I didn't know, but on the other hand I thought it likely that I too had now a minor advantage. He could hardly have known of the presence of that ring in that hole. He had been round his house covering up pictures, drawing blinds and removing the key from the cellar door, and would certainly not have left that ring where it was had he known it had been there. It had been put there since he had last seen the hole. The event, as you will see, showed that I was right in this, and that in one of his main objects he had broken down badly. *A bon chat bon rat.* I laughed softly.

"Done with you, Philip," I murmured. "I'll send you the packet of sketches, and you shall know how your precious picture-framing's going on. But that's all you are going to get for the present."

And so I sought the little shop with the bisected Old Master in the window, one half cleaned up like day and the other dingy as night.

Dadley was not doing anything in particular except sitting among his molding-patterns eating an apple. The door of his workshop beyond stood open, and when I told him my errand he led me into these back premises, leaving the greater part of the apple on the shelf beneath his counter but bringing small portions of it in his gray beard. The pictures were going on very nicely, he said, but he was waiting for glass; I wouldn't believe how difficult it was to get glass; like asking for the moon, it was, trying to buy glass. It was as he talked about the price and scarcity of glass that I drew my own conclusions about those two pictures. Obviously a job given out of kindness. As obviously it followed that I myself was being used to serve a turn.

"A fine painter, Mr. Esdaile, it's a pleasure to work for him," the old man ran on; and I did not reply that in my experience few pleasures in the world lasted quite so long. I was thinking of other things, the nature of which you may guess at.

For I wanted to know, by no means for the purpose of passing the information on to Philip, how Mr. Harry Westbury had fared since I had last seen him, and whether his friendship with Inspector Webster prospered. I also wanted to know the latest news of Monty Rooke. I decided that it was better to begin with Rooke, so did not hesitate to ask Dadley whether he had seen him.

"Oh, yes, he was in here last Thursday—no, Wednesday," the old man replied. "Paspertoos. Six of them, or else eight; no, six; I think the other two are Mr. Hammond's. I can't show you them because they're all glued up in the press. And I can get the glass for small things like that. It's the large plate that breaks my heart."

"Then Mr. Rooke is working again?" I said. "The last time I saw him he told me that his removal had rather interrupted his work."

The lids dropped over the kind old eyes. "Yes, sir, and I understand Mr. Rooke's had trouble as well."

This, if he meant Mrs. Cunningham, I did not propose to discuss, and he went on.

"Well, you get over these things when you're young, but it seems hard at the time. And troubles seem always to come together in a lump. I sympathize with Mr. Rooke, which some doesn't. He's always been a very pleasant gentleman to me."

"Oh? Who doesn't sympathize with Mr. Rooke?" I asked.

He hesitated for a moment. "Oh—there's a few here and there—but it will blow over—it will blow over. I think it's blowing over now as a matter of fact."

It was at this point that I suddenly decided on a measure of candor. He was a likeable old soul, long past even such innocent relish of contest as that I entertained towards Philip, a lover of peace and the least mischievous of gentle gossips.

"Do you mean the affair of that parachute that morning?" I asked him. "I was there, you know."

His ivy-veined old hand smoothed the edge of his mitering-machine.

"Yes. I know you were," he said. "Yes, I know you were. But I think it'll blow over now that Mr. Westbury's taken this turn he has."

"Mr. Westbury? Yes, I remember. What turn has he taken?"

"Well, sir, as a matter of fact, that's what some of us is waiting to hear," he replied.

II

From the point of view of my profession the story he told me was not without interest. I give it for what it may be worth, not as an instance of mental abnormality, but merely as it bore on our Case.

I have said that Westbury was about thirty-five, which means that he was still under thirty when the war broke out. It is no man's business, certainly not mine, to enter into the question whether he should or could have joined up, nor whether he would have been of much use if he had. His interest to me lies in the fact that he did not. For all I know he may have been of far greater use to his country in his brown check than in a khaki jacket, for his experience of his complicated profession was considerable, and I understand that he became a person of some little temporary importance when the commandeering of hotels and other properties got fairly into swing. Therefore he did not attest under the Derby Scheme, and his subsequent applications for exemption were allowed.

I repeat, I wish to be perfectly fair to him. During a few London air-raids he probably saw as much of the actuality of war as many thousands of uniformed men who spent their year or two years "in France." We see these things a little more clearly now. "In France" may mean much or it may mean very little. Of our millions, I have been informed that only about eight per cent. went "over the top," and that this eight per cent. consisted largely of the same men over and over again. Later the gunners' casualties approached those of the infantry, and I believe there was a time when the losses of the Flying Corps were twenty per cent. per week. Granted that there was no arm that did not suffer its proportion of loss; but—we know now by whom the brunt of the fighting was borne. Mr. Harry Westbury may claim, if he wishes, that he did as much of it as many and many another whose allowances were credited to them at Cox's.

But there was a strain of resentment in his nature, by no means uncommon among his kind save that he experienced it in an uncommon degree. I myself had heard him say of our flyers, "They're paid for it, aren't they—they know the risks, don't they?" but it went much further than that. According to Dadley, he showed suspicion and mistrust towards any who had given an eye, a limb or life itself. He seemed to think that in some obscure way these people had wronged him. And, Dadley went on, in some cases this mistrust became positive dislike and hate.

"If the war was to begin all over again I fancy Harry'd be in it next time," he said. "Speaking for myself, I should say it worried him. Got it on his mind like. Maybe it's that that's stopped him going about very much except to a few places. Sometimes you'd think he'd quarreled with the whole world."

"From the little I've seen of him I can't say I found him a prepossessing young man," I observed.

"Well, myself, I can't help feeling a bit sorry for him," the old man continued, with a shake of his head. "Many a man without a leg's happier than what Harry is. He isn't even the man he was two or three weeks ago. He thinks everybody's got their knife into him. Nor that inquest he was on didn't do him much good neither. He's moped and muttered about it ever since. Talks to himself, he does, up and down the streets and play-acts dreadful things he's going to do, as you might say. Says he won't stand this and that and the other. Any little thing sets him off. Then there was that about that bullet. I expect Mr. Esdaile told you about that?"

"Yes."

"Well, he goes clean off his head about that sometimes. Has the kids downstairs—fetches 'em out of bed—and makes 'em tell him it all over and over again. Says somebody tried to murder 'em. Oh, and a whole lot more nonsense. What he ought to do is to get away into the country for a bit, but when the doctor tells him that, he glares and says it's all a conspiracy to get him out of the way so things can be hushed up."

"What things?"

"Oh, I can't tell you half the rubbish. I keep out of his way now—go somewhere else. I like to have my glass of whisky in peace, not with all this muttering and fist-shaking going on. Yes, he ought to get away for a bit."

"You say a doctor's attending him?"

"Well, he is and he isn't, in a manner of speaking. The doctor goes round—Doctor Dobbie of Carlyle Square he is—but Harry won't do what he tells him, so he might just as well be without one. He'll neither go to bed nor get about his business, as you might say. He's got a couch pulled up to the bedroom window, and he sits there by the hour together staring out. That's the bedroom where the bullet came in. And he writes scores of letters, but I don't think his missis posts all of them. They're to all sorts of people. He gets 'em out of directories."

"What are the letters about?"

"All about miscarriage of justice, and one law for the rich and another for the poor, and lots of them's to the newspapers. Oh, he's going downhill is Harry, I'm afraid. Downhill he's going. He was never any particular friend of mine, but it isn't a pleasant thing to see a man you've chatted with over your glass of whisky going downhill. Not much more than a boy by the side of me neither. I can give him getting on for forty years."

I mused for a moment; then: "You said something about his not being sympathetic to Mr. Rooke. What do you mean by that exactly?"

But at that moment the most astonishingly unexpected thing happened. A customer came into his shop. And so, as Dadley grabbed incredulously for his spectacle case, my question went unanswered.

III

One thing at any rate now seemed fairly certain, namely, that if what Dadley told me was true it was not likely that a man of Inspector Webster's penetration would pay much attention to the mutterings of an incipient megalomaniac. For, if I could guess at the signs at all, it was megalomania. I have not made a systematic analysis of those infinitely intricate mental states that we speak of conglomerately as "war nerves." I am not prepared to say that one man may bitterly grudge another something from the taking of which he himself has drawn back his hand, nor yet (to turn the case the other way round) that there is not on occasion just as heady and overweening an egotism on the part of the envied man. It is useless to generalize on these matters. It is also not quite decent. The least we can do is to mind our own business, the most to consider the given instance on its merits. It is simply as yet another curious by-product of our Case that I am speaking of Westbury.

Quite the most curious thing about it was that he was the only one of us all who had, in the sense of public duty, been wholly and entirely in the right throughout. But a little reflection showed me that it was precisely therein that the germ of his malady lay. It was *because* of this consistent technical rightness that he was now in process of arrogating to himself all the rightness in the world. No doubt he had been technically right when he had decided that his special knowledge of estates was of more solid use to his country than his skill at arms would have been. He had been technically right if, in the very uncommon circumstances, having reason to believe that a pistol had been moved that should only have been moved by the police, he had taken steps to ascertain that it really was a pistol Rooke had carried in his pocket. He had been right when, finding a bullet in his own house, he had instantly reported the matter to Inspector Webster. He had been right in demanding a post-mortem; right when Mackwith had all-unconsciously thwarted this; and oh, how right when, in that Chelsea back street, he had broken furiously out on me as an accomplice in the suppression of things that should have been brought to the light of day! Yes, it was all this rightness that was precisely the trouble. It is not good for any of us to be right so often as that. Personally, if I am right twice running there is no living with me. The real cure for Westbury would have been for him to find himself a few times in the wrong.

So, as I left Dadley's shop, I pictured him sitting there at his bedroom window, his furious eyes fixed on Esdaile's roof, his furious heart brooding on his rightness, and bearing the whole of the burden of our collective offense. What a contrast between this just man and our malefactor away in the country, Charles Valentine Smith himself—courting, care-free, and in a danger that appeared to be lessening with every hour that passed! Truly the Princes of this World seem to have the Kingdom and the Power and the Glory, and the Westburys to be persecuted like the prophets before them! I could understand old William Dadley feeling sorry for him. At the same time, I had not one single atom of sorrow for him myself.

For we are not ruled by these municipal virtues. We say we are; it is as much as our lives are worth to say anything else; but we know better. Wonderful Case, to bring all this out, to present so dramatically that single Question—the first man had to answer it and the last man will have to answer it—without which there is no society nor state nor government at all! Westbury had the whole weight of intellectual approval—and nothing whatever else! Unreservedly our whole nefarious conspiracy was to be condemned—yet something bade us stand unflinchingly by our friends!... I was wiser than I knew when I wrote that we all do precisely what we want to do and look for reasons afterwards. And if it be said that Society cannot be run on these lines, the answer is that it is our business to see that it is run. We *have* to serve God and Mammon though the God be the God of Injustice and the Mammon the

Mammon of Righteousness. We *must* face both ways, square law with force. There is *no* escape from worshiping tradition even when we break it, from giving revolt our acknowledgment even as we trample it down. The world has got to go on and we to take sides.

Do you see why I laughed to see the hay our Case had made of the merits of our respective sides?

I was ruminating thus when a bodily collision brought me with a shock back to earth again. I had scattered somebody's armful of parcels, a tissue-paper bag with a couple of eggs in it among them. Instantly I was in a consternation of apology. Diving, I managed to rescue a small loaf from rolling from the kerb and to save from a passing foot a packet of cooked ham. Then, flushed and humbled, I heard a laugh.

"Look here—I don't so much mind your upsetting my grub, but I do mind being cut," said a voice—Rooke's voice.

IV

What a change for the better! He had shaved, his boots shone, the soft collar round his neck was a clean one and his gray tie was fastidiously tied. His face had a brightness again, he was engaged in the pleasant ordinary task of buying groceries, and Dadley had just told me that he was framing "paspertoos" for him. Was another of the clouds of the Case breaking up?... On the spot I decided to lunch with him, and told him so.

"All right, but the eggs are up to you," he said.

Inside his little den in Jubilee Place the improvement was no less marked than in his person and demeanor. There was not a spot on his little red-and-white checked table-cloth, his crockery shone, his bed was neatly made. He had faced the new situation and had ceased to mope.

In my waistcoat pocket was a ring he had once given to Audrey Cunningham. Seeing his cheerfulness, I had not the slightest intention of reopening matters by telling him anything about that ring. If Audrey dropped rings as casually as he picked up pistols, very well; it was not my business to mar this cheery new beginning.

"Lightly boiled, or how?" he said, my egg poised in a teaspoon over the saucepan on the gas-ring.

"Yes—lightly boiled—anything," I replied. "Got any mustard for this ham?"

That too he had, and he had taken care over the preparation of his jug of coffee. He was entirely the old Monty again.

I don't know when I have enjoyed a lunch more, not even excepting the washing-up, which he insisted on doing the moment we had finished. "If there's one thing I loathe it's coming in to a lot of unwashed things," he explained. "Not a ha'porth of trouble once you get the habit."

Then he showed me the work on which he was engaged. That too had energy and movement again. One small sketch I liked and bought on the spot—a little thing, neither black-and-white nor color, or both if you like— a crayon sketch of a couple of infants in the Flower Walk in Kensington Gardens, one of them with a shining round sixpenny balloon touched with a whiff of pink, the other with the doleful rag of one that had just exploded— the slightest, sweetest little bit of treasure-trove of the eye picked up in an afternoon's stroll.

"But not the copyright," he stipulated with a quick sideways glance at me. "I might be able to reproduce."

"Right; not the copyright," I agreed. I didn't mention it to him, in case it shouldn't come off, but I thought I might be able to help him with reproduction-rights. We have a good many side-shows on the *Circus*.

Then, in the middle of turning over further sketches, he broke suddenly into a gesture of remembrance.

"By the way—I knew there was something I wanted to tell you! A funny sort of thing happened the other day. You remember that police-sergeant or whatever he was, who came into Esdaile's place that night?"

"He was an Inspector."

"Inspector then. Well, I've seen him. Had a talk with him. Funny sort of talk too—I've been puzzled about it ever since. I was loafing round Sloane Square. There's a flower-woman there, interesting type of head—this sort—" He turned over one of the sketches and on the back of it his pencil flowed into a few swift assured lines. ("That's rather like her, by the way," he said in parenthesis, "regular cast-iron gypsy.")

"Well," he went on, "her face struck me as rather an interesting contrast with a lot of silly mimosa she had in her basket—I hate mimosa; so I was taking peeps at her, not sketching, you understand, when I heard somebody behind me say, 'Well, Mr. Rooke!' and I turned. I jumped rather. It was this Inspector fellow, and he'd a funny sort of expression on his face, not laughing exactly—sort of quizzing—I can't describe it—

"Then he said something that I thought the most infernal neck.

"'You aren't thinking of adopting a flower-woman's baby this time, are you, Mr. Rooke?'

"Damned impudence, wasn't it? Fancy the beggar knowing that!"

Monty was ruffling up at the recollection. I could not resist a smile.

"Chelsea knows that exploit of yours as well as it knows the Albert Bridge, Monty," I assured him. "Go on."

"Well, then he said, 'You'll have to get out of that habit of adopting things, Mr. Rooke. You never know where it ends.'

"'What do you mean?' I said. He *was* smiling now, but I felt a bit uneasy. We did stuff him up a bit that night, you know. He's a dark horse, that fellow.

"'It doesn't do, Mr. Rooke,' he said. 'Different men take different views of their duty, and you'll be striking one of the other sort one of these days!'

"'I don't know what you mean,' I said. 'Oh yes you do,' says he. 'I'm dashed if I do,' says I. 'Then you're lucky not to be dashed a good deal worse,' says he; 'you take my advice, Mr. Rooke, and stop adopting things, babies or what not. You might burn your fingers. You might—ahem!—blow 'em off'....

"And he nodded and marched off.

"Now what the devil do you think's his game?"

I know of no more exciting mental pleasure than that of finding your *a priori* guesses taking shape and substance in the realm of actual things. I suppose it is the triumphant cry of your deeper self telling the other self "I told you so!" Remember how little I knew of Inspector Webster, yet with what instinctive reserve I had hedged my impression of him. "A dark horse?" Yes, of quite the darkest kind. I recapitulated the degrees of his darkness. He had come round to Lennox Street that night, probably fresh from his talk with this fellow Westbury; he had put a whole series of questions, but of implications so guarded that in writing that portion of the story I had to itemize and underline what I surmised to be their real purport; and he had instituted a search of Esdaile's premises—twelve hours later! Why twelve hours later? Why not on the spot, there and then? Why give Philip this law, that as a matter of fact he had made use of to drop that pistol into the river?

Could it be that he knew his House and Estate Agent better than we did—knew his vanity, dullness, and the risks of basing a charge on his unsupported word? No doubt he had questioned Westbury in terms far more explicit than those he had used to us. Unless Westbury had actually put his hand inside Rooke's pocket, probably all he could swear to was that the pocket contained something heavy. Not until late in the same afternoon had the bullet been found. Suppose Webster had said to Westbury, "Not so quickly, my friend; you said nothing about a pistol at the time; it only became a pistol when the bullet was found; we can't go putting the cart before the horse like that; evidence is evidence; you can't let half a day pass and then remember things to fit the Case; *you* may feel sure of a thing, but could you make a jury sure?" Suppose he had said something like this? The police too are bound by the probabilities of conviction. It is no credit to them to fail on a charge.

And a man who can say, "Was it indeed, sir?" when informed of the identity of a distinguished King's Counsel who has expressly announced himself only a few hours before is emphatically not the man to think that he can make a jacket for a large gooseberry by skinning a small-sized flint.

V

"Now what was his game, do you think?" Monty asked again.

"He was giving you a piece of wholesome advice," I answered promptly.

"But 'You stop adopting things; you might—ahem!—blow your fingers off.' He said it like that. I haven't put in the 'ahem.' That was his. It looks to me as if he knew about that pistol."

"It has very much that look," I agreed blandly.

"But how? I can't understand yet how Esdaile knew, but this Police Inspector—!"

"'Oh, what a tangled web we weave when first we practice to deceive,'" I murmured. "You never can tell, Monty."

"Oh, stop burbling. How do you suppose he did know?"

"Let me see. You told Philip it was his keys that made your pocket bulge so, didn't you?"

"Oh—if you're just going to rot me—"

"I'm not rotting you. I've a feeling that if you'd told Inspector Webster the same thing he'd have been happy and delighted to believe you."

"But how does he know *any*thing about what's in my pocket?" said the bewildered Monty....

Should I tell him? Why not? I had studiously avoided anything that might have reminded him of Mrs. Cunningham. Pluckily as he had taken himself in hand, I did not think that that wound was healed. But the episode of the pistol was another matter. I felt singularly and perhaps not quite justifiably light-hearted about that. The mists of the Case were perceptibly thinning. What he had just told me about Inspector Webster let still a little more sun through them. To all appearances the Inspector had dismissed Monty with a quite characteristic admonition. And that being so, it was perhaps his due that I should not leave Monty altogether unarmed in the event of any contingency with Westbury.

And so I told him how his pocket had been fingered as he had descended that ladder.

He was furious. "Damned pickpocket!" he broke out. "I should have thought these sharks made enough out of their filthy premiums nowadays without putting their hands right *into* your pockets!"

"I didn't say he did that exactly."

"It's the same thing. And anyway, how did he know? What made him think—?"

"Perhaps he saw you pick it up. Could he have done that from down below?"

"Might. I shouldn't have thought so though. Of course, I was flurried."

"But you wouldn't have thought it in Esdaile's case either," I reminded him.

"No, that beats me," he admitted.

"And I wouldn't be *too* virtuous about it, Monty. In any case you'd no business with the thing, you know."

"Oh, stuff!" he scoffed. "It's you that's being virtuous."

And, with that ring in my waistcoat pocket that I had picked up with no more justification than he had the pistol, he might have added that I was hypocritical too.

VI

To tell the truth, that ring was beginning to worry me a little. I don't mean my possession of it, since I had no intention of pawning it, and was prepared to hand it over to its rightful owner as soon as I felt that that course would not do more harm than good. My concern was about the severed relation of which it had been a symbol. I wondered whether I was not perhaps a little excessively delicate on Monty's behalf. If my eyes, wandering round his tidy room, had encountered a copy of the *Era* or been given any other excuse for introducing Audrey Cunningham's name, I think that after all I should have risked it. But "When in doubt cut it out" is a safe motto, and I remained silent.

I had had, however, an idea. Mrs. Cunningham might be "fed" with men, but it was not likely that she had broken off her engagement without saying something to Mollie Esdaile about it. What was the harm in writing to Mollie, not necessarily mentioning the ring, but asking for her version of whatever had happened?

The more I thought of it the more I liked the idea. Match-making is rather out of my line, but I am not entirely indifferent to the happiness of my friends, and I had not forgotten poor Monty's anguished cry of "Dawdy! Dawdy!" the last time I had visited him in Jubilee Place. I do not call it match-making merely to inquire whether a possible obstacle may not be removed. If it was the Case's doing, the Case's solution ought to get matters right again. A little prematurely, perhaps, I was growing to the belief that the question was not whether the Case would settle itself, but how.

Before I left him, which I did very shortly afterwards, I had determined to write to Mollie. I did so indeed that very night. I did not mention the ring. I simply gave her a faithful picture of the two Montys, the first one so distressing, and the second so enheartening, and asked her what about the other side of the affair.

It was nearly a week before I received her reply, which, when it did come, contained that invitation to spend a month at Santon that I have already anticipated in this story. It was a curious letter in some ways. Parts of it, even certain parts that touched Audrey Cunningham directly, were as free and frank as I have always found Mollie to be; but other parts were noticeably the other way. For example, she wrote:

"The engagement is certainly 'off' as far as I can make out, and whether there's any chance of their coming together again I really can't say. She gave me to understand not, but it's three weeks since she wrote, and Philip hasn't heard from Monty at all."

That seemed frank enough, but, on the very same page, was this:

"I don't think it's absolutely impossible they'll make it up. Perhaps I oughtn't to say this, and I'd rather not give you my reason, but I don't think it's altogether out of the question. But the circumstances are so peculiar. Everything's really most awfully mixed, and I don't want to raise even my own hopes. I can't see why you didn't ask Monty," etc., etc.

"I'd rather not give you my reason"—"the circumstances are peculiar"—"things are most awfully mixed"—those were the dubious parts. I was certain that she, as well as Philip, was holding something back. The letter, in fact, seemed to confirm the opinion I had formed on finding that ring so fantastically embedded in the studio floor, namely, that before shaking the dust of Lennox Street from her feet Audrey Cunningham had made some sort of a discovery, which she had since shared with Mollie and Mollie now declined to share with me. In this, as you will see, I was partly right and partly wrong.

In the meantime, suppression for suppression. I had not been candid either. I had said nothing about finding the ring. Perhaps after all my letter had got the answer it deserved.

But the invitation to visit the Esdailes at Santon tempted me extremely. Quite apart from the Case, I hungered and thirsted for the air of my own country. And there was the Case itself. Now that, with Glenfield's countenance, Westbury's deterioration and the merely admonitory attitude of Police Inspector Webster, it was becoming almost a jocund affair, its center of gravity had shifted away from London to the country. It was in the country that our young slayer was demonstrating murder to be the way of happiness. It was in the country that Philip Esdaile was apparently machinating to get the half-escaped strings back into his own controlling fingers again. And it was from the country that Mollie was now writing her interesting blend of candor and reserve.

And what was there left of much interest in London? It seemed to me very little. In Lincoln's Inn Fields and the Temple the lawyers were no doubt busily getting up their briefs for *Scepter Assurance Corporation v. Aiglon Aviation Company*, but I could depend on Mackwith to keep me posted on all that. In the columns of the *Circus* I had awakened quite a lively, if somewhat rambling, correspondence, in which the name of Charles Valentine Smith had not definitely appeared, but for the appearance of which, if the Case demanded it, I could arrange at a moment's notice. All the life and interest seemed to have passed out of these things. That is the worst of this intangible operation of Publicity—it possesses you in spurts, with gaps of complete listlessness.

It is super-heated, and at a change of atmosphere condenses into a few chill drops. Then, when you have brought it up to the proper state of rarefaction again, you find that the popular interest has shifted leagues away. Already my correspondence showed signs of becoming as much beside the mark as had that nine-days'-wonder that one morning had filled Lennox Street with a gaping crowd and had set mysterious rumors circulating with the morning milk-carts. Publicity, like lightning, never strikes in the same place twice. Nobody now cared a rap whether an aeroplane had crashed in Chelsea on a May morning months ago, nor how, nor why. Nobody was going to drag the bed of the Thames for the identification-number of a useless Webley and Scott pistol. A spent bullet, flying in at an open window, had *not* killed an Estate Agent's child, and Inspector Webster had far too much work on his hands to dream of applying to the Home Secretary through the proper channels for an Exhumation Order. Cases left long enough unanswered answer themselves. The scene changes, the circumstances alter, the world moves on.

I too felt like moving on. Glenfield had offered me a holiday, and I had my book to finish. As well finish it at Santon as anywhere else. Santon—its cornfields and skies, the cliffs for ever a-racket with the seabirds' clamor, the dappled fawn of its sands! I was there in my heart already.

I wrote to Mollie that very night.

PART VIII

AT SANTON

I

"For goodness' sake, Joan, stop chattering just for a few minutes!" Philip broke out testily. "If you don't want to sit, say so and have done with it. This is enough to drive anybody mad!"

I had been wondering how much longer his patience would hold out. When an artist is in difficulties with his canvas, motor-bicycle talk for an hour on end can be extremely wearing.

Joan looked up with aggravating sweetness. "What, Philip?" she inquired.

"I say if you don't want to sit, off you go on the confounded machine and I'll start something else."

"But, Philip darling, you know the sparking-plug's broken, and it will be three or four days before we can get another. Do you think Wellands will stock that make, Chummy?"

Charles Valentine Smith knocked out the new Captanide pipe and proceeded to refill it with the Dunhill Mixture.

"Well, if they don't I think I know a fellow who has a spare. That's the worst of the Beaver," he went on. "Now with an Indian or a Douglas ..."

And off they went again, she as well as he, both talking at once: big-ends, plugs, magnetos: Beaver, Indian, Douglas.... In my younger youth I used to ride a tall ungeared ordinary; except for one hellish five minutes in which I had clung, ardently praying, to Smith's back-carrier, I know nothing about these modern machines; and how Joan managed to keep her sideways seat on that grid of torture over his back wheel passed my comprehension. But ever since the arrival of the hideous thing she had hardly been off it, hair all over the place, ankles stiffly out, skirts rippling like a ribbon on a ventilating-fan, and cauliflowers of dust trailing for a hundred yards behind them. I could only conclude that modern love, besides being blind, is deficient in the tactile nerve-centers as well.

It was ten o'clock in the morning, and Philip had set up his easel on a sheep-nibbled slope of the cliff-tops. Joan, in her old tweed skirt and new canary-colored silk jumper, was stretched luxuriously on the thymy bents. The amber beads about her neck matched the potentilla on which she lay, and I give you your choice which was the bluest—the aimlessly fluttering butterflies, the nodding harebells, or her demure and reprehensible eyes. Philip had deliberately excluded the blue of the sky from his canvas. The picture was simply of Joan herself, the crewel-work of flowers on which she lay, and behind her, red as the habitation of dragons, the midsummer sorrel that massed itself up the slope.

The talk continued, a fitter's romance: clutches, brakes, front-drives: Minervas, Excelsiors, de Dions....

In my day we played croquet and read "Maud." ...

And then Philip exploded again.

"Oh, *do* dry up! How do you expect me to paint? Pull that book a bit closer, Joan, so it throws the light up on your face, and hold your chin a bit higher—"

As if she spoke to herself I heard Joan's murmur: "Why did the razorbill razorbill?"

As softly Charles Valentine Smith murmured back: "So the sea-urchin could sea-urchin"; and this last flippancy was too much for Philip. He put his palette down on the turf and turned to Smith and myself.

"Look here," he said politely, "will you two fellows oblige me by pushing off? Right away somewhere else, please, and now."

"Oh," Joan wailed, "and I shan't have anybody to talk to!"

"You can read your book."

"But it's such a stupid one—all about an old artist, over thirty, who fell in love with his model and bought her alpaca blouses and thread stockings—"

"You shall have a motor catalogue tomorrow. Now sheer off, you fellows."

Obediently I got on to my feet and turned to Smith.

"Come along. We'll give him till midday. Here's your stick."

And I helped him to his feet and bore him off.

II

Ordinarily I do not find it easy to talk to very young men. I have been as young as they, but they have not been as old as I, and I know this but they do not. Young women—that is another matter, and I will make a very candid confession. I now envy these youngsters their youth. I envied Smith his youth. Despite his limp, I was conscious of his tallness and lissomness as he hobbled by my side. And I will add that it is not an unmixed joy to be asked to do a young goddess's shopping for her because you are "quite the kindest person she knows."

It would hardly be true to say that my acquaintance with young Smith had made no progress at all. I had made quite a number of interesting observations on his idyll of petrol, love and crime. But he for his part was still at the stage of apology for his "neck" in asking Joan to ask me to buy his pipes and tobacco for him, and by way of leveling up the obligation had actually sent for a copy of that dandy book that I as a novelist must on no account miss, *The Crimson Specter of Hangman Hollow*. But I was still "Sir" to him and he hardly "Chummy" to me, and our small-talk was quite small. It was certainly small enough as we left the thymy hollow and slowly made for the cliff-tops.

"Tell me if I walk too quickly for you," I said. His hurt was to his right ankle, and his stick left a trail of little round holes in the turf.

"Oh, that's all right, thanks, sir," he said cheerfully, pegging away; and he added with a chuckle, "I say, between you and I, old Philip was rather in a paddy, wasn't he?"

"Between you and me he was," I said. I corrected him quite deliberately. Now that the failure of the sparking-plug had put this opportunity into my hands I was determined at all costs to know more of him. Hence my—well *grossièreté*. But he noticed nothing. Instead he broke out with a feigned enthusiasm.

"I say, these pipes are turning out jolly well! Lovely bit of straight grain this one! You do know how to choose a pipe, sir! Are they French or Italian briar?"

"French."

"Jolly nice bit of root!"

"I'm very glad."

"Cool as a nut. Joan's quite right about my smoking too many cigarettes. They're all right for the street—I hate to see a fellow smoking a pipe in the street—and gaspers smell a bit sickly to other people sometimes, don't you think?"

I agreed with this too.

"I suppose the *Specter* hasn't turned up yet?" was his next effort, as he sat down to rest for a minute.

"Not yet."

"I do hope it isn't out of print. How soon does a book go out of print, sir—on an average?"

Weakly I thought of "Why does the razorbill razorbill?" and, I am afraid, found nothing to reply....

Then, as he continued to babble laboriously across the gulf that separated us, I remembered again certain tubular parcels that arrived for him by post, which, when stripped of their wrappings, turned out to contain the *Transactions* and *Proceedings* of this Society or that. Seeing these left lying about I

had peeped into them, and had been brought up standing against such intimidating fences as the following:

"*Aerofoil Sections in relation to Speed Range.*"

"*Influence of Wave-friction on Aerodynamic Resistances.*"

"*Notes on Lateral Stability.*"

My simple literary mind faints in regions such as these. His presumably
did not. This apparently was his ordinary reading, the *Specter* his relaxation.

"—amber beads," the words came across the void that separated soul
from soul. "Just the shade I meant—neither too yellow nor too brown—I'm
afraid it took up an awful lot of your time—"

It was here that I took my plunge.

"What," I said, looking steadily at him, "is the Influence of Wind-friction
on Aerodynamic Resistance?"

His jaw dropped, as well it might. I knew that for a moment he was wondering whether I had taken leave of my senses.

"Eh?" he said.

I repeated the question. Of course, I no more wanted information about
Aerodynamic Resistance than I did about briar pipes and amber beads. It
was information about Charles Valentine Smith that I wanted and intended
to have.

I date my possession of him from the moment that that look of consternation came into his face. It broke upon me that I had put him into some
position that he felt he must immediately explain. Indeed he half rose, as if,
having obtained my acquaintance under false pretenses, he must set himself
right or leave me.

"Oh, I say, sir!" he broke anxiously out. "Do you mean those Journals
and things?"

"That's what I had in my mind. Especially the blue-covered ones."

"Oh lord! You don't suppose I can make head or tail of *those*!"

"Not make head or tail of them? But I've seen you reading them."

He seemed positively sick to extricate himself from my too flattering
opinion of him.

"*Me* understand all *that*! I could kick myself if you think that! Why,
that's all designers' stuff—they've got brains, those chaps—shiploads of
them—why, I should never have heard of the things but for—" He checked
himself.

"But—" I began, puzzled.

He was blushing—blushing like a young girl.

"I know," he said. "I feel a most awfully ass. The fact is, sir, I just moon
over those things, lose myself in 'em, sort of. I don't know the first thing
about 'em. Of course, there are bits here and there—engines and practical

flying and all that—I know a bit about that—what I mean to say is, a fellow doesn't want to miss anything—it's hard to explain—"

On the contrary: it was not at all hard to explain. Simply, I had caught him day-dreaming. That vivid color still in his cheeks told me that I had stumbled on a privacy. A young girl approaching womanhood knows these soft *oubliances*, these shy yet hardy excursions of the spirit that lead nowhither and die of their own over-sweetness. It is love of which she dreams; and this was his equivalent. He just "mooned." It was not understanding—he "didn't want to miss anything." His was not a technician's, but a poet's nature. And caught unawares he blushed.

"Of course my real job would be one of these Expeditions," he mumbled.

I pursued him relentlessly. "Which Expeditions?"

"Well, between you and I, they've started work on several of them. In Africa and India and places. You see I'm awfully keen on Air-geography. If this dashed ankle of mine ever gives me a chance again, that is. Bobby always said that was my line of country. He was the chap for the technical end. Thought in surds, Bobby did. He put me on to all those Journals and things, and—after—well, I sort-of keep it up. *He* was your man for that."

"By Bobby do you mean your friend Maxwell?"

"Yes. Bobby," he replied, his eyes far out over the sea.

III

He spoke the name with the most perfect readiness and simplicity; there was neither tremor in his voice nor the faintest sign of pain in his dark and steady eyes. He was not even self-conscious under my (I admit) prolonged and deliberate gaze. By what mystery of self-absolution he had expunged the sinister fact for which Esdaile vouched I could not tell. He repeated Bobby's name.

"Yes, Bobby was your man for all that. Fearfully hot stuff. When Bobby opened his mouth I used to dry up."

Then, still without removing my eyes from him, "I never knew Bobby," I said. "But I know a man who did."

He turned to me swiftly. "Who was that?" he demanded.

"A man called Hanson. An Australian. He says he knew him in Gallipoli."

His brows were knitted. "Hanson? Hanson? What was his other name?"

"Dudley."

"Hanson? Hanson? Did he say he knew me?"

"He wasn't sure. He thinks he ran across you. He knew you by sight, anyway, for he described you to me."

"Hanson? No, I give it up. Don't remember him at all. You met such crowds of chaps, you see—sometimes it's just like a dream—"

I appreciated that; but there still remained one thing that was no dream. This was Philip's explicit declaration, "Oh, he remembers all right—it was the other I didn't tell him—that anybody else knew." Philip might now be resolved to let the whole affair sink into oblivion, but Philip after all had not shot anybody. On that morning when I had had my talk with Mackwith I had been rather pleased with my acumen in pointing out that whether our Case had legal consequences or not its moral consequences were inescapable. Yet here, if I could believe my own eyes, was a man who was escaping them in their entirety. He continued to order Journals that Bobby had "put him on to," and could speak of his victim apparently out of some transcendental state of mind where sorrow was an anomaly and regret beside the mark. It all appeared to be admirable, but I found it quite incomprehensible.

"But," I came out of my reverie presently, "you haven't yet told me what 'it' was that Bobby knew all about."

"Do you mean those books?" he asked.

"No, I don't mean the books at all. I know a good deal about books. You can get so soaked in them that you make a whole artificial world out of them, quite self-contained, logical with itself at every single point, and absolutely out of touch with anything that really matters. Do you see what I mean?"

I wasn't sure that he did, and here was I, who do not talk easily to young men, quite anxious that he should.

"Well, let's put it another way. You say Bobby knew all about these equations and diagrams and things. Did he know what it was all *for*—*really* for— not just wind-resistance or whatever you call it, but something more—why there should be aeroplanes *at all*, for example?"

I had said it badly, but I saw his brow clear. There was a kindling in the eyes he turned to me.

"It's funny you should say that," he said in a rather low voice, "because that's just what Bobby himself used to say. He used to say that anybody who'd passed his matric. could do what he did, and he always would have it that *I* was the whole show. I didn't agree with him, of course, but—is that what you mean?"

"It is so far," I said. "What else did he say?"

"Well, he always said it was a jolly good thing I wasn't technical. And I did see what he meant by that. I mean to say things *are* simple really, the big things I mean. You take the sea—" again his eyes wandered far out over it. "People talk an awful lot of bunk about the sea. They think bases are just harbors and ports and coaling-stations and so on. That a base is something fixed. Why, that's exactly what it isn't. You've got to get your coal and oil and stores, of course, but that's only like going into a shop and coming out again as quick as you can. It's only then that the job really begins. I'm afraid I'm talking an awful lot, sir, but I got it down to this: that a ship's only a ship when she's moving. She's no better than a stupid old breakwater when she isn't. I mean to say her real base is her course. Just an imaginary line to make a dash from and turn up where the trouble is. Focal points I believe they call 'em. At least that's the way I worked it out for myself."

"And do you mean the air's the same, or going to be?"

The look that I have ventured to call discontent came into his eyes.

"Well, nothing's quite the same as anything else, of course. But I do think this. There's Germany. Over there—," he nodded out to sea. "North Sea or German Ocean we used to call that, and that was there she said her future was. Well, it isn't, of course. She hasn't got any coast to speak of, and isn't going to have any. But—"

And this time his eyes went aloft to the immeasurable fields of the air.

"She's got just as much of *that* as anybody else. Taking a perfectly sound line about it too. And what's the good of our saying she shan't build aircraft as long as the damn dog doesn't know? Of course she'll build aircraft. That's where her future is now, and she can afford to hand over ships. But every Zepp or plane you get out of her you'll have to get with a pair of pincers. Then ... swift? Swift won't be the word.... Oh, don't I wish I could get on one of these Expeditions!"

I made no comment on this, since I know nothing about the air. These were merely the words of Charles Valentine Smith, who did.

IV

He knew very little about himself—hardly seemed aware that there was anything of importance to know. It was all Maxwell—"Bobby was the whole show." And I had a very keen sense of the honor the dead man had done himself in denying this. "Frightfully hot stuff on maths," said Smith; and the world is full of men who are "frightfully hot stuff on maths," in that sense; but it is rarely that you find one of these not too absorbed in the technique and detail of his own activities to be aware of a vision beyond. I know this in my own business. I see men working with an appalling intensity, a new and wild and squandering energy that has long ago passed from me; but for their Muse I look in vain. An altar is set up, not to any god known or unknown, but to itself. I speak diffidently, but I seldom see that any flame from Elsewhere descends upon it. This is hard to say, since I too rub my two sticks together with my fellows, hoping they may kindle. I should not say it except that I was now trying to arrive at some comprehension of Maxwell, the competent and efficient man, exposed to all manner of temptations to narrowness and complacency and inertia, but who could yet see in this unsuspecting youngster something he himself did not and could never possess.

And add to this that quasi-religious bond of the air that makes of two men twins in one womb....

I repeat, Maxwell did himself a quite radiant honor.

"What sort of a fellow was Maxwell to look at?" I asked by and by.

The answer was almost startlingly ready. This lad who had bolted from Malvern, forced his way into an Embassy and demanded to be taken in the service of a foreign Power, unbuckled the watch from his wrist.

"Here he is," he said.

I found myself looking at a young but curiously worn face, with a great width of brow, eyes that seemed to hold I knew not what nameless expression of disillusion and fatality, and a firm and sweet mouth. That face had certainly lost nothing spiritually by its ungrudged and generous homage. Yet he too had probably jazzed and pink-ginned and drummed ragtime on cases of stuffed birds. Strange days! Wisdom and experience under young brilliantined hair, and the bald and reverend dome accepting the result on hearsay! Slang, and an undreamed-of valor; Magalhaens' vision, and a lark at a Grafton Ball! By being "frightfully keen on Air-geography" Smith merely meant what Columbus and Cabot and the Navigator had meant; by wanting to "get on one of these Expeditions" he was willing to dare for discovery's sake some monstrous Baffin's Bay of the air. "Not to miss anything," he fumed and fretted over Maxwell's equations and made them part of the Dream and the Desire. He was brooding over it now as we lay there together, I with his watch in my hand.... And all this, I ought to say, was at the time when the last of the Santon hay was barely stacked, and John Alcock and Whitten Brown had just flown the Atlantic in sixteen hours. It was when the headland was pale cloth-of-gold with the ripening corn, and the R. 34 had crossed to America and returned. It was when the ditches were yellow with hawkweed and the copses pink with campion, and no man living could have told you what the intentions of the Air Ministry were. Smith was lying there brooding, not on the carriage of a few pounds' weight of letters nor on prizes of £10,000, but on the problems of man's unchanged and warring heart. He dreamed of Imperial Defense. He was "keen" on making India and Egypt secure. He was "dead nuts" on the safety of Africa, "all out" for Australia's protection, and "tails up" if any other nation jolly well interfered.

And this was his next remark:

"I say, sir, I think Joan got that Dunhill number wrong after all—I'll swear there's latakia on this—don't tell Joan though—this is *entrez nous.*"

Entrez nous! Between you and I! O modest flower tossed to the welcoming hands of the Entente!

I handed him his watch back.

Strange, strange days!

V

Why did I not say straight out to him, "Look here, my young friend, this is all extremely interesting, but what I don't understand is why you shoot a man and then carry his picture on your wrist. In plain English, now, why did you shoot him—always supposing you did?"

Well, I was trying to put myself in his place—trying to picture a friendship such as he had had with this wistful, self-effacing young fatalist whose picture I had just handed back to him. I have told you how the more poignant of these experiences between man and man have been denied me; a flying-friendship I could never by any possibility have had; but I could reach out to it in my fancy. I could imagine with what fierce jealousy I should have guarded a treasure so rich. Not a word, not a breath from outside would I have suffered with regard to it. It was not a question of mere impertinence. It was rather one of the violation of a sacred place.

And it seemed to me that I now owed him no less than I would have claimed for myself. It made no difference that he was twenty-four and I within hand's-reach of fifty. Less than an hour had swept these conventions aside, and thenceforward he was entitled to the full honors of friendship and respect. He might tell me what he chose. Ply him with questions, however, I could not.

Nay, it even seemed to me now that I should have to drop my point before Philip also. However much I had been put on my mettle by those discoveries I had made on that Sunday afternoon in his studio, to drag them up again now would merely be to attack Chummy at one remove. If I could not have it from himself I could hardly have it at all, and the Case, which had unfolded as a conjuror's pilule unfolds into a flagrant and morbid-hued passion-flower, looked like shutting itself up again and being as if it had never been.

Yet the discoveries of that Sunday had been much on my mind. Especially that gold ring that had once belonged to Audrey Cunningham had been on my mind. That the circumstances in which I had found it were directly connected with the rupture between her and Monty I could hardly doubt, and several times, as a mere man, I had been on the point of confessing my share in the incident to Mollie Esdaile.

If Mollie has a little dropped out of the picture, let me now bring her in again as she brought herself in as Chummy Smith and I lay on the turf that morning.

I forget for what delinquency Alan and Jimmy had spent some hours in disgrace; I think they had been cutting one another's hair. But apparently all was now expiated. With joyous cries they dashed over a low brow, Mollie's head and shoulders rising behind them, and flung themselves upon us with the jubilant announcement that they were good again and that the hens had laid eleven eggs.

"One's a duck's—"

"Two's duck's—"

"I'll bet you—"

"I'll bet you my purple pencil—"

"I'll bet you my Bible an' all my shells—"

"Where's daddy?"

"Hasn't he finished painting Auntie Joan yet?"

Mollie was laughing and telling Chummy not to get up. She "goes to pieces" a little in the country in the matter of dress, and wore her mallow-flower of an old sunbonnet and her gray sandshoes. As Smith reached for his stick and got up on to his feet she caught my eye and laughed again. She had suffered from big-ends and magnetos too.

"Did Philip bundle you both out?" she asked.

"He bundled this man out. I was behaving myself."

"Well," quoth Smith, "we only gave him till twelve o'clock, and it's five to now. You coming, kids?"

They were not merely coming; they were already twenty yards on the way, with Chummy pegging after them. Had Mollie and I followed, Philip would merely have commandeered us for the carrying home of his painting-tackle. Instead we turned along the cliff-tops in the opposite direction, towards the zigzag path that dropped steeply to the beach.

Since that impetuous dash of hers to London she had shown herself from time to time—I will not say brooding (that is too strong a word), but frequently withdrawn, pensive, *rêveuse*. She was as brisk and practical as ever about the house or in the arranging of picnics and excursions, but somehow the routine of her daily life struck me as a series of detached and separate efforts, that for some reason or other never acquired momentum. I admit, however, that it would be easy to make too much of this change in her, if change there was.

"Shall we go down?" she said as we paused at the top of the path. "I haven't seen the sands for two days. 'Man works till set of sun—'"

"Come along," I said, giving her a hand; and we began the descent.

The Santon sands were a rather wonderful sight that morning. The tide was at its farthest out, and some mysterious wave-action had rolled out the wide spaces, not to an even flatness, but into regular parallel striations of wet and dry, the wet so mirror-like and shining that the sky was perfectly reduplicated in it and the flight of the seabirds far under our feet could be distinctly seen, the dry portions the intervening footings from one to the next of which we stepped. Our feet left no prints on the firm surface, so that looking behind the illusion was still the same—the dry stripes, the sudden brilliant chasms in between, everywhere the interrupted inversions of blue and white and dazzling sun.

"Well, I've been having my first real talk with your Chummy," I remarked as the alternations slowly flowed under our feet.

"Oh? What about?" she asked.

"About his aims and so on—what he wants to do. Apparently he wants to get on some sort of an Expedition. But is it likely he'll ever fly again?"

"I don't know," she said; and walked a little way before adding, "I shouldn't think he'd want to."

"He does."

She looked straight before her, as if to rest her eyes from the passing immensities underfoot. There was indeed a fantastic sort of consonance between flight and the phenomenon of the shore that midday. I do not know, however, whether this vague association prompted the huge implication of her very next words—an implication which I now had from her for the first time.

"You know what I mean," she said quietly.

I tried to steal a glance at her face, but saw only the folds of the sunbonnet.

"And that it isn't the kind of thing anybody wants to talk about," she added, leaving me to take the hint.

"No," I agreed mechanically; but for all that I needed a few moments in which to think.

Obviously I was not there to get out of Philip's wife something that Philip himself refused me; but the immensity of her quiet assumption had pulled me up short. I was assumed to know the whole—the whole—of "what she meant." It was left to my good sense to see that it was not a thing to talk about. There was to be no argument; she merely expected an equal simplicity in return, and with a woman like Mollie to expect such a thing is to get it. I watched a cloud of sheldrake that wheeled and broke over their own images a few yards away to our left, and then I turned to her.

"My dear, I'm not sure that I do understand altogether, but we certainly won't talk about it. I should, however, like to mention one little thing that I don't think even Philip knows."

She turned quickly. "What is that?"

"Nor Smith."

"What is it?"

"Nor, I should say, you yourself."

"If only you'll tell me what it is—!"

I looked into her eyes. "Where is Mrs. Cunningham now?" I asked.

VI

Her start could hardly have been more sudden had I asked her where Alan was a few moments after he had been seen playing at the cliff's edge.

"Audrey Cunningham? She was at Harrogate last, I think—or Scarboro—why?"

"Why was her engagement broken off?"

She made an abrupt, impatient gesture. Evidently I had plunged her back into an older mood.

"Oh, I don't know! I'm tired to death of—of everything! Why do you want to remind me of it? I was just beginning to forget a little. Oh, why didn't we leave London a week earlier! We nearly did—Philip was only waiting for Billy to get those pictures back—we should have escaped everything then!"

I soothed her. "Yes; but about the engagement. I could make very little of your letter. You said things were tangled and difficult and so on. What did you mean, Mollie?"

She was silent.

"Do you mean that you won't discuss Mrs. Cunningham with me?"

Still she did not speak.

"Because you have discussed her. I had your letter. You said you'd heard from her. That was since you last saw her. What happened in between?"

She found her voice. "Nothing that I know, except that it seems to have been definitely off."

"By that do you mean that she returned Monty's ring?"

"She didn't say what she did with the ring."

"Well, she neither returned it nor kept it. I have it. I don't want it. Will you take it?"

I fetched it from my pocket and held it out to her.

Her hand found my sleeve, almost as if that brilliance underfoot unsteadied her head. Her eyes had closed and there was a little hard crumple between her brows. I put my other hand on her shoulder.

"Let's get up the beach—this is too dazzling—it's making you dizzy," I said.

Faintly she murmured, "Yes—it does get in your eye—"

VII

On the hot loose sand above the highest seaweed I made her sit down. Presently she had recovered a little. Her manner was now undoubtedly that of a person on whose back a half-withdrawn burden is reimposed. But she shouldered it.

"Where did you get it?" she asked, her eyes on the ring in my palm.

"Do you remember Philip asking me to pack up some sketches for him and sending me his key?"

"He did say something about it. Monty had left."

"I found the ring on the Sunday afternoon I went for the sketches. It was in a hole in the studio floor."

"In a hole.... Ah-h-h-h!"

I looked sharply at her, but continued.

"Stuck quite firmly in: in fact, I had to prise it out with a screwdriver. I didn't know which of them it belonged to—I don't know now—so I slipped it into my pocket. Perhaps you'd better take it."

But she made no movement to do so. She was picking up handfuls of sand and allowing it to slip through her fingers again. She made quite a number of little heaps, which her eyes attentively watched, but her mind was elsewhere—perhaps on that last letter of Audrey Cunningham's, when apparently the engagement had been neither off nor on. She made no sign when I placed the ring in her lap. I had to speak.

"Queer, wasn't it?"

Her murmur was so low that I scarcely heard it. "Of course a thing like that *would* make it definitely off."

"A thing like what?"

"Losing it like that—after all the other."

"Come, she can hardly have 'lost' it, since I had to get a screwdriver to prise it out!"

"I don't mean 'lost' in that way—be quiet and let me think."

The fingers began to make a fifth sandhill.

I hope I have made it clear that I was confining myself quite strictly to Monty Rooke's affair. If it was simply a misunderstanding I did not think I was going beyond my business in discussing with Mollie whether that misunderstanding might not be removed. But it now seemed to me that I was once more on the verge of far more than this. That deep long-drawn "Ah-h-h-h!" that "A thing like that *would* make it definitely off" were enough to convince me of this. Evidently my words had meant more to her than to myself who had uttered them. Therefore if Mollie claimed time to think, so did I.

And first of all I recalled my firm persuasion of that Sunday afternoon that Audrey Cunningham had made some sort of a discovery. It might have been an accidental one, or she might merely not have rested until she had made it, but a discovery she had made, and it had to do with the hole in the studio floor. I remembered too my own pacings, eye-measurements, judgment of angles, and my slight chagrin that Philip had frustrated my further investigations by his removal of the key from the cellar door. And it seemed to me that again everything seemed to come round to that cellar of Esdaile's—the cellar on which Hubbard had instantly fastened as holding the answer to the riddle, the cellar in which Philip had spent that unaccountable half-hour and over which he had since so jealously watched, yet the self-same cellar into which both Rooke and Mrs. Cunningham had since descended and found ... nothing.

Yet instantly all my former objections rose again as vividly as ever—the extreme physical improbability that Philip could have seen anything through that peep-hole, the utter unlikelihood that he should have had his eye at it at that particular moment of time, the virtual impossibility that he should have thought of the hole at all on hearing the crash.

And yet in this hole had been tightly jammed the ring now lying in Mollie's lap.

Suddenly Mollie surprised me by looking up and almost brightly smiling. She smoothed out the sandhills and picked up the ring from her lap.

"Well," she said in a tone of relief, "that makes an immense difference. I'm awfully glad you told me. Shall we be getting back?"

But this, it struck me, was rather rushing matters. I thought I had a right to know just a little more than that. Therefore I did not rise.

"One moment," I said. "I should like to know why you said that 'a thing like that would make it definitely off.'"

She smiled again, with a sort of affectionate raillery.

"Oh ... and you're supposed to understand women!"

This I warmly disclaimed. "In any case I only know Mrs. Cunningham very slightly," I protested.

"And you formed no impression of her?"

"I didn't say that."

"Not even that she would be just the woman to take a—hint—of that kind?"

She was gently but quite plainly laughing at me; but, glad as I was to see the cloud disappear from her brow, she was not going to have everything her own way.

"Then she did make a discovery, and received a hint, as you call it, in doing so?"

"Did she?" she parried.

"*Did* she?"

At that she laughed outright. She patted my sleeve almost as if I had been a child.

"You men *can't* know how funny you are sometimes!" she mocked me.

VIII

It struck me even then that the moment Mrs. Cunningham's name was introduced there was introduced also something of that sex-antagonism—perhaps I had better modify that and say sex-difference—for which her personal story had given her such bitter reason. Here now was Mollie, suddenly and in the middle of our *tête-à-tête*, abolishing me as an individual and saddling me with the collective qualities of men in general. And I must remind you once more that as a matter of mere historical sequence I was still unaware of what had passed between her and Philip on that night when she had put Audrey Cunningham to bed, and Monty had spent half the night in wandering through the dark Roehampton lanes.

"Well, let's take it that we're funny," I said rather shortly. "I don't quite see the joke myself, but that's neither here nor there. The point is that if I can do Monty a good turn I want to. Whether patching it up between him and Mrs. Cunningham is a good turn is for you to decide. I only met her once in my life, and hardly exchanged a dozen words with her."

"You shall presently if I can lay my hands on her."

"What do you mean? That you're going to have her down here?"

"Of course I'm going to have her down here if she can come," said Mollie in her most matter-of-fact tones. "How slowly you think! She must come immediately. I shall see about it this afternoon *même*."

"And Rooke too?"

"We'll see about that."

"And Hubbard? And Mackwith?"

"No. What have they got to do with it?"

"Merely to make the party complete. We should be just where we started then."

"Oh, I think we can dispense with that side of it," she answered lightly. "Let me see: was it Harrogate? It was Buxton, and then Matlock, and then either Harrogate or Scarboro...."

I wonder whether the surmise has dawned on you that was now beginning to dawn on me? I admit that I had none but the very slightest grounds for it, and that even these were more exclusions than affirmations; but in the absence of anything more positive they had to serve. Think for a moment how we men, solemnly, ponderously and sure that we were doing the decent thing, had decided that at all costs certain facts of our Case should be kept from the womenfolk. To that end we had evaded, temporized, shuffled. And now suppose—just suppose—that all our care and concealment had been wasted, and that two of the women at any rate knew as much as Philip Esdaile knew and far, far more than any of the rest of us? Mind you, I was only guessing; but I began rather to fancy my guess. If there was little for it, I could see nothing against it. Certain things, moreover, were distinctly in its favor. Why this remarkable brightening in Mollie's manner, this change from her dizzy little stagger over those strips of inverted sky when I had first produced that ring to her air of lightsome raillery now? Why this quick instinctive taking of sex-sides, this sudden practical decision to seek out Audrey Cunningham this very day and to have her down to Santon? It was not the ring at all; it was—could only be—the place in which the ring had been found. Always, always we came back to that hole in the studio floor at which Philip's eye could not possibly have been at the moment of the crash that May morning. Somewhere between the hole and the cellar the elusive explanation lay. I had been thwarted, Mackwith knew nothing about it, and Hubbard could only grunt and mumble about periscopes and sound-ranging and selenium cells; but Mollie, I was persuaded, knew.

And what I had just told her, which she had not hitherto known, was that Audrey Cunningham shared the knowledge with her.

PART IX

WHAT PHILIP KNEW

I

The other day, accompanied by an engineer acquaintance, I was pottering about certain new excavations in the heart of London, and came upon a number of heaps of crushed and broken-up concrete, evidently the remains of old foundations. Yet those foundations could not have been very old, since I myself could remember the buildings of which they had been the support, and these had been old-fashioned rather than old. One of them had been a theater, another an hotel; and I stood there with my friend, looking over the waste of rubbish and barrows and wheeling-planks and thrown-up London clay, trying to evoke in my mind the exact plan of those vanished streets of thirty-odd years ago.

I found it difficult. Had these streets been older streets there would have been remembered records to help me. Prints would have jogged my memory, maps and plans have come to my aid. The seventeenth or eighteenth centuries would somehow have come nearer home than that unnoteworthy period of hardly more than a generation ago. Particularly when I tried to picture the huge new palaces of ferro-concrete that will presently arise, that intermediate epoch seemed ephemeral and without significance.

And so, even already, I find this record of our Case to be. There is a strange blank, full (I know) of all manner of busyness and bustle and restless effort, but without either the security of history nor yet the full brightness of new discovery. The *Scepter* action seems somehow more remote than the Armada, the findings of this high-sounding Committee or that farther away than Trafalgar. All is still too near to be seen, and by the time the dust has settled another pen than mine will have to take up the tale.

Indeed, I have more than once felt inclined to hand over the pen now, for, when all is still to prove, a younger faith and vision than those of my day are needed. For example, Cecil Hubbard tells me that the man who nowadays does not know at least the elements of all this lore of wave-lengths and directional wireless has no business to say that he belongs to his age at all, and sadly I believe him. Yet Philip Esdaile contrives to keep abreast, not by joining in the banging and burnt-cork of so much contemporary painting, but by virtue of something else, often temporarily hidden, that will still be quietly there when the whistles have ceased to scream and the tom-toms to thud. He too maintains the continuity, sharing with his forerunners that quality, whatever it is, which makes the old centuries modern and the novelty of yesterday afternoon musty and stale before the sun next rises.

Therefore, it should be understood that the rest is more theirs and less mine than ever. In the *Scepter* action Charles Valentine Smith, speaking (thanks largely to my friend Glenfield) from the witness-box and not from the dock, with wreaths and garlands and the glamour of his Embassy adventure almost visibly about him, made this abundantly clear. Easily, familiarly, and with pronouns all over the shop, he dealt with matters so far above my head that I will make no attempt to report him. If you are interested, there are *The Times* Law Reports in which you can read it all. And similarly with the whole crop of associated actions and inquiries and investigations. My own interest in them is no more than that something has been born in my time whose infant strugglings and gaspings I witnessed, and about which I shall doubtless become garrulous all too soon.

II

So that conjuror's passion-flower to which I have likened this case all but folded itself up into its original pilule again. That it did not do so was due to a series of small happenings which I will now relate.

The first of these was my leaving Santon before Mrs. Cunningham arrived there. Mollie, despite her energy, did not discover her friend's whereabouts so easily as she had anticipated. It took her, to be precise, a fortnight, at the end of which time I had to leave. But so narrowly did I miss Mrs. Cunningham that I believe her train passed mine on the way.

But I did not leave Mollie without that sort of smiling salute that accompanies a fencer's "en garde." If (I told her flatly) she held herself free to accept information from me and to give nothing but pitying looks of sex-superiority in return, I for my part should also consider myself at liberty to do as I pleased should further information come to light. What I had in my mind was that if she and Audrey Cunningham were going to put their heads together in the country Rooke and I might do the same thing in town. I may say that I was quite conscious of the feebleness of my retort, and did not for a moment expect that Rooke would have anything fresh to tell me.

"Very well," Mollie laughed gayly from the platform. "But you can tell Monty from me that I'll look after this end of it. Don't tell him anything about the ring though, or you may spoil it So long, my dear—see you in September—"

And the waving hands of the Santon party slid past my carriage window.

I gave Monty her message, though strictly without prejudice to myself as its bearer. He was not caught up into any sudden transport of joy. Instead some cheerful confidence of his own seemed to envelop him.

"I fancy that will be all right now," he said.

"Do you? Well, I'm very glad. It's a great improvement on the last time."

"Oh, I've had rather a bit of luck since then," he replied.

His "bit of luck" seemed to me slender enough grounds for his confidence that all would yet be well. It appeared that he had been sent by a weekly paper down to Hounslow to make certain sketches (he was in full harness again), and there he had got into conversation with a ground official, an ex-R.A.F. man. He had rather "palled up" with this man, and had seen him several times since. Indeed, Monty was a little inclined to impart recently acquired information with regard to the organization of "dromes" and similar matters, and had quite a number of yarns that were "absolute facts" to tell. His conversation also had become noticeably slangier.

"You see," he remarked casually, "I think I'm on the track of why that pal of Philip's shot the other chap."

I found myself staring blankly at him; but, as often happens in moments of shock, I did not at first feel the full force of what he said. I interrupted him.

"I say—I hope you haven't been talking too much about that?" (I knew his weaknesses, and a perfectly open candor was one of the gravest of them.)

But "Lord, no!" he instantly reassured me. "Talking about it? Do you think I'm a—" the initials he used were those of the words "blind fiddler."

"I'm glad of that," I murmured.

And then it was that the full weight of what he had said began to sink into my mind.

"Then why did he shoot him?" I asked presently, when I was a little more master of myself. This conversation, I ought to have said, took place on the top of a bus going eastward down Piccadilly. I was on my way to the office, and I had found Monty with a finished drawing which he also was taking to Fleet Street. He looked away over the Green Park.

"Well, I'm not perfectly sure I'm right, of course," he replied, turning to me again. "In fact, I might be miles out—right off the map. But I *did* see him on the roof that morning, you know, and I've been trying to piece it all together again, and I must say it fits in pretty well."

"What fits in, and with what?"

He dropped his voice. "Well, you see, this fellow Smith waved his hand the way I told you—like this—" On the bus top he made that same aimless and wavering movement of his hand that I had seen him make in Esdaile's studio, that I had seen Mr. Harry Westbury make in the Chelsea public-house. "I think now he wanted the pistol back again, but of course I didn't give it him."

"What did he want it for?"

"Might have wanted to shoot himself," Monty replied.

I pondered deeply, my eyes on the passing façade of the Ritz. Certainly Monty, as the first on the scene that morning that now seemed such ages ago, had the right to collate his original observations with anything he might subsequently have learned, and the resulting conclusion would probably be a strong one. But that Chummy had possibly wished to shoot himself was no explanation of why he had shot Maxwell. Indeed, another explanation was far more probable. Having realized that he had in fact shot him he might merely have wished to take the shortest way out himself, and I drew Monty's attention to this.

"I'm coming to that," Monty answered. "You see this fellow Wetherhead is a jolly interesting chap. You remember the July push on the Somme? Well, he was in that—Bristol Fighter—and then he went up the line to Wipers. He told me that one time when they were in Pop—Poperinghe that is, you know, and we'd a lot of heavy guns there—" (but I think I may safely omit the rather lengthy second-hand recital of Wetherhead's movements and experiences). "Extraordinary yarns he has to tell. Did you know that a first-class pilot can drive another one down with the wash of his propeller? He can, Wetherhead says. He gets above him, and maneuvers for position, and then—I forget exactly how Wetherhead put it, but he showed me with a couple of models they have there—"

"Yes, yes, but you were going to say—"

"So I was; I know I'm rambling a bit, but it's awfully interesting, and you must meet Wetherhead. Well, when he was with the infantry (Northwold Fusiliers) he says quite a number of their fellows used to carry little doses of poison about with them, just in case. He'd heard awful yarns of the way some of these Boches used to treat their prisoners. So they had this poison to be ready for anything, like Whitaker Wright with his cigar."

"Monty, if you don't come to the point—"

"Why, I'm there now; don't have a vertical gust, old thing. Well, just in the same way Wetherhead says some of these pilots and their observers had an arrangement that if one of them got it in the neck the other one was to finish the job for him. And the other way round, of course. He and his observer—he's going to introduce me to him—they had it all fixed up, but luckily it never came to that. So it's not impossible that these two fellows were like that. What do you think? It fits in with my end all right, and you've been down there and seen Smith. What about you? I'm inclined to have a bit on it myself."

A bit on it! ... A bit! Instantly I would have had all I possessed on it. Our bus was standing at the Circus end of Lower Regent Street when Monty at last came out with it, but it had reached Waterloo Place before I next became conscious of my physical surroundings. A bit on it!... Look at Monty as I have tried to describe him to you. An unworldly and lovable and gentle sort of donkey he was in some ways; now that he had finished with his dummy trees and linoleum infantry he was apparently beginning to learn a little about other aspects of the war; and Wetherhead (whoever he was—already Monty had so crammed him down my throat that I was resolved to put the width of England between us rather than meet him) suddenly stood for the whole of the Air Force to him. But behind all his sweet credulity Monty was no fool. He was aware of his ground. He *had* been the first on the roof that morning. He *was* in the last event capable of putting two and two together and of scoring a bull. Do you know these flashes of the absolute and unalterable rightness of a thing? One of them blinded Saul of Tarsus on the road to Damascus; something of the same kind blinded me for the whole length of Lower Regent Street. I had no longer one single shadow of doubt. Nay, I had a certitude that even Monty didn't share. *He* "wasn't perfectly sure." But *I*—!

For what else could it have been? What else in the whole realm of man's created spirit? For what other reason could Esdaile, up to then wavering and swayed by doubts, have visited the hospital where Smith lay, have been back in his own home again within half an hour, and then have straightway borne his exonerated friend off into the midst of his family? Why, from that moment, had he immediately set about to get his own half-confidences to the rest of us back into his possession again? Why, at Santon, had my own questions been met with a silencing stare? Of all the things conceivable to have been told, could Smith have told him anything but this?

And Smith's own demeanor on that uplifted Yorkshire headland? Was not that too explained? I thought it was, and could only marvel—marvel— that not as much as the smell of the fire had passed upon him. That white and welding heat of war had not merely made his pact with Maxwell a thing to be honored in the last emergency without a further moment's thought, but it admitted no sigh nor compunction nor regret afterwards. Compunction? Sigh? Regret? For what? It had had to be done, and it had been done. As gladly would he have accompanied his friend's spirit on that last flight of all, but, that denied him, unsorrowing he remained behind, ground-officer henceforward to an angel. What more than this is death to those who for four years have been crucified all the day long? What else is life, their own life or that other-own their friend's, when it is held at this instant readiness? The coil about it all is not for them, but for us, who peer about for bullets and cartridge-cases and holes in the floor. Chummy's every breath would not have been his absolution had he *not* laughed with Esdaile's children and, with Joan perched on the carrier behind him, cheerfully fouled the Santon roads with the stench of his exhaust. He had *no* burden to assume. He had, on the contrary, an urgent task to carry on. And in the carrying-on of it he knitted his uncomprehending brows over Maxwell's *Transactions* and *Proceedings* and carried a dead man's portrait on his wrist.

III

Instead of going straight to the office that morning I waited in some ante-room or other while Monty took in his drawing. Somebody else waiting there, who may or may not have known me, observed that it was a fine morning, but I am not sure that I replied. I was in no mood for exchanging casual remarks about the weather.

For while I still marveled—and I need hardly say rejoiced—admiration and joy must wait for the present. It might be some little time before I saw Monty again (he had told me he was making business calls during a great part of the day and working until late into the night), and another point had struck me. This was his new confidence that it would presently be "all right" between himself and Audrey Cunningham. I had had a glimpse, if not yet the full revelation, of where Smith stood; but I did not yet clearly see how this affected Mrs. Cunningham. Yet in Monty's mind a connection obviously existed. He came out of the editor's den again, folding up the brown paper that had enwrapped his drawing and putting it carefully into his pocket.

"Brown paper's scarce," he said. "I've used this piece four times already. And I undo all the knots in my string too. Well, which way are you going?"

We left the office and, barely a hundred yards away, turned into the Temple. Presently he resumed our previous conversation by asking me what I thought of his guess; and I told him. I told him also my difficulty about what his own engagement had to do with this.

"Do with it?" he repeated as we began to pace backward and forward along King's Bench Walk. "It's a good deal to do with it—if that about Smith's right, of course. You see, you hardly know Dawdy. She thinks you don't like her very much—"

"Then I hope you'll take the first opportunity—" I began hurriedly, but he waved his hand.

"Oh, don't you worry about it. I don't suppose she means it. And whether she does or not it seems to me this is exactly where I come in."

"Then you see more than I do," I remarked.

"Don't you? I mean her taking sudden fancies of that kind. I'm not superstitious myself—silly I call it—but she's a mass of it. Theatrical people are, I've heard, and anyway she is. I think that beast Cunningham started her off. When she used to sit up at night waiting for him to come home she used to do all sorts of stupid things—sit there counting slowly, and if he didn't come before she counted a hundred he wouldn't come at all—counting the taxis that passed too—watching the clock—beastly. Filthy time she had. I hope I'm somewhere near that brute at the Resurrection."

Presently he swallowed his anger and continued.

"Well, about when Philip offered us that studio, that accident happened, and everything was at sixes and sevens. Philip began it, stopping all that time in the cellar and behaving like a lunatic when he did come up. What his game was—well, you can search me. So first Philip starts playing the goat, and then there was all that fuss about Mrs. Esdaile going away, and Philip staying on day after day, always saying he was going and everything was perfectly all right but never budging an inch, mind you. Well, it began to get on Dawdy's nerves. And I began to catch it too. She said *I'd* something up my sleeve as well, and of course I had, about that pistol. And then there was that time when we took her wardrobe down into the cellar."

"Yes, tell me about that."

"Absolutely nothing to tell. That's all Dawdy's fancy too. If there'd been anything funny he wouldn't have left the key in the door, would he?"

"He took it out afterwards."

"It was there for some days anyway. In fact, I took another box of Dawdy's down, but I came straight up again. You're all wrong about that cellar."

"Hubbard doesn't think so."

"What does he say?"

"He doesn't actually say anything; he doesn't know; but he wouldn't be surprised if it turned out Philip had some sort of a portable installation down there. But don't take this from me. I know nothing about these things."

"Wetherhead knows about them," Monty mused....

"Go on about Mrs. Cunningham."

"Well, as I tell you, it got on her nerves. She began to say she was fed up with men and silly things like that. Didn't want to get married at all; wanted to go and live with some girl. And then one day—"

But here he suddenly stopped, and for a reason I could easily guess. Undoubtedly at this point she had made independent investigations, which Monty either knew or suspected and didn't want to talk about. His hesitation over, he continued.

"Well, so it dragged on, until one evening I met her after rehearsal, and that was the finish. Absolutely done in she was; ten hours that day and nothing but a bun and a glass of milk. Of course, I saw she was all tuckered up, and I didn't want to take much notice of what she said—just gave her something to eat and tried to calm her down. But it was no good. When I called at Oakley Street the next morning she'd gone—gone to stop with this other girl; and in a week the Company was off."

In spite of Mollie's injunction I ventured to ask a question.

"Did she return the ring you gave her?"

"No, and that's one of the reasons why I think it might be all right yet. But the chief reason's this. She's got it into her head that it all started with that crash. Superstition, but there was no arguing with her. Well, suppose I'm right in what I told you, and Smith didn't really shoot that chap at all—didn't shoot him in the way we thought at first, I mean. It would be just like Dawdy to say that took the bad luck all off. She's always either up or down, poor darling. A rotten life she's had."

I nodded, remembering Mollie's words: "She *would* be just the woman to take a hint of that kind." Although Monty didn't know it, Audrey *had* lost her ring, *would* regard the loss as an omen, and the loss had probably taken place shortly before Monty had met her at the stage-door.

It *did* seem to follow, even as Monty said, that with the removal of the whole Case out of the regions of ordinary crime, there might be an end also of the nightmare shadows that had oppressed Audrey Cunningham's soul.

IV

This record has already taken so many turns and windings, anticipations and doublings back upon itself, that I cannot see that one more excursion will either make or mar it. Many pages ago I wrote that the Case *was* a Case, complete, self-contained, and independent of the larger issues and forces in which it is nevertheless paradoxically rooted and involved. And though the Case as an entity is approaching its close, the outside influences continue. The *Scepter* decision, for example, is being appealed against, and Mackwith tells me that there is every likelihood that it will end up in the Lords. The Press, from which I shall shortly retire, seems to be attaining something like a real policy with regard to the matters of which I have spoken, and, encouraged by certain signs of Ministerial yielding, has taken still better heart. Cairo to the Cape has for the present failed, and Charles Valentine Smith did not succeed in becoming a member of that gallant Expedition; but other great projects are in meditation, and this very day the announcement is made of an impending flight round the world itself, for which Cooks and Ansons and Drakes and Dampiers of little more than half my age will eagerly flock to enter. The gloomy forebodings of Hills, my fellow-clubman, that attack and defense will presently become a matter of black typhus cultures do not at present seem likely to be fulfilled, not altogether for the reasons publicly given, but for quite other ones; but the chances are that he is right about gas, and that one day we may have to carry fans and box-respirators as we now carry umbrellas. What must come must come, even as it came to our fathers before us, and we, like they, can only do the duty of our day. The rest is out of our hands, and it is impotence and vanity even to dream too far ahead. So to our immediate business, of which my own present portion is the final putting to bed of our Case. With the permission of Philip Esdaile, A.R.A., and the others, I bid you to yet another breakfast. This time it is a wedding breakfast, and a double one. Hardly an hour ago Joan Merrow, spinster, became Mrs. Charles Valentine Smith, and Audrey Cunningham (*née* Herbert) Mrs. Montagu Rooke. Joan was married at Holy Trinity, Sloane Street, and wears her full bridal attire; but Audrey Rooke wears the gray costume and the black satin hat (that sticks out on each side of her head like the serifs of a capital "I") in which she walked from the Registry Office. And there is present the same party, with the addition of Chummy, with which this story opened.

V

Again the breakfast recess was full of charming light. About the walls the love-making butterflies danced when carafes were moved, and only the flowers on the table were different—for it was early in a halcyon autumn, and the mulberry outside had already begun to turn. The faces of the Esdailes and the Rookes were enviably brown, for Monty and Audrey had spent three weeks at Santon and the whole party had returned together; and Joan, who knows perfectly well that I adore her, had very simply and sweetly come over to my side of the table and linked her hands for a moment round my arm. Then, after a warm little pressure, she had returned to Chummy again, who had risen. He was staying at an hotel in Gloucester Road, must get out of his wedding garments, and would then return to take Joan away.

"Don't change your mind and not come back," Joan called after him; and he waved his hand from the door and was off.

"What about Joan? Isn't it time she was changing too?" Philip hinted.

Mollie gave him a sidelong look. It was understood that Philip was willing at last to explain himself, and that look was Mollie's comment on the situation. Mingled with its fondness were faint pity, irony, wonder at us. It said, as plainly as need be, "That tiresome business all over again! What a sex!"

But all she openly said was, "Come along then, Joan—you too, Audrey—never let it be said we aren't properly submissive—"

And they too departed.

Instantly Cecil Hubbard swung round his chair to face Philip. Philip gave a backward glance through the French windows. He seemed to derive some reassurance from the sunlight that made vivid the garden outside.

"Well...?"

"Well...."

The words came simultaneously from the two men. As for the rest of us, we were content for the present to let Cecil Hubbard make the running.

VI

"Well, you know what the first question is," said Hubbard.

"Let's have it," Philip replied. "Better not take anything for granted."

"Very well. About that other morning. What were you doing down below all that time?"

"Moving furniture," Philip replied.

"Moving ... what for?"

"I'll show you that presently."

"Good.... Next, when you did come up again, what made you march straight up to Rooke in the way you did?"

"Because he had that pistol in his pocket."

"How did you know he had a pistol in his pocket?"

"Because I saw him put it there."

"Because—you say you saw—?"

"I saw everything—practically everything that happened."

The blue eyes stared. "How ... but you say you're going to show us. What's the next? Ah yes—After you'd fooled about with that candle and liqueur-jar you went into the studio and we followed you. You hadn't even put the candle out; I had to take it from you if you remember. Well, the next thing you did was to tell us you were going to tell us all about it. But you never did."

"Steady on, Cecil—that wasn't the next thing I did."

"What was, then?"

"I drew the studio blinds."

Hubbard nodded. "So you did. The police were getting those chaps down. I remember."

"That wasn't my reason."

"Then what was?"

"Well, I'll show you that too presently. But let me make something else clear first. I was all excited and upset, and really didn't know half I was doing. I'd just seen that crash, remember, and one man shoot another, and then another fellow altogether slide his hand out and pouch the pistol. It was rather much to spring on a fellow without any warning at all. I'd simply gone down to get something to drink, you know, not to—" He failed to find words for it, and motioned to Hubbard to continue.

"Next," Hubbard went on, "you packed your wife and children off but refused to go away yourself."

"Naturally. When you get a downright facer like that you want to see it through."

"And when Rooke here wanted to sweep up the studio you told him not to."

"I did. And not to go into the cellar either."

"But he went into the cellar later?"

"Later—yes. The blinds were drawn then."

"Then are people only to go into the cellar when the blinds are drawn?"

"Oh no, not necessarily. A rug—or a bit of paper or a halfpenny—would do just as well."

Here Hubbard seemed suddenly to give it up. He leaned back in his chair. "Here, somebody else carry on for a bit," he puffed, almost as if he had been running; and instantly I took up the catechism.

"Of course, you mean the hole in the studio floor?" I challenged.

"That's it," said Philip, smiling. "So you discovered that, did you?"

"It had been discovered long before I discovered it," I said.

This time it was Philip's turn to stare. "By whom?" he asked quickly.

"Rooke's here. Ask him to ask his wife."

"Dawdy!" Monty ejaculated, wide-eyed.

"I imagine so. At any rate you might ask her."

"Good—Lord!" said Monty, puffing as the Commander had puffed.

"And," I continued to Philip, "I don't think the blinds were drawn then. The key was in the cellar door too."

"The devil!" Philip breathed softly. "I didn't bargain for that! It did occur to me, of course, but I chanced it—never dreamed—I had to do something, and it seemed safest to be perfectly open...." And then suddenly he gave an awkward little laugh and met my eyes. "Well, evidently you know all about it?"

"Indeed I do not."

"What, you're as warm as all that and can't guess the rest!"

I frowned, a little annoyed. It is a little annoying to be told that something is under your nose that you don't see.

"As for that bullet-hole in the roof—" I hazarded.

"Bullet-hole in the roof? There never was a bullet-hole in the roof. The branch did that. Westbury had the bullet all right. By the way, I saw him last Sunday morning. Going great guns. He'll end up as our first Bolshevist Premier. Quite the biggest crowd in the Park."

Here Monty chuckled. It was he who had first discovered the final effect of the Case on the House and Estate Agent. He had come upon him one Sunday morning in the space just within the Marble Arch, standing on a box and holding forth passionately on social inequalities and equal opportunities for all. I am afraid he had never got over the unconscious trouncing Billy Mackwith had administered on that coroner's jury, and the collapse of his righteous cause, ending in Inspector Webster's refusal to have him hanging about the Police Station any longer, had completely upset his mental balance. He declaims from his box until the opening-time of the public-houses, and then adjourns, box and all, to the establishment near the Marble Arch Tube Station. Here he is as well known as he formerly was in the King's Road; but whether he has his private billiard cue there I do not know.

"Well, I give it up, Philip," I yielded at last. "I claim my single point, though—that it was news to you that Mrs. Rooke knew."

Philip rose.

"Then come along," he said. "We must get it over before Chummy comes back. Light the candle, somebody."

He led the way to the cellar door.

VII

"Why, you've changed it all!" was Monty Rooke's first exclamation as Philip stood there with the candle held at arm's-length.

As for myself, I was looking round the dark, clammy place with a positive passion of curiosity. That it had been rearranged I knew at once from Monty's former description of it. The dust-sheeted furniture and packing-cases had been pushed back against the walls, leaving the middle of the floor clear, and once more the candlelight barely penetrated into the gloomy recesses. It showed Philip's face, too, serious, but not to the complete exclusion of a certain quiet satisfaction and triumph. And in Hubbard's sailor eyes I fancied I already saw the dawning of comprehension.

"No I haven't—that is, I've only changed it back again as it was," Philip replied. "I told you I'd been moving furniture that morning.... Well, do you want to lose a bet, Cecil?"

Hubbard spoke oddly quietly. "No. I'll win one," he said.

"Ah! Then you're barred.... Take this, somebody, and you fellows wait here. I shall be back in a minute."

He thrust into my hand the candle, which he instantly blew out, leaving us in sudden and pitchy darkness.

I confess to a light creeping of the skin of my face. This may have been due to the chill, clammy air, to my stimulated imagination, or to both. Nobody spoke, and so still were the others that I had no difficulty in doing what in fact I was already doing—putting myself months back, alone down there, as Esdaile had been alone when he had descended for the jar of orange curaçao that morning. I seemed to myself to be standing there waiting for a sound of splintering glass, the muffled thud of two falling bodies, the faint murmur of half Chelsea running out of doors. I was conscious that the candle shook in my hand, and suddenly I wanted to relight it. I am not sure that my fingers did not go to my pocket for a match.

But it was another light that irradiated us as we stood waiting there—a soft bright cone that all at once spread down from the ceiling above. Up went my startled eyes as if at some trick of thaumaturgy, some imposition on my credulity. Down as if through a funnel streamed that circular shower of pale brightness, outfanning from its small orifice—the hole in the floor.

The hole in the floor! It was that to which my thoughts, following that instinctive movement of my eyes, turned like a flash. The hole in the floor! With my body still in the cellar, I seemed in some transcendental way to be upstairs at the same time, stooping over that hole as Audrey Cunningham had stooped before me. We seemed to be stooping inherently together, yet at the same time independently, so that, I was able to watch her. I saw her in my imagination pallid and hysterical, putting forth one honeysuckle finger half-way to the hole, and then, seized by a wild and baseless urge to put some torturing fancy to the test, changing her mind and putting forth another finger—the finger that bore her engagement ring.

"If he does not come before I count a hundred he will not come at all...."

"If I thrust in that finger and anything happens I shall know what to do...."

And then her cry as the ring jammed and the finger was withdrawn without it.

But understand that all this did not take a moment, and that I was still down in the cellar, looking up at that hypnotizing cone of white light.

The glimpse suddenly vanished, and I heard Esdaile's voice. I had not heard him come down.

"Stand back a bit," he said, his hand on my sleeve.

Then it was that my eyes fell on the floor.

VIII

On the floor? Rather on the roof itself, for, spread out over the floor, was a perfect image of that glazed studio roof high above us. The divisions between the panes were marvelously penciled there, and about one of them, though not the one I had expected, the browning branches of the mulberry crept and played. Something darted across and was gone—a bird.

And it was too late to bet now, for the book was closed. By merely seeing that the roof-blinds were open, and then pushing away a rug with his foot, Philip had confounded us all. Again I hardly heard his words: "House simply a big pinhole camera, you see...." Once more I was seeing what he had seen that morning so many months ago.

His mild astonishment at witnessing that phenomenon for the first time (for it was the first time)—

His interested realization of the cause of it as he had stood there with the bottle of liqueur in his hand—

And then the half-heard shock and the light tremor of the house and the whole astonishing scene instantly enacted before his eyes!

But I had little time to marvel anew. He was speaking.

"... so down they came, not at this end, but over there, in reverse, you know. And of course I'd no idea then it was Chummy; didn't learn that till the afternoon; I simply saw him point that pistol at the other man, who crumpled up. That was a shock, you understand, but you could have knocked me down with a feather when I saw another shape crawl across and pick the pistol up!... Eh? Oh, with the light above they were silhouettes more or less; we'll send somebody up and try if you like; but I knew it was Monty the moment I came upstairs and saw him."

"And then——?"

"I'm afraid I can't give you any very clear account of it. Time didn't seem to exist, if you know what I mean. But I know that all of a sudden I was moving furniture about, to break up that beastly picture, a bit on a box top and another bit on a sofa-end and so on. It didn't seem quite decent, somehow, all spread out dead flat like that. But I don't wonder you fellows were puzzled."

"But," said Mackwith presently, as we still stood looking at that moonlike radiance spread across the floor, "why couldn't you tell us all this sooner?"

"What for?" Philip retorted. "It didn't take me long to realize that I'd told you a dashed sight too much as it was! I had to have it out with Monty and Chummy, of course; but the less said after that the better. Suppose it *had* been a common Murder Case. I saw it, and could have hanged a man straight away with a word. You didn't, so why fill you up with a lot of hearsay? Don't you think I was right?"

"Hush! Listen!"

It was the tinkling of the street door bell. Chummy Smith was back already.

IX

He had a taxi waiting, and the driver was getting the boxes on as we reached the annexe again. Philip carried in his hand the jar of orange curaçao.

"Get the liqueur-glasses out, Monty," he said, and the words sounded remotely familiar.

"Where are my darling babies?" Joan cried, darting out into the garden where the Esdaile boys played beneath the mulberry. Philip and Mollie had decided that the best and cheapest thing to do with them was to pack them off to a preparatory school, and for a month past Joan had been impressing on them the dignity of this promotion.

As Philip busied himself with the jar of curaçao I found myself by Audrey Rooke's side. It was a little on my mind that she had the impression I didn't like her. Very charming and graceful indeed she looked in her filmy black tulle, and the hat with the little jutting-out serifs admirably suited her. The ring that I had prised out of the hole in the floor with a screwdriver was on her finger again, above her wedding-ring.

"May I say how sincerely glad I am this has all ended so happily?" I said in a low voice.

She lifted the large dark eyes to mine, and I fancied I saw a grateful look in them.

"Thank you," she said; and added, "Mollie told me what your share in it was."

"The merest fluke," I said.

"But you were quick to understand," she replied; and we let it go at that.

"Got those glasses, Monty?" Philip called. "Fetch Joan in, Mollie—there isn't much time—"

We pressed about the tray of glasses filled with the pale liquid gold.

"Well—extraordinary good luck, everybody—"

"Here's how—"

"Cheerioh—"

"God bless," said Chummy, with a little jerk of his glass aloft. "No, Alan, liqueurs are not for little boys—not till after their first term—"

"The best of luck, Mrs. Rooke—"

The glasses were set down again, and we bustled into the little hall.

"Gear all aboard?"

"Right—so long, Mollie, and ever so many thanks—"

"Good-by, darling—"

"Good-by, Commander—"

"With your permission, Chummy—"

"Here, I say, let them get off—they'll miss their train—"

We flocked down the path after them, and Philip closed the taxi door.

"Paddington," he said.

Waving hands, handkerchiefs, blown kisses; and the taxi glided away. As it did so it showed a tall figure in police uniform who had been standing behind it.

"Good morning, Inspector," said Philip.

Inspector Webster gravely saluted.

www.ingramcontent.com/pod-product-compliance
Lightning Source LLC
Chambersburg PA
CBHW011445170626
46816CB00008B/2532